IMPERFECT
SOLO

IMPERFECT SOLO

a dark
comedy of
random
misfortune

STEVEN BOYKEY SIDLEY

ARCADE PUBLISHING • NEW YORK

First North American Edition 2019

First published in 2014 by Picador Africa, an imprint of Pan Macmillan South Africa

This is a work of fiction. Names, places, characters, and incidents are either the products of the author's imagination or are used fictitiously.

Arcade Publishing books may be purchased in bulk at special discounts for sales promotion, corporate gifts, fund-raising, or educational purposes. Special editions can also be created to specifications. For details, contact the Special Sales Department, Arcade Publishing, 307 West 36th Street, 11th Floor, New York, NY 10018 or arcade@skyhorsepublishing.com.

Arcade Publishing® is a registered trademark of Skyhorse Publishing, Inc.®, a Delaware corporation.

Visit our website at www.arcadepub.com.
Visit the author's site at www.stevenboykeysidley.com.

10 9 8 7 6 5 4 3 2 1

Library of Congress Cataloging-in-Publication Data

Names: Sidley, Steven Boykey, author.
Title: Imperfect solo : a dark comedy of random misfortune / Steven Boykey Sidley.
Description: First North American edition. | New York : Skyhorse Publishing, Inc., 2019.
Identifiers: LCCN 2018022712 (print) | LCCN 2018024535 (ebook) | ISBN 9781510731837 (ebook) | ISBN 9781510731806 (hardcover : alk. paper)
Subjects: LCSH: Love stories. | Domestic fiction. | Divorced people—Fiction. | CYAC: Coming of age—Fiction.
Classification: LCC PR9369.4.9.S57 (ebook) | LCC PR9369.4.9.S57 I66 2019 (print) | DDC 823/.92—dc23
LC record available at https://lccn.loc.gov/2018022712

Cover design by Erin Seaward-Hyatt
Cover illustration: iStockphoto

Printed in the United States of America

To musicians who can really play—
even when no one is listening

IMPERFECT
SOLO

CHAPTER 1

I AM FILLED with dread.

This realization has come to me slowly, because dread creeps—it does not announce. Different than fear, which is sharp and pointed, and generally shrieks a lot. Dread is dull and gray and cold and nebulous. It's not depression either. I am a smiley sort, given to exuberance and inappropriate optimism. Which, surprisingly, coexists quite nicely with dread. A sort of a yin-yang balance, or something.

Van, who has been filled with dread since he was born about forty years ago, is unimpressed.

"Fuck your dread, you newbie. Don't come crawling to me—you who have demeaned and insulted me all these years. I own all the dread in the world. You are stealing from me. There is not enough space for both of us."

Bit harsh, I thought. He's my best friend, after all. Male friendships are entirely about insult and one-upmanship, as long as there is unstinting loyalty somewhere in there. But really, that was an overreaction. Morose shit.

He's right, though; an attitude of blackness and despair cloaks him constantly, and has carried him quite nicely through life. Particularly in those days when we sought nothing more than uncomplicated sex with some accommodating collaborator. My approach would be pure charm, deep intellect, humor, virtuoso displays of arcane knowledge, generosity, politeness, interest. My success rate was, well, best described as piddling. Van simply sat silently and looked gloomy as he got progressively drunker. Then he went home with the girl.

Of course, we are all grown up now. Sort of.

Los Angeles is a good place to feel dread. It is not a dreadful place at all—that is a non sequitur—it is simply a place where dread can exist without being harassed. It is warm in LA, there is a seaside, it can be pretty if you know where to look, there is a fantastic tiny Mexican restaurant in the run-down part of Hollywood owned by a grumpy Chinese couple who can speak neither English nor Spanish. After the burritos and refried beans, they bring those little white Chinese rabbit sweets with the check. I once tried to engage the owner in conversation, asking how a Chinese man got to own a Mexican restaurant. He looked at me as though I was loco. The food is stupidly inexpensive. There are only five tables, which rock alarmingly on unbalanced legs.

I am terrified the place will shut down. It increases my dread load. Along with the certainty that my house will burn down during one of those periodic brushfires in Beachwood Canyon. Where I was stupid enough to buy a house when real estate was a steal. So that I could stare at the Hollywood sign and have deep thoughts about the transient nature of celebrity and combustible wood-framed construction materials.

Krystal, my soon-to-be-ex-girlfriend, says I swear too much. Although that is not the reason I expect her to be an ex-girlfriend. She is leaving me because she considers me insufficiently ambitious. Which is a fucking lie. The problem is that my ambitions and hers have nothing in common. For instance, I have an ambition to play better saxophone. I play reasonably good saxophone. Some people think I play great sax. Charlie Parker and Michael Brecker and David Sanborn would beg to differ. What I would like is for Michael Brecker to come into the bar and listen to a solo of mine, and walk up to the stage during the break and say— damn, that was pretty. Michael Brecker died a few years ago. So he is not coming in. Neither is Sanborn, although he is very much alive and plays in a totally different genre than Brecker. It's just a matter of the odds. I am a great student of the odds. I was a math major at college. The whole damn universe serves the odds. From quantum mechanics and the chances that some little particle is here or there, or moving this fast or that fast, all the way up to the chances of us getting whumped by a meteor, to the chances that Sanborn will come to the restaurant one sunny Saturday, and say—damn, that was pretty, to the chances the Krystal will stay. Which are apparently zero. She is right, though. I swear too much.

Krystal is confused about the sax thing. She thinks I want to become a star. Which I don't. At least not anymore. Any musician who is over forty and still wants to become a star is touched. A sad victim of not understanding the odds. I don't want to become a star. I simply want to play a sax solo well enough that the guys who are never going to come and hear would be moved to come up and say—damn, that was pretty.

Besides, I am not even a proper musician. I play at a bar on weekends. That's as far as this is ever going to go, after some promising moments in front of stadium crowds some decades ago. My real job is as a computer programmer. Software developer, if you will. I work at a big company that makes stuff. I write code that helps them make and market and sell and ship and track the stuff they make. I am a great software developer. Write code in my sleep. Symphonies of computer-linguistic elegance. Here is where Krystal and I clash again.

"If you're so good, why don't you write an iPhone app or something? We could be rich."

"Firstly, I don't want to write an iPhone app—the odds of a winner are terrible. Secondly, I would get rich, not you. Thirdly, I earn an excellent salary; don't need to get rich. Fourthly, why do you want me to get rich?"

And, in addition to the whole ambition mismatch, I also tend to piss her off. For instance, she thinks I am too argumentative. She doesn't understand the difference between argument and reasoned debate. Even when it is carried out in a loud voice. Some years ago, I accused Isobel, my precocious daughter who was eleven at the time, of being argumentative.

"I am not argumentative. I am right."

I know what she means. Isobel is now fourteen. She spends every second weekend at my house. She likes Krystal. They gang up on me. Go shopping. Talk about young boy TV stars whose names I barely know. Take opposing positions against anything I say. Laugh at jokes I haven't heard, or don't understand. Female bonding. They probably have their periods in sync. Although Isobel thinks I play great sax. Krystal, on the other hand, is tone deaf.

"How can you like that song?" I shriek at Krystal as she turns up the radio in the car. "The singer is off-key, and the song has only two chords. It is a fucking blasphemy. You can't be serious."

"It speaks to me," she answers. "In a way that you don't understand. And you swear too much."

Maybe she should move out. I cannot live with a tone-deaf person. I could live with a fire-breathing Republican, an idiot brain-dead liberal, even an anti-Semite—and I am Jewish—if her anti-Semitism was just occasional. And benign. And good-natured. But I can't live with a tone-deaf person. This, for me, is a capital crime.

Krystal is going to move out. I am never going to play sax like Coltrane. My other ambitions are out of reach, not even visible really. Isobel is going to grow up and go out with boys and try drugs and start having sex and drive drunk. My second ex-wife, Bunny, wants to get remarried. I didn't include the cash payments from our gigs in my tax returns. I think I left the stove on. The front left tire on my car is bald.

I am filled with dread.

CHAPTER 2

THIS IS A reasonably new phenomenon, this dread. Like most men at the tail end of their prime, I am occasionally beset by regrets and psychic discomforts, and even sharp but vaguely articulated fears, buried, I assume, in the same metaphysical slime that has always attracted the attention of thinkers more able than I.

This dazzling city by the sea in which I have plied my various trades is terra flora for narcissistic wonderings. They are, indeed, the stucco of life here, under which stories and plots are developed. They reach their acme on the billboards of Sunset Boulevard, where the great questions of life are reduced to clever taglines in giant typefaces, towering over citizens stuck in endless traffic jams, a blunt metaphor for their lives.

None of this is new. Though this dread thing, damn, this is a whole new ball game. My psychologist friend Farzad has a patient with agoraphobia, which, among other things, sometimes renders the sufferer unable to leave home, so overwhelming is the fear of being trapped in strange territory without means of escape. I don't suffer from that, but I empathize. It has become common cause for me to duck and cover, as the sky falls. It wouldn't help to simply stay home, because apprehension awaits there too. It is ubiquitous, like ether.

Take, for example, the twisted complexities of multiple wives, multiple children, maddeningly closely missed musical aspirations, and a suspicion that bad things are seeking me out.

Van, again, is unimpressed.

"You're a self-obsessed whore. A slave of solipsism. You would embarrass even Narcissus."

That sort of ends the conversation with Van, not because it didn't open a slew of conversational possibilities potentially leading to epiphanies and palliatives, but because he has smoked the joint so hard he burned his lip.

"Ow. Shit."

He is only partially right. Los Angeles certainly breeds this sort of introspection. Peruse your local bookstore and you'll see that the shelves are pregnant with advice for the lost and self-absorbed. In any neighborhood there will a mushroom-like infestation of yoga studios, replete with sanctimonious undercurrents of spiritual peace. A trip to Whole Foods, a corporate behemoth mutant born of a tiny well-intentioned Texas store in 1980, will convince the uninitiated of the danger of an unexamined diet, and raises food shopping to the plateau of survival therapy.

However, I am no more than everyman, and I defend myself from Van's accusation of exaggerated conceits. It's just that it has become self-evident to me that doom waits around every corner, patiently picking at his toenails, which, in my imagining, are long and filthy.

We are sitting in my modest wood-frame stilt house in the Hollywood Hills, the "D" of the Hollywood sign looming in the window. Visitors find it glamorous. For me it now stands for Dread, Death, Doom, Destruction, Desperation, Disorder, Dire, Disaster, Disease, Dreck. The sign used to read "Hollywoodland" in the 1920s. It was a real-estate gimmick to attract house buyers, leading to the great irony that this hillside icon of global entertainment was born of crass commercial hucksterism, now a self-fulfilled prophecy.

It is dusk and Van is visiting because he wants to smoke a joint, a pleasure in which I now rarely indulge, given that its effect on me has morphed from all-purpose fun house to soporific, which I take to be a function of aging. Van's girlfriend disapproves, believing it to be his way of escaping the mandates and sacrifices of a relationship, so he occasionally skulks up to my house like a teenager to feed his guilty pleasure.

He picks up a guitar, a number of which are strewn around my house, testament to stoned and forgetful musicians who have passed through over the years. He starts noodling, ricocheting vaguely related chords off each other until he finds a sizzling 8-bar groove. It is a basic minor I IV II V pattern, but with each chord spiced with unusual altered notes.

"Cool." We still talk like this.

"Get your horn."

I go and grab my antique alto and slot in, pushing away cobwebs and distractions until I have sliced a simple but damning melody through the groove.

"Cool," he says.

"Very cool," I respond. This is all said without any hint of irony.

We continue in this way for a while until the moment fades. Which, I have discovered over many years as a nearly musician, it always does.

"We should make a CD," he says, rolling another.

"What era do you live in? No one listens to CDs anymore."

"Ah, right. We should post a video to YouTube."

"Uh huh. Looked in the mirror lately?"

"Ah, right. Aren't there any music sites that we can download stuff to?"

"We do covers, remember?"

"Ah, right."

He thinks for a minute.

"Why can't we download our covers?"

"I'm not sure anyone will listen to them. Besides, I'm sure we will have to pay someone for something. Isn't there a royalty issue?"

"Why don't we compose some stuff?"

"Because the passion has died."

"Ah, shit. Forget it."

"OK."

Being a once-upon-a-time nearly successful musician over forty has its simplicities.

CHAPTER 3

MY FAVORITE FICTIONAL character, *Catch-22*'s Yossarian, was filled with dread. The Germans wanted to kill him. That's why he didn't want to go on another bombing run. The fact that they wanted to kill everyone else was irrelevant. They still wanted to kill *him*. Fucking luxury, being able to define your dread with such precision. I should be so lucky.

Krystal, my soon-to-be ex-girlfriend, has grown tired of my doom-laden prognostications. This is a great pity. She used to find me funny, smart, perceptive, unusual. But unusual slowly morphed to oh-please-get-a-life.

We are sitting in my living room. When I met Krystal, she swept me off my feet. Taller than me (a good thing, I thought—any girl untainted by my stature must be able to see into my soul, which I imagined to be far taller than I was). We were at a bar on Western. The Dresden Room. She was drunk. I was drunker. I was at the bar, alone, musing, a hopeful ruminant, waiting for a chance to unleash my charm. She sat down next to me. It was Monday, there were plenty of other seats. She looked amused. I tried my luck.

"You're smiling. Lend me your smile."

"Fuck you, you piece of shit, don't you dare hit on me just because I choose this seat. I like this seat. It has nothing to do with you."

But she was smiling.

And our little flirtation was a marvel of clever banter out of a 1930s movie—parry, thrust, imply, innuend, insinuate, euphemize. She made me feel smart. I made her feel smart.

"So why are you smiling?"

"Because my boyfriend just left me."

"And this is amusing?"

"You should have heard his exit speech."

"Yeah?"

"He said, 'It's not you, it's me.' He actually said that—with a straight face and an earnest little frown around his stupid hairy eyebrows."

"That's pretty funny."

"That's what I thought. Buy me a drink, before it stops being funny."

"First you have to comment on my eyebrows. Nobody else has ever done that."

"They look like question marks."

"Uh huh. What typeface?"

"Sans serif."

"French eyebrows?"

"No, honest eyebrows, without unnecessary flourish."

So it went.

And she came home with me and has not moved out since. It never did get any better than that night. Instead, slowly, it got worse, the initial sparkle shedding its light slowly, slowly, in drabs and stutters, like embers in a dying wind, until we were habit, and now we are bad habit.

But even habits have function. The sex is great, no matter that its frequency has diminished to a faint pulse, like a distant celestial body. She still looks good. She still talks smart. She remains tall and imposing. She just doesn't seem to like me much anymore, and I smart under the indignity of it.

Did I ever like her? Hard to tell. I enjoyed her company—she made me laugh, I suppose. Tickled the intellect. Made me work at sounding smart. Not the same thing as liking her. And light-years from loving.

Who is she, I wonder. The girl who rode her height and confidence and eloquence to lonely triumph at high school, scaring the crap out of football players, whose easy access to local celebrity did not require challenge of the tongue.

So we sit in the living room, at noon on a Sunday, eating pasta and pesto and drinking shitty wine. We think of something to say, fail, so we stare out of the window, trying to ignore the "D."

"How is Innocent?" she asks, after the silence thunders.

Innocent is my son from my first marriage. He arrived unplanned when I was way too young. My then girlfriend, Grace, was a Zimbabwean who—like many of her white compatriots— had to flee her family's farm when Mugabe's henchmen went from merely menacing to beating her dog to death and cooking it. She ended up in LA.

Grace was also too young and she named him Innocent because it is apparently quite a popular name among Zimbabwe's rural people. This may be a good idea in the Zimbabwean hinterlands. Not such a good idea in LA, where he rebelled against his name, eschewing innocence in favor of everything but. Grace and I got married, but that lasted no more than a year. She was good with him, though. She did not rebel against her name. I should have tried harder with her. Ah well. We are all young and foolish for a time, some of us for longer than others.

Innocent is now in his early twenties and has emerged from the trauma of his name a wiser and stronger man. He was born with my ear for harmony. When he was about twelve, and I was finally resigned to the fact that I was not likely to make a living as a musician, let alone ride the supernovae of celebrity (those damn odds again), I once snuck him into a club at which I was playing. I think it was Cherokee, off one of the Boulevard side streets in Hollywood. It was a studied dive, with muted lighting and black paint and mismatched furniture determined to advertise its street cred, in stark contrast to the high-flying dreams of its hopeful young denizens. We had a strange little band, a mash of Dixie and funk, with enough chord changes to keep me focused. I had already given up on trying to play bebop licks, it was not in my blood, and I had wasted years trying to be Charlie Parker-derivative, to sound intelligible on "Giant Steps" and "Scrapple from the Apple." Still, I wanted my lines to move smoothly from chord to chord, wanted to sound like I was composing, not improvising.

Innocent watched me intently from the inconspicuous corner table where I had hidden him. At six he understood the structure of the twelve-bar blues, at eight he was experimenting with altered chords on the piano. At ten he could hear things that I never would. Part of his general rebellion against his name and the parents who bestowed it on him was disinterest in ever becoming a professional musician, a circumstance for which I am eternally grateful.

I finished the set and sat down with him.

"What did you think?"

"You're trying too hard, Dad."

"The hell you say."

"You're trying to play right. Just play easy."

The little tyke had me.

At UCLA, when I was a bright-eyed and freshly minted BS graduate migrating to a Master's program, I had become interested in the study of Artificial Intelligence, and specifically the omnipotent mind-machine that sits inconspicuously behind acts of creativity, whispering instructions so quietly that the protagonist doesn't even register them. I was aided by a very short, very fat, very old Frenchman, a longtime professor of Computer Science, a Holocaust child, an intellect of breathtaking dimensions.

"Do you believe in God?" he asked me when I sought him out as an adviser for my Master's dissertation.

"No, I don't think so."

"A question of a belief does not allow a 'don't-think-so' answer. If you are not sure, then you believe in God."

"I don't believe in God."

"Are you sure?"

"Yes, why?"

"Because the study of Artificial Intelligence presupposes that we can analyze the very essence of what it is to be human, learning, empathy, emotion, creativity. And it presupposes that we can reduce it to algorithms. And it presupposes that we can code these algorithms and, ultimately, create a species superior to ourselves. If this bothers you, go to Professor Ixtapa and study Database Design."

So I tried to find out what it was about Diana Krall that made me weep. What it was about Tatum, Peterson, Davis, Fisher, Brecker, Pass, Ellington, Marsalis and Norah Jones and Dixie Dregs and Sting and Steely Dan and Quincy Jones arrangements and Bach and Mozart and Stravinsky and Chopin and myriad unheralded singers and guitarists in all the end-of-the-line bars in Las Vegas and Lubbock and Albany that tore me to shreds, that made the universe larger, more filled with wonder.

Which led me to a set of algorithms. Underpinned by probabilities. This note with that chord played with this degree of prior proximal rhythmic repetition and preceded by this or that is less or more likely to be boring, dissonant, tense, expectant, unresolved. I set values on these, fine-tuned, created secondary relationships with intervals, pitches, relative keys, tritone substitutions, altered chords, vocal limitations. And produced, well, a kind of music, somewhat otherworldly, but haunting. Even real. And correct, composed within the boundaries of hundreds of years of classical, jazz, and popular music academia.

It never made me weep. But I suspect that if I had kept at it, it may have, one day.

It was enough, though. I published a paper in the journal of the American Association for Artificial Intelligence Press. My one and only. Now framed and on my wall. A testament to peaking too early. A great sax player would not have known what the hell I was talking about, nor would he have cared. And when I played, the algorithms interfered. Don't play right, play easy, the boy said. Nailing me to the wall.

Still, there were things he didn't realize, perhaps even now. Playing on a stage for people was never that pure for me. Nobody, except for Brecker, perhaps, who would never come, nobody would ever have the faintest idea whether I played a good solo or a bad one. Wouldn't notice if I played a bum note, or even if I played in the wrong key.

Listen, listen, I would silently plead. Listen to how clever these notes are. Did you hear what I just did with that note over this chord? How I set up the tension and resolution? How I left a question mark at that end of the phrase? Aren't you all just stunned into mute admiration? No, nobody gives a fuck. You are all looking to drink and forget, to get laid, to find love, to make the score, to beat the odds, to be heard. To be noticed.

As was I. As am I.

I look at Krystal's face, a long composition of thin straight lines, all of which I have often seen conspire to rearrange themselves into sharp distaste.

"Innocent is fine, thank you."

Another silence repeats like an echo.

"So, Meyer . . ."

"Yup?"

"Remember that thing?"

"What thing?"

"With the silk scarves?"

The thing with the silk scarves. That was long ago. But not that long ago to forget the heat of it. She liked soft restraint then. She doesn't like much of anything now.

"Uh, yes I do."

"Want to try and push it?"

I feel a spike in blood pressure. A surge of blood to familiar places. She continues.

"I'm thinking we add rubber bands and a candle. A thick one."

Rubber bands and a thick candle.

"What do you mean rubber bands and a thick candle?"

Her eyebrows swish up and down, like a sigh. Then she stands and walks up to the bedroom, raising her skirt to reveal an uncovered butt cheek.

Fuck. I am just a pawn in a complex chess game. Love has nothing to do with it.

I follow like a brainless supplicant.

CHAPTER 4

I AM SITTING in the boardroom of the company for which I work, the company that makes stuff. It is a big boardroom with an oval table that shines and stretches almost to the horizon. There is large expensive-looking art on the wall, peering on in mute disbelief at what transpires here.

The CEO walks in. Everyone stands, so I do too. He stops when he sees me.

"Good morning, Mr. Meyer, why are you here?" the CEO asks. The same question every damn time.

"I was invited, sir." He hates it when I call him sir, I think. Or maybe he likes it.

"Why?"

"I don't know, sir."

He turns to one of his executive sycophants. "Why is he here?" At this point I have morphed from Mr. Meyer to a distasteful object in his boardroom.

"We are going to be talking about how to leverage social networking for enterprise marketing. Meyer may have some input—he understands this stuff," the fat fuck COO offers.

Leverage social networking for enterprise marketing. Anybody who uses that phrase should have an iPhone shoved up his ass. Generally, these meetings are very long, with a signal-to-noise ratio of about 1:10. So they are generally ten times longer than they could be. Most of the time is spent on slavish and verbose agreement with the CEO, or the CEO offering other people's good ideas as his own, or the CEO offering the most stupid and irrelevant and loquacious of ignorant opinions, or the CEO shrieking and yelling at somebody.

And Krystal wants to know why I am not ambitious enough to climb up to the corporate suite.

I have been at the big company that makes stuff for fifteen years. In this day and age of career-zigzagging and job-hopping, this makes me somewhat unique. And quite valuable to the company, being a rare recipient of fifteen years of institutional knowledge, particularly in the arcane processes that govern the complex information paths that are taken from making stuff to getting it to the people who buy stuff.

Along the way, there have been a number of attempts to interest me in taking management roles. Had I acceded to the whims of earnest and well-meaning HR professionals, it's likely I would have been at the top by now, sitting on all manner of committees and boards and eating at fine restaurants. But I didn't want to. Not my game. Krystal, no doubt, would put it down to lack of ambition. I, of course, put it down to a need for a stress-free life so that I can pursue other plans. Originally it was music, but as that tailed off into melancholy resignation and semi-retirement, I have replaced it with others. Which are going to come into focus any day now.

So anyway, my extended tenure here sometimes results in invitations to sit in meetings of the bigwigs, who will occasionally look stupid and turn to me for some wisdom about *processes* or *IM governance*, or *work flow*, or *new media trends*. Mostly I am silent, though, a witness to the crushing boredom of long meetings, and the sad state of American corporate leadership. And it is through this occasional privilege that I have gotten to know the CEO. He is an abrasive, vitriolic, spitting, angry, arrogant, vituperative, friendless, dictatorial, talentless piece of shit who should be put in stocks and drawn and quartered by cackling employees.

OK, maybe not talentless; the company does, after all, make lots of money. But the world, on average, would be a better place if he was locked in a dark hole for the rest of his life. This is a guy who likes making waitresses cry, which I have seen firsthand.

"Waitress. WAITRESS! Did I or did I not ask for medium rare?"

"Yes, sir."

"Does this look like medium rare? Do you have eye problems?"

"I will have it put back in the grill, sir."

"How many university degrees do you need to be a waitress? None that I can think of. Therefore, I conclude that it takes little or no skill to get an order right. It is the only requirement of your job. How is it possible to fuck it up?"

"I am sorry, sir."

"No, I don't think you are. Do you know who I am? If you worked for me I would have you frog-marched to the door because you would be useless to the enterprise. Do you understand? Do you hear me or are your ears as bad as your eyes?"

This was at a "morale booster" dinner, organized by the Human

Resources people. No one really wanted to be there. I watched the waitress's eyes start filling with tears and the sycophant executive committee stare into their salads.

I leapt across the table, shoved my fingers into the CEO's nostrils, and ripped his nose off.

No, actually, I stared into my salad. That's what you do if you have a high-paying job. You compromise. You sacrifice. You bring home the paycheck. You hope that your children never get to witness your cowardice.

Van has no sympathy.

"Why don't you just hit him?"

Van is a big guy. He has never hit anyone. He likes to think that it is a simple matter. Also, he has never worked a day in his life. He is a trust-fund baby, somehow connected to the Velcro fortune, or maybe it's the earbud fortune, I forget. So the prospect of losing a good job has no emotional resonance for him.

I, on the other hand, am not a big guy, but I have hit plenty of people. Almost all of them have hit me back harder. Except for the kid with the broken leg at grade school who I knew couldn't catch me.

"Van, he is a big guy, he works out and he owns a Maserati."

"So what?"

"Any guy who owns a Maserati can beat up anyone who doesn't. It's just a natural law."

"Horseshit."

"Besides, he would sue me so hard, he would impoverish my entire extended family. Perhaps my entire tribe."

"You can't impoverish all the Jews in the world. Even if you own a Maserati."

"Yeah, maybe. But I would probably end up in jail for aggravated assault or something."

"I will bail you out."

"Yes, but not before my sweet white butt has been raped by a big black guy. Or worse, a white biker gang."

"So you're just going to suck it up?"

"I guess."

Van is a simple man. He reads and plays guitar and doesn't spend much of his money. He tries to fend off the incessant attacks of his ever-vigilant neo-feminist girlfriend, Marion, who secretly believes that he has the makings of a closet misogynist wife-beater, which doesn't prevent her from insisting on proposal ultimatums, which he ignores. He plays guitar well. We have been playing together for twenty years. Great sense of rhythm. Great composer. Terrible soloist, so he doesn't even try. No stage presence. Leaves that to me and the others. He has a keen ethical sense of right and wrong.

"We should have him killed," he offers.

"Nah, been there, done that."

"Who did you kill?"

"The beast within."

"Then you must steal the thing that he loves."

"What's that?"

"His money."

Not a bad idea.

How did I get here, to this point? The trajectory of my life fills me with fucking dread.

CHAPTER 5

DREAD CAN BE wrestled to the ground. It is a quiet portent, full of vague menace. It can be exiled to dark corners of the mind, where its dull moans and thumps can be barely heard. It is manageable. But once it breaks free, once dread morphs into the sharp incarnation of its promise, beware.

Bunny, my ex-wife most recent, calls. Her voice is raw. "Meyer, Isobel never turned up at school today. They just called. Is she with you?"

Like most people I know, she calls me by my last name. This strange appellation now seems disrespectful. My beautiful daughter is kidnapped, dead, raped, tortured, overdosed, drowned, run over, smoking meth with people with black teeth. Why the hell is she calling me by my last name?

"What do you mean she didn't turn up at school?"

"I dropped her at the bus stop. She didn't turn up at school."

"You dropped her at a FUCKING BUS STOP? ARE YOU KIDDING ME?"

"Meyer, calm down. I have been dropping her at the bus stop for two years. I am sure there is a simple explanation."

"THERE ARE NO SIMPLE EXPLANATIONS. SHE DIDN'T ARRIVE AT SCHOOL. THERE ARE ONLY COMPLEX EXPLANATIONS."

"If you don't stop shouting I am going to hang up."

I pull the phone away from my ear. Stare at it. Breathe deeply.

"OK, what do we do?"

"I have already called the police. They are not that interested unless a child has been missing for twenty-four hours."

"WHAT DO MEAN THEY ARE NOT THAT INTERESTED?"

"Meyer, I am giving you one more chance."

OK, dread. You win. You took my daughter, leaving me to a life of misery and regret, possibly to self-hate and suicide, a painful one. Swallowing caustic soda. Self-immolation in front of some awful country's embassy (yeah, that'll help). Drug addiction and overdose. Cirrhosis of the liver from booze. Finding Jesus and thanking him for the excellence of God's plan.

This is not amusing. I start hyperventilating. I sit.

"Meyer, are you there?"

"What do we do?"

"Let me call some of the moms. Maybe she's playing truant with a friend."

"She doesn't play truant. She doesn't smoke. She doesn't lie. She doesn't do this stuff."

"She's fourteen. You have no idea what a fourteen-year-old girl does or doesn't do. Neither do I."

"Fuck. What does the school say?"

"They think she is playing truant. Notwithstanding nearly five years of perfect attendance."

"OK. OK. OK. Let's think. Bunny, you make the calls to the moms. I am going to drive around near the bus stop. Where is the bus stop?"

"Pico and Lincoln."

"OK, call me or I'll call you."

I hang up. It was always going to come to this. A wise man once told me that a life without tragedy is a life well lived. How does one avoid tragedy? It's the fucking probabilities again. You can't control them. It decides to visit or it doesn't. It's the mother of black swans. An unlikely event at the extreme end of the bell curve tail, whose consequences are a lifetime of sadness and horror, undiminished by the passing of time. And it can start with a simple phone call, a passing of information. Small sentences suffice. "She's missing." "There was an accident." "It's about your daughter, your son, your mother." "I am sorry to inform you." "I got the test results back." Here it is then, the great divide between one life and another, announced to me by an ex-wife on the phone. I am rooted to the spot. I can't move. I can't breathe.

The phone rings again.

"Meyer?" It is Krystal.

"Krystal. We've got a problem. Isobel's been kidnapped."

"What in the world are you talking about? She's with me. She just turned up at my office. She's fine. Didn't want to go to school."

"ARE YOU FUCKING KIDDING ME? PUT HER ON."

"No. She is crying, and you are just going to rip her face off."

There are tears rolling down my cheeks. I am as happy as I can ever remember.

"OK. OK. Fuck. Sorry for cussing. I just died a few deaths. Why is she upset?"

"She was cyberbullied."

"Cyberbullied?"

"Yes."

"Krystal, don't move. I'm coming to pick her up. Don't let her out of your sight."

I call Bunny. She is more angry than relieved. I tell her to hang tight—I'll drop Isobel off later.

Cyberbullying. Strangers are being nasty to my little girl, and I will find them and hurt them. I will beat them to the ground with hard objects and snap their vicious little spines, so that they spend the rest of their miserable lives eating through a straw and contemplating their cruelty to my baby.

Cyberbullying. What the fuck? Before all of this, before the stuff from which I earn my keep insinuated itself on the march of civilization. Before communication leapt from its primitive perch into a wild tumult of options. Before the Cambrian explosion of networks and devices and email and tweets and statuses and digital bulletin boards and texts and VoIP and video chats. Before that, you knew your bully. There he was standing in the schoolyard, in your face, his ugly eyelash-less pig eyes bulging as he roared with menace and spittle, "Fucking Jew, you want to go a round with me, momma's boy, huh? Huh?"

Then it was simple. Reptilian brain decision, a binary option, fight or flight. And only three outcomes. If you fought, you won or lost. Worst-case scenario was the hospital for a stitch or two.

If you didn't, then you were toast. A wuss, coward, lower than sharkshit slime. You retreated into silent corners to congratulate yourself on your wisdom, your moral height, while trying hard to avoid the stares of contempt and disgust from your peers.

But you knew your bully.

Now Isobel has had her dignity stripped by faceless beasts, impugning her reputation, spreading lies and rumors, posting image-processed pictures of her head on porno stars' spread-eagled bodies. They have savaged her, an innocent, with damage, possibly irretrievable, instantaneously spread to hundreds of thousands, maybe millions, of cackling teenagers, their lust for victims and scapegoats insatiable.

"Honey, I'll find out who did this. This is my business. There are technologies that can track—"

"I know who did it, Dad. It was Cheryl."

"As in Cheryl, your best friend?"

"My ex-best friend."

"How do you know?"

"She put a message on her Facebook status."

"Saying what?

"Saying I'm a slut."

Oops. The gray and angry masses of anonymous cyberbullies disintegrate. I love technology, such a boon to humanity. A slut. The queen of schoolgirl insults since the dawn of time. Call a girl fat, ugly, stupid, nerdy—they all sting. Call her a slut, and it is ruinous. Interesting thought, though. Could it be that some of these girls are having sex already? Surely not, says the dad. You're naive, say the stats. Surely not my daughter. Surely not with enough frequency or recklessness to be called a slut. Surely not.

"Cheryl called her a slut?"

Bunny is fuming. I remember her outrage well. Usually directed at me. Usually with cause. Although sometimes not.

"So it seems." I am treading lightly here. This is not my core competence, females accusing each other of sexual indiscretions, even if they are fourteen.

"Cheryl's the damn slut, not Isobel."

"Ah."

"I've heard things."

"Ah."

"Bad things."

"Ah."

"Is that your total contribution?" Her tone is a warning. I know it well.

"Uh . . . what things?"

"Cheryl. Dark corners. Blow jobs."

"I don't think I want to hear this."

"And drugs too, hard ones."

"Aaaargh. I am covering my ears now."

I sing for a while into the phone. Loudly.

"Bunny, you still there?"

"What are you, nine?"

"Who told you?"

"Isobel."

"So Isobel tells you that her best friend is giving blow jobs and shooting crystal meth, and calls her a slut on Facebook. Sounds to me like we should stay out of this."

"Meyer, you really don't understand anything, do you?"

"No, not really."

Not at all.

CHAPTER 6

"WHAT THE HELL do you know anyway?"

I am asking this important question of Farzad twenty-four hours after my daughter scared me to death, which is approximately how long it has taken for my heart rate to settle. We are sitting in a café on a Saturday morning on the Venice boardwalk. Which has, of late, become so upscale you would think you were in the middle of an ersatz film set, if it wasn't for the fact that the hundreds of homeless people populating the grassy verges are not extras. The palm trees, rollerbladers, and sunny Pacific beach backdrop make me want to do something inappropriate, vulgar. But it's just a thought.

Actually, Farzad knows a great deal. Although I don't want him to know I know. An Iranian immigrant, fled from the grand idiocies and brutalities of the theocratic revolution in Iran decades ago. Only to reach the USA and face the daily indignities of a swarthy skin and accent and obvious Al Qaeda–bestowed American-hating name. Actually, Farzad and Innocent could swap notes about appellation and identity. He is a Harvard-trained psychologist, ministering to foreigners and immigrants who failed to find the American dream. I met him in a laundromat in Boston when I briefly attended Berklee, trying to kick-start my jazz career. He gave me a quarter for the dryer because I was skint. This endeared him to me for life.

"I know many things, Jew."

Farzad is allowed to say that to me. I don't know why.

"All you know is how to say 'there, there' to swarthy immigrants from medieval autocracies who still believe in beating their wives."

"Perhaps, but if you think you have the lock on dread, my Semitic friend, you are wrong. It is the human condition du jour."

"Yeah? Well fuck you, my dread is unique, and far more refined than that of your idiot patients."

"Au contraire, my beloved Hebrew."

"Stop with the French, you fucking towelhead. It doesn't fool anyone."

"You are an ignoramus, Lansky, I am a Persian, not an Arab. We do not wear headgear."

"You are in the US now. All people east of Spain and south of Gibraltar are known as towelheads. This is taught to us by Fox News. Didn't you learn anything at Harvard?"

"I was not studying Geography, Metro Goldwyn."

"Wait. Have you read Joseph Heller?

"Who is he?"

"You're kidding."

"I never kid, Cohen."

"That's his gag."

"What gag?"

"Calling a Jew by any old Jewish last name. Haven't you read Heller's *Good as Gold*?"

"I do not do that, I call everyone by their correct names. I am a doctor. And who is Heller?"

A particularly statuesque specimen of bikini-clad California womanhood drifts by on wheels, blonde hair trailing behind her, various tanned muscles peristaltically undulating for us. The tiny white hairs on her legs give her skin a glint sheen, like a seal. We maintain a respectful silence until she passes.

"That's what I mean, Farzad."

"What?"

"That girl. She will never, ever notice me."

"Why should she? You are twenty years older than she is. She is also beautiful, while you are, how shall I say . . . ?"

"Exactly my point. This is what I mean by dread."

"What exactly?"

"That's the problem with dread. It coats everything. Especially her. Or rather the fact that she will never, ever notice me."

Farzad is a deeply wise man—on rare occasions when I can get him to take me seriously. A sage really. He is also married to a woman who looks just like the rollerblader, a fact that has always left me uncharitably short on generosity toward his views on women. A deep racist strain rears its ugly head when I see them together. Swarthy ethnic heathens stealing our blonde women.

"Farzad, I want you to take me seriously."

His head is swiveled around like Linda Blair in *The Exorcist* as he sucks in a last sight of her glowing buttocks as she disappears. I am looking at the back of his head. He turns around.

"You want me to take you seriously?

"Yes."

"Seriously?"

"Yes."

"OK, Meyer. What is troubling you?"

"Dread."

"I would not take it too seriously. It is very fashionable now."

"See? You don't take me seriously."

The waitress arrives to take our order. She has skin the color of a peach sunset. I want to lick her face, while simultaneously avoiding the metalwork in her nostril, lip, ear, eyebrow, and tongue.

"Good morning, young lady. This is my friend, Meyer. Would you say he is dreadful?"

She looks at me, and then back at Farzad, confused.

"Uh . . . no. I guess."

Farzad slams his palm down on the table.

"There. I told you there wasn't a problem."

I glare at him, and order a burger. Studface retreats. I glare some more.

"OK. OK. Meyer. Stop being such a crank. Here is what it is, my little Christ-killer. My patients, many of them, have seen horrors that you cannot even imagine. The lucky ones have lost or left everything: money, home, culture, loved ones, hopes, ambitions. And have washed up on these fine democratic shores through good fortune or bribing or cheating or begging or desperation or the graces of our do-gooders in government. And most of them live sad lives of deep melancholia, depression, and ungoverned and undirected anger, asking themselves every day, why me? The unlucky ones have had their children tortured in front of them, been forced to rape their daughters on videotape, have had their extremities amputated. And for these people, melancholia is not enough. To this they must add guilt, the sort of guilt for which I can offer only platitudes as a poor substitute for healing. These people understand dread. It is not a subject for conversation at the beach. It is a living thing for them, weighted like lead. So that breathing and walking and eating and living is a task of onerous dimensions, requiring great courage and pain. They do not talk of dread; they are its living incarnations, walking ghosts of tragedy.

"And then there are other patients—people much like you— born in the land of the free, every waking moment since you were born awash with opportunities and rainbows and hope. And somehow, you conspire to summon up dread, to incarnate darkness and despair against all odds. Why is this, I ask? Why does my friend Meyer feel dread? The gods that dispense mental health and illness are fickle, smiting even the most unlikely of candidates. Like you. With delightful children and friends and a great job and some creative talent and relative youth and health and, it pains me to say, some intelligence. Why then, does my friend Meyer feel dread?"

"It's because—"

"Shut up, I'm not finished."

He does this a lot, Farzad. Shuts me up. I assume it is an Iranian thing. I find it endearing, in an irritating sort of way. He continues.

"It is because the world has changed. The opportunities for our undoing have proliferated explosively, even comically. Not too

long ago we lived in a time when we feared cancer and car accidents and upset stomachs. Now every event on the planet is
massively intertwined, chaotically bound by laws and relationships no one understands, conspiring to hurt us, kill us, rob us,
diminish us. Nuclear-armed Iran and Korea, climate change,
meteors, microbiological plagues, irradiated Japanese fish, Internet pedophiles, irrational dictators with chemical stores, deranged
individuals with explosive belts filled with nails, irrevocably
addictive drugs, metastasized financial systems gorging on hard-
earned citizens' money, ubiquitous and friendly technology that
strips us of our privacy, religious fundamentalists from the Dark
Ages armed with hate and bile.

"I could go on, Meyer, but here is my diagnosis. You are full of
dread because it is the only mental condition that is appropriate
to the educated, well-read person. It is, in fact, the only healthy
response to the world around us. I congratulate you on your mental acuity and well-being."

He pops a fry into his mouth.

I stare at him.

"Why do you never take me seriously?"

He calls for the waitress. We will down a few beers today.

At least.

CHAPTER 7

THE WEEK PASSES slowly. I avoid the CEO and all my coworkers and bury my head in the opiate of bug-fixing, a demented cousin of software development that has always appealed to me in the same way that Sudoku enslaves otherwise perfectly reasonable people. The weekend approaches with a rush of possibilities. Escape beckons.

I feel like Richard Gere as Dr. T. Too many women in my life. Isobel, a teenager who will soon be too embarrassed to hug me. Krystal, my tone-deaf, soon-to-be ex-girlfriend, who thinks I am not ambitious enough. Bunny, mother of my daughter, who wants to get remarried, procuring a new father for Isobel in the bargain. Grace, mother of my son, who was better than me at the important stuff.

"Van, there are too many women in my life. Let's go away for the weekend."

"We're playing this weekend."

"Fuck the gig. We can tell them we got sick. Simultaneously. Ate the same irradiated Japanese sushi. We were rushed to the hospital in the same ambulance. Out of ICU, both stable. Back on stage next week."

I am at Van's house on Thursday night going through a new song with him. Van studiously ignores the temptations of his trust fund. It is a modest little cottage from the '20s near Silver Lake, the LA skyline clearly visible from his living room window. We don't rehearse much, but occasionally Van or I hear something that we want in the repertoire. The others just sort of rehearse when we play live, so it takes a few weeks to get it right. Of course, the audience doesn't know or care. This is a Piazzolla tango Van discovered. Soaked in tradition. Lots of minor flat 5ths and dominant flat 9ths. A melody of passion and loss.

"Nah."

"What do you mean 'nah?' You and I haven't been on a boys' weekend for ten years, Van."

"Wasn't much fun then either, if I remember correctly."

"You're not adventurous anymore."

"I never was."

"C'mon, we'll go to Vegas, cheat on our girlfriends."

"You never cheat on your girlfriends, Meyer."

"OK, you cheat on your girlfriend. I'll watch."

"*Marion* is my girlfriend, remember? She will have me followed. Then she will have me castrated. Broadcast the event on the Feminist Channel."

Marion doesn't like me. Thinks I am not politically motivated enough. Which I am not, of course. But then she clearly likes Van, who is even less politically motivated than me. Perhaps it had to do with the time I got into a drunken argument with her and called her a feminazi. Which wasn't inappropriate given that she had just defaced my latest issue of *The National Review*, which I only get because the previous right-wing owner of the house failed to send a change of address when he moved. Her defacing technique was unique, I will grant her that. She found the magazine in the little rack in the bathroom. She pissed on it and gave it to me, soaked.

"Van, why are you still with her?"

"She likes to be tied up and spanked."

"Really?"

"That's all I am giving you."

"So, no weekend romp then?"

"We have a gig."

The gig is a disaster. The drummer, Mike, a man of immense talent and immense drug intake, has taken it upon himself to lose his temper with the accordionist Tim, a man of immense talent and no drug intake. The reasons for his opprobrium are a bit opaque but, man, is he pissed off. He leaps off his kit on the last note of the last song of the set, and takes three long strides across the stage toward Tim, face red, upending his snare drum along the way.

"I WILL SHOVE THAT ACCORDION UP YOUR ASS."

Tim smiles, expecting a joke.

Mike's eyes bulge further. A couple of punters at the bar take notice.

"YOU DO NOT STAND UP IN FRONT OF MY BAND AND PLAY A PIECE OF SHIT SOLO LIKE THAT EVER AGAIN."

It is not, and has never been, his band, but I split hairs here. Tim looks at me. I shrug. Tim looks back at Mike.

"Huh?"

Mike, breathing and perspiring heavily, decides that further explanation is redundant, and lunges at him with a drumstick, apparently trying to stab him. Tim steps deftly aside and Mike loses his center of gravity, falling heavily into the PA system, causing irreparable damage to both his hand (which snags on a music stand and gets sliced open), and to the electronics, which hiss and die.

After the set, Van had disappeared into the alleyway for a cigarette. Upon hearing the ruckus, he sticks his head in from the exit door, sees Mike on the ground holding his bleeding hand, the upended snare drum, the smashed PA speaker. He blinks, poker-faced, and returns to the alleyway to finish his cigarette.

I walk over to Mike, who is lying on the stage, on his back. He looks like a flipped turtle.

"What's going on, Mike?"

"That little shit doesn't take his music seriously. He fucks around. He fucks me off."

"How fucked up are you, Mike?"

"Maybe a little bit."

"What?"

"What what?"

"You know what I'm asking, Mike."

"Crystal meth."

"Oh, wonderful."

"Shit. Shit. My hand is fucked. Can't play any more tonight, Meyer."

"Fuck you. I'm not paying you anything. Why can't you get stoned or drunk like a normal fuck-up?"

We finish the next set without him and without a PA. Unplugged. The chatter of the audience is many times louder than the instruments.

It is rather enjoyable.

After the gig, Van drives along Hollywood Boulevard, on our way to my house, where Krystal is probably asleep. She used to come to my gigs, sit at the bar, her eyes alight with promises of unspeakable bedroom acts as I played. Now she doesn't even bother. Her faded interest in my music is another nail in our relationship coffin. Back then, I looked to her like a fascinating and anguished artist, playing eclectic music with panache and passion. Now I suspect that I look like a pathetic has-been.

"So, Krystal is moving out."

"No shit? Why?"

"The music has died."

"Huh?"

Van lights a smoke.

"You OK with that?"

"No. Yes. I have no fucking idea."

"Time you settled down, Meyer. You're forty already. Ask her to marry you."

"No."

"Why?"

"She'll point out my failings until I die."

"Ah, right."

"And while you're calling the kettle black, why aren't you marrying Marion?"

"Trust-fund babies are not required to get married. It's in the Bill of Rights."

We are silent for a while.

"I would prefer it if she didn't move out right now."

"Why?"

"Dread, Van, dread. Not a good companion for being alone."

CHAPTER 8

I NEED TO pause here, develop some context. I am in danger of creating for myself an embarrassing midlife crisis. It's not that. It cannot be that, it is too much of a cliché. A midlife crisis, as dissected by countless movies and books and shrinks, happens when a man hits a certain age, beyond the blush of youth, beyond the rigors of adolescence, beyond first careers, love affairs, and marriages, and enters that part of life where the future is now less compelling than the past. Where possibilities are no longer endless, where the certainties of aging color and limit everything. Reactions to such existential realities generally range from affairs to divorce, from fast cars to drugs, from shedding careers to newfound spirituality.

Pah. That's not me, I tell myself. My problems are far more poetic than that. In fact, to be fair, I have no problems—at least not internal ones. I have issues, doubts, questions, bewilderments, resignations, bemusements, sure. But not problems. I am not concerned by my age, which is at the top of the roller coaster, heading downhill from here. Not concerned about the metaphysics of it all, the big questions—Why are we here? What's it all about?—and other such nonsense. Too much introspection on these matters can lead to early-onset depression, followed by dementia and death. Not to mention loss of libido. It's just my life, really, no need to go all Sartre about it.

No. My issues are more narrowly narcissistic than that. For instance, how come I don't stand up to the prick CEO? I like my job and all, but somebody has to do something about this guy. For instance, why can't I accept the end of Krystal? Why can I not stop worrying about my kids when the odds say everything will be fine? Why didn't I stay with Grace and build an uncomplicated life? Why did I marry Bunny, when we had nothing in common except sex? Why don't I marry Krystal and work on the things in my personality that irritate her? I refuse to see a psychologist because I do not consider myself in need of paid help; I mean, after all, I'm generally a functioning, happy individual, beset by the onset of justifiable dread.

Farzad would have all sorts of palliative advice, but he's my friend, so he can't charge me, so he is never going to give me the sort of quality expert advice that his paying clients get. He can offer amateur advice only, which by definition is bargain basement. This is an odd thought. Perhaps I should ask him for a four-week crash consultation for my next birthday. Wait. In normal circumstances, he might buy me a book for my birthday. Or a CD for my old car. This costs him, oh, about $15. Which would buy maybe five minutes of his time. Not even enough time to exchange a few good insults.

"Hi, Grace. It's Meyer."

I don't speak to Grace much. Occasional calls to swap stories and concerns about Innocent. An email exchange on birthdays and Christmas. She moved on easily after our fleeting little dalliance. She still lives in LA, but the size of this city can make a mere neighbor a foreigner. Having a child with someone like Grace creates the sort of bond that does not necessarily tie, but always connects. She brought Innocent up, while I did drugs and had late nights and bad relationships and tried to find the door to adulthood. She raised him despite the deprivations of single motherhood, the constant shortage of time and money, the competing calls for her attention from Innocent and work, the need to combat the loneliness of dependency. Innocent always came first. She triumphed in the mothering department. I tried to help where I could, but I was hopeless, bewildered, unskilled. She didn't need me.

In parenting there is only failure. That failure is simply a matter of degree. One can never do enough, never lay the perfect groundwork, never set the best moral foundation, never create an environmental hermetically sealed cocoon against the exigencies of a child's constant need for independence. It is an imperfect world, and within that I was an imperfect father.

"Hi, Meyer. What's up?"

I'm not sure why I am calling.

"I'm sorry."

"Huh?"

"I'm sorry."

"For what?"

"For not being better when Innocent was young. A better dad, I mean. I left you with the burden."

"Are you serious?"

"Yeah."

"Meyer, that was twenty years ago. It's history. Innocent is fine, I am fine. Apologies are not required, I assure you."

"Even so . . ."

"OK. How are you? How's Chrysalis?"

"Krystal."

"Right."

"She's fine. We're fine. No, wait. I am pretty sure she's moving out."

"Damn. I thought you were finally going to, you know, concretize your life?"

"Concretize my life? What am I, a building site? What the hell kind of word is that?"

She giggles. I love her giggle.

"I am about to get my PhD in Contemporary American Fiction. Weird words have crept into my vernacular. Sorry."

"Really? So quick?"

"Not that quick. Three years."

"Mazel tov. I'm proud of you."

"Thank you."

"You seeing anybody?"

"Sort of. Not really. None of your business actually."

"I fucked up with you, Grace. You were the one that got away."

"Nonsense. Nobody got away. We were kids. We made a mistake, Meyer."

"But we got Innocent."

"Yep, that we did."

"How's he doing?"

"Oh, you know. College boy. Hardly see him anymore. But he calls me every day."

"He calls you every day?"

"Yes."

"What does he tell you?"

"Got another A today. Love you, Mom, bye-bye."

"He tells you he loves you every day?"

"Has done for twenty years. At least since he could speak."

"Huh."

"D'you speak to him?"

"Every few weeks. He doesn't say, Love you, Dad."

"Gender thing. What do you speak about?"

"Stuff."

"What stuff?"

"Boys' stuff."

"Like what?"

"Sports. Politics. Girls. And music, of course."

"Since when is politics boys' stuff?"

"We should have lunch."

"Why? The last time we had lunch was about ten years ago."

"Um . . . no reason. Can't I have lunch with the mother of my son?"

"OK. You all right, Meyer?"

"Yes, mostly."

"Mostly?"

"I need to punch my CEO, and I can't."

"Why?"

"Because he'll fire me."

"No, why do you want to punch him?"

"His face irritates me."

"I see."

I spent years not really thinking about Grace, other than via the exigencies of our shared child-rearing activities. Then gradually and somewhat aligned to my recent onset of dread, I started thinking about her more and more. Perspective is difficult at the best of times, although perspective with the benefit of hindsight is a gentler hill to climb. Twenty years of plodding mediocrity has sharpened my recollection of our relationship, its colors and edges sharpened in ways that I might have missed at the time. As soon as I hang up, I am sorry—I should have talked longer, reminisced with wit and sparkle, been funnier, entertained her, impressed her, made her want to see me. My apology should have been more sincere, should have left some residue of future intent. She sounds so self-assured, so over me and our premature and barely remembered year of marriage. That hurts. Men are assholes about this. They expect they will always be missed. The truth is often inverse. I expect that if men rifle through all the women who have passed through their lives, from the onset of prepubescent romanticism onward, they would flagellate themselves at the memory of so many opportunities missed, misread, arrogantly ignored, or just plain fucked up. I have become increasingly convinced that Grace was all that and more.

I am sitting at my desk, in my little office. Which I guess is a privilege in this day of shared workspaces and business school–researched communal and collaborative business practices. My laptop is blinking at me. I hibernate it.

Bunny pops into my head. My ex-wife. Courted and married and impregnated when it seemed that settling and sustaining was the way to go. When it became obvious to me that I was becoming a loser and a prick. I met her at some activist event or other. Climate change or something. She was there to be active. I, having discovered the attractive gender ratio of left-wing causes, was there for the wine and the girls. Not to say I wasn't worried about the environment or global warming or tuna. I was. But I was also a lot more worried about other things. Like how not to end up bitter and alone. So I used these events as, well, dual-purpose hunting grounds—women and self-sanctimony. I met her at the bar, where I was onto my fifth cheap Chardonnay. She ordered a water. Tap water. Which stamped her bona fides as authentic. She saw through me immediately.

"So what do you think of his theory?" she asked.

The he in question was a famous Clinton-era science adviser.

"Um . . ."

"You haven't a clue, have you?"

"No, sorry. Is that bad?"

"Yes. Why are you here?"

"I'm interested."

"In what?"

"Well, right now in you."

That got me through the door. The rest was plain sailing. And she actually did drag me into her causes. They were good causes too. They still are. Doomed, of course, by realpolitik. But even intentions have value.

Good causes like these were a marker of social status. Not only did you contribute time and energy to causes that seemed, so, well, obviously upstanding, but you could make friends along the way, agree enthusiastically with each other, easily identify Satan's armies, and sleep with swell of breast. As for myself, my basically liberal bent was bruised and deformed by raging skepticism. I remember a presentation by a scientist who berated the earnest crowd for diluting their efforts. The Amazon, he said, the destruction of the Amazon outweighs all other warm and fuzzy causes by orders of magnitude, because if the destruction continues, we will have no oxygen. Be bold, he said, be realistic, prioritize your energies, turn away from lesser causes.

I suppose. But in the great maelstrom of competition and connivance for your time and money, even science gets damaged. Remember how AIDS was supposed to decimate Africa by 2015? The unraveling of the food chain because of various industrial food technologies? The end of energy? Whales, dolphins, tuna, rhinos, rents in the ozone layer, cloying mercury, electricity pylons, cell phones, pollution, global warming, genetic engineering? The Club of Rome, for fuck's sake?

Who has the time for all of this? Well, Bunny had time. My attitudes of doubt and cynicism and barely concealed boredom were utterly unpalatable to her, and unraveled the fabric of the marriage.

I am in a calling mood. I call Bunny at work, a verdant, predictably earnest environmental lobbying group. She doesn't like to get personal calls at work. Especially from ex-husbands who think Gaia is a stupid word.

"Hi, Bunny, it's Meyer. How's Isobel?"

"Fine. She's made up with Cheryl."

"You're kidding."

"She's fourteen. They make up easily. Me, I haven't made up with Cheryl. Little slut."

"Now look who's nine. How are you? How's work? Are we in danger of killing the planet yet?"

"Always. Why are you calling?"

"Besides Isobel, no reason."

"You know I can't talk at work."

"What sort of husband was I?"

"Really, Meyer? It's two p.m. on a Thursday."

"I thought I was a pretty good husband."

"OK, Meyer, what's up?"

"Just shooting the breeze."

"Sure you are."

"How's it going with whatsisname?"

"You know exactly what his name is."

"How's it going with fuckface?"

"OK, Meyer, goodbye."

"No, wait. Sorry. How's it going with your boyfriend, Daniel?"

"Fine, thank you. Why are you interested?"

"You can't marry him."

"I can do whatever I want."

"Mostly. But you can't marry him."

"Why not?"

"It will be confusing for Isobel."

"How so?"

"You know, two father figures and all."

"Nonsense, happens all the time. You're just scared she will bond with Daniel."

"Am not."

"Then what's the problem?"

"She is a nearly sexual young woman. We can't have a full-grown man walking around the house in his underwear. It could damage her."

"Bye, Meyer."

"Wait."

"Bye, Meyer."

CHAPTER 9

I GO OVER to Van's house to take a look at some new stuff we want to try out. We are starting to experiment with strange stuff—7/8 time signatures, songs based on nontraditional scales, reworked gypsy mash-ups of old pop songs. Most of it, I assume, unlikely to find favor with audiences. Never mind, it is fun to fuck around. Reminds me of being in the sandbox at nursery school when I was a tyke. You fuck around, and then you go home for a nap. If only life were so.

Marion arrives while we are playing, and pops her head into the bedroom-cum-studio we are using for the fuck-around.

"Hey, Marion."

She looks sourly at me, but manages a thin smile. "Tea?"

It is a tiny olive branch in a small war that we have never declared. Only the very question deserves its own bitch slap; only pseudo-intellectual Anglophiles offer tea. This is America, for God's sake—we don't drink tea, we drink coffee. I realize that I have completely unreasonable enmity toward Marion, but it is mainly because she does not like me, and I have thin skin about that. She retreats without saying a word to Van, which he doesn't seem to notice.

"Van, I need to ask you something. Seriously."

He puts down his guitar, and looks at me apprehensively.

"I smoked a doobie earlier, I don't do serious. Even if I hadn't smoked a doobie, I don't do serious."

"Why does Marion dislike me?"

"Um . . . what d'you mean?"

"Your girlfriend doesn't like me. And it's affecting our relationship."

"What relationship?"

"You and me."

"We don't have a relationship. We're men."

"Yeah, you're right. Fuck her."

"Hey, you can't talk about her that way."

"Why not?"

"I don't know. She's my girlfriend—I have her honor to protect."

"Oh, horseshit. You don't even like her that much."

"True, but even so . . ."

Van is a dark soul, with occasional pinpricks of light. These are, in order of priority, his friendship with me, music, and his disinterest in his trust fund. The dark part of his soul is impenetrable. I am rarely allowed in, except when we are under the influence of something, in which case he tends to open up, revealing all manner of colorful moving parts. He is the one person I know for whom drugs allow the better part of him through. When he is straight his face is placid, no emotion can be gleaned from the usual markers of lips, eyes, and eyebrows. He is startlingly handsome in a Johnny Depp sort of way, sort of angular and haunted and dangerously sexual. He is also tall and broad shouldered and athletic looking, graced by the munificence of good genes. I know this because he has never as much as raised a sweat in all the years I have known him.

He talks little about his life before we connected, but I have met his fabulously rich parents a few times. They came into the club once, clapped enthusiastically at his solos, greeted the band politely. I couldn't fault them. They were sweet and interested in me. They disturbed my preconceptions of the superrich. Even their house, perched in the Holmby Hills and nestled among ostentation and excess, is understated and tasteful. I once asked him about his upbringing, hoping to excavate terrible dysfunction—incest, abuse, neglect.

"So what was life in Holmby Hills like? I mean growing up?"

"It was OK, I guess."

"Thanks, Van, I'm much more informed now. Give me something I can work with."

But he didn't. He remains, even now, a small riddle, with only occasional hints as to the answers that may be his core. We all hide parts of ourselves, I suppose. Not necessarily out of shame, but simply for the joy of privacy. Some more than others. Van is the most private of men. He is my best friend, and I try to take him as he comes.

I press. "But why doesn't she like me? She makes it obvious."

At that moment, Marion arrives with a tray of tea. With scones and jam, for fuck's sake.

"I heard that, Meyer. What makes you think I don't like you?"

"Signs and semaphores, Marion. I have a degree in those."

"I wouldn't go as far as to say I don't like you, but you are a typical misogynist."

I feel my hackles rise. "Is that a fact?"

"Yes."

"How so?"

"You have a history of many failed relationships and superficial sex. You are a serial philanderer. I don't trust you."

"Do you trust women who have a history of many men?"

"That happens less frequently, but yes I do. Sexual politics gives them a greater right."

This conversation is on the edge of rapid expansion, like a science lab experiment that will surely end in an explosion. I weigh up the options. Sarcasm. Reasoned debate. Complete surrender. Spirited defense. Insult.

"Maybe we should have a threesome after tea."

She stares at me dully and retreats. My brand of humor has never quite gelled with her.

"Thanks for the tea, Marion," I say to her retreating form.

She probably has a point. No need to be impolite.

Van and I head up to the Beachwood Cafe for lunch. It is a landmark lunch restaurant, perched halfway up the canyon. Those people below the café are almost exclusively apartment renters, those above are generally homeowners, among them residing some of the feted and famous. The restaurant acts as a metaphorical fulcrum, on any given day feeding both the aspirant and the arrived, the scrabblers and the players. The waitresses have been there for decades, their faces now weathered, their dreams dulled in the cast of their eyes. The clientele is the story of Hollywood, if not America, if not the whole Western world.

The menu is quaintly old-fashioned; I suspect it has not changed since the days when studios actually made movies instead of out-sourcing them. We order the special, meat loaf.

"So, Van, what's the story with Marion?"

"Haven't we just had this conversation?"

"Yeah, but I am soon to be single and you owe it to me to break up with her so that we can be her imagined philanderers."

"No."

"Why? And don't tell me about the sex."

"I dunno. We don't argue. We like the same movies. We don't have many friends. I still find her attractive. She doesn't really want my money. She wants sex about as often as I do. What more do I need?"

"How often?"

"What, sex?"

"Yeah."

"Often enough. We don't break records. When the mood strikes."

"You're not going to give me any more, are you?

"No."

At that moment, one Astor Grand walks in. I haven't seen him in ten years. At the time he was the top keyboard player in LA, most in demand in the studio and onstage, supporting everybody who was anybody. He had his own band too, made up of studio luminaries hungry for the chance to stretch in front of an audience without charts and headphones and producers and divas. Every time they did a gig, which was never advertised, the who's who of the muso world turned up.

He looks shocking, aged, beaten. The lush hair has thinned to a malnourished colorless fuzz, his skin sallow, and there is sag of tired skin below his chin. I call him over, he sits down.

"Astor, long time. How've you been?"

"Yeah, OK. I see you guys play weekends at The Beast Belly. I should come by."

"Anytime. Bring your ivories."

I glance at Van. He looks uncharacteristically openmouthed, shocked. He is obviously speechless.

"So, Astor, where you playing these days?"

"Not playing much anymore." He does not meet my eyes as he says this, his gaze bouncing around the room.

"What you up to?"

"I'm gonna be putting a band together soon."

The tense, the phraseology, the delivery tells its own story. He was dead center ten years ago, sitting atop the mountain, gazing down upon the less fortunate. There was nobody who came through LA for a gig or recording session or concert who didn't want him. He could play in any genre. He could shine or support. His stage presence was amped up or restrained in deference to the personality of the headline star. He made more money than he could spend, and he was married to Star, a uni-named songwriter of distinction who churned out hits for almost any young singer passing through the brief portals of MTV fame. I vaguely remember a divorce announcement in one of the music rags some years ago.

He suddenly stands up. "Hey, nice to see you, I gotta run."

"Come by the club." It is the best I can manage.

"Yeah, yeah, this weekend maybe. You got a keyboard I could use?"

Fuck. He doesn't even own a keyboard. After he is gone we are silent for a while.

"Huh," say Van with typical loquacity.

"There but for the grace . . ." I say.

"Wonder what happened?"

"Sure it's the same old sad story. Drugs. Ego. New talent. Indiscipline. Whatever."

"This is the advantage of a trust fund."

"This is the advantage of being able to program computers."

"Yeah."

"Yeah."

After lunch, we head out into the parking lot. The tire of my car is flat.

"Fuck, why me?"

"C'mon, not a big deal—let's get the spare on."

I open the trunk. Haul out the spare. Haul out the jack. Start the whole rigmarole.

It starts to rain. Hard.

"FUCK! Didn't I just say why me?"

We get the spare on and lower the jack. The spare is flat.

"FUCK FUCK FUCK." I am dripping. I reach into the car to get my cell phone. It's dead.

"FUCK FUCK FUCK FUCK FUCK. What are the chances? What are the fucking chances? JESUS!"

We head back inside, drenched, to make a call. It is then that I realize that I have just locked my keys in the car.

Van starts laughing. It feels like someone is out to get me. The universe, perhaps. I am not amused. I am really not amused.

CHAPTER 10

IT'S A MONDAY morning, I am a salaryman, and I must earn my keep.

I go to the gym before work, just as I have been doing for over fifteen years. Although it goes against my lifelong tendencies toward sloth, which I overcome only with extreme effort and berating and occasional illegal stimulants. At the time I started working out, contemplating a music career that had certain visual requirements onstage, I considered it a business decision. Now it is habit.

I suspect there are two types of people who go to the gym on a regular basis. Those who do so for health reasons, believing with fetching optimism that three sessions of light exercise per week will allow them to live longer and more sparkling lives, and those who go to look better. The narcissists. Who wish to attract a better class of mate, or to have something to preen about in the mirror, or to lord it over their flabbier citizens. This is where I belong. Wallowing in guiltless and indulgent narcissism. To which I must add, it is not now the narcissism of beauty and youth, it is the narcissism of wanting to be able to peer over my stomach and still see my dick. Without that, we are nothing.

I wish I could say that I love going to the gym. Wax eloquent about zinging pheromones, or the wonder of the fit and the firm, or the joy of sweat, or the conquering of pain or some other splattered and broken cliché. But I don't. I hate it. You know that feeling as you walk into a dentist for some potentially life-threatening tooth rot that can only be palliated by extreme pain delivered by torture-chamber implements? That's what I feel like when I arrive. Every morning. But I do it, grim-faced, self-flagellatory, and cursing the convergence of cultural spandrels and memes that have led me here.

Actually, to be honest, the whole rock-star-onstage image was only a part of it when I took my first hesitant steps through these portals of vanity. I was—to be kind—what one would call an unathletic kid, not graced with bulk, height, or speed. And here I must get into the dark secrets of male attitudes toward their own. . . . I began to notice, at some point in my early twenties, that not only was the weak and skinny thing a demerit on the girl front, but it was clear that men, in manly places like bars and sports stadiums and hardware stores, would view me with a tiny tremor of disgust. I was letting the team down. Worse—beneath that disgust, there was a message of violence. You are a bloodless ninny and I can take you anytime I like. This runs deep, even for a failed liberal like me. I remember the first time I moved up the rank from skinny nerd to not-so-skinny nerd, after about three months in the gym. I went to a club. And in walks a girl I know. With her is a guy. Undernourished, sunken chest, shapeless arms. My first thought was not, how do you do, nice to meet you. It was—I can take you, you weak pathetic motherfucker.

It wasn't overt, you understand. Just under the surface. I had moved up a rank, like from Private to Private First Class. That's the real reason why I started working out. To be sure that there was someone, anyone, to whom I could give a good ass-kicking. That's all we are. Mere aspirants, clambering over weaker bodies toward the vaunted pedestal of alpha male. The rest is disguise.

And then there's the inner sanctum. The men's locker room, where sexual social science reveals its dark logic. The point of the locker room is, primarily, to wash and change. The logistics of changing very often involve a degree of nakedness. This is where dick swinging comes in. It is a big moment for the well-endowed, their moment in the sun. These guys can't wait to strip off. At which point, they strut—quite literally. Their actual gait changes, from a normal walk to a rhythmic tilting of the hips, hither and thither, setting up what is known in engineering as sympathetic resonance, the phenomenon that causes bridges to sway and collapse. Except in this case the desired effect, available only to the long schlongers, is for the fascinating appendage, usually at rest halfway down the leg, to start swinging, left right left right, until, like a heavy length of chain, it is swaying from horizontal to horizontal, displacing air with each oscillation so that the whole locker room can hear this unearthly sound—woosh, woosh, woosh, woosh—and all eyes are drawn down to pelvis level, affording the proud owner full accolades and envy. On the other side of the coin are the less fortunate, those who shed their clothes like magicians, where they can go from fully clothed to naked and then towel-bedecked without revealing even a nanosecond of view of what is presumed to be their shame. Eyes downcast,

expressions of grim resignation, they make their way to the show-
ers, limp towels strategically hung to protect their reputations.

I am at my desk by 9 a.m. Crack my fingers and plunge in, writing an extension to an ancient piece of institutional code that will
allow smartphone access to the application. This amuses me
greatly. Most companies spent fortunes in the 1980s and '90s buying and developing and installing large lumbering pieces of
software that colonized powerful servers, pushing and pulling
information from users tethered to their desks and PCs. Then,
wham! Mobiles. Most of these pieces of software were conceptu-
alized and developed before anyone had ever heard of a cellular
network. And in every boardroom in the world the cry went up—
MOBILITY! Let's get this software working on the mobile phone,
so that our guys can be productive on the subway, at the amuse-
ment park with their kids, in restaurants, in toilets, after sex with
their partners. They pay large fortunes for the grand new capabil-
ity. For me, guaranteed employment, as usual.

After an enjoyable hour of wrestling the API—which is fancy
jargon for the doorway that original programmers had built into
their bloated architectures to allow future explorers like me to
extend the capabilities of their software beyond their original
intent—I head over to the canteen for a coffee and a brain reset.

I spot two of my colleagues, Ellen and Eduardo, sitting and
chatting. They are IT support people, meaning that they take calls
from angry employees whose passwords have been reset. It is a
thankless job, akin to janitorial services. They are an item now,
having moved from vague flirting at the help desk to the tipping
point of our last IT strategy session, where they got bat drunk at

the cocktail party and were spotted fornicating in the server room behind the printer. I was the spotter. We keep a camera in the on-site server room, a security monitor. I recently fed the video stream to the cloud, and have programmed it to stream to my iPhone if there is undue and anomalous movement. I can't say I wasn't gratified to see a porno movie rather than a mute set of computer hardware. I didn't tell them—that would have been too cruel and would have opened me up to all sorts of legal trouble. Or perhaps a beating from Eduardo. Or perhaps a firing.

"Yo. E and E. What's the gossip?"

Eduardo doesn't talk much. He's from Chile. He prefers to smolder. Ellen smiles at me.

"Meyer. Sit down, we were just talking."

"About what."

"Getting married, maybe."

"No shit?"

"What do you think?"

"How old are you?"

"I'm twenty-four, Ed's twenty-eight."

"Are you still virgins? Have you done the deed?"

Eduardo smolders hotly at me. Ellen giggles.

"OK. Have you agreed on a child strategy?"

"Yup. When I turn thirty."

"OK. Have you agreed on a cheating strategy?"

Eduardo now smolders threateningly.

Ellen raises a suspicious eyebrow. "What d'you mean?"

"If someone cheats, is it over, or do you get a mulligan?"

"This is obviously why you're twice divorced, Meyer."

"Only kidding. Do it, my children. Tie the knot. Make roots. Become a nuclear family. Go forth and multiply. Commit. Lest you become like me. An elder, trapped in loneliness and disquiet. Contribute to the world. I bless you, my children."

And I mean it. I was always happier married. At least it seems so now.

I head off back to my office. As I turn into the main corridor, the CEO strides past, face purple and apoplectic. He stops outside the Human Resources director's office.

"I WANT HIM FIRED."

The small voice of Jim, the HR guy, trickles out.

"It is quite difficult to do that. We need to show cause and prove guilt, and go through due process."

"HE IS AN INCOMPETENT JACKASS, AND HE IS TOO OLD. FIND A FUCKING WAY. I DON'T WANT TO SEE HIS UGLY FACE AGAIN. AND FIRE HIS UGLY GIRLFRIEND TOO."

The CEO turns on his heel and flies down the corridor. I am rooted to the spot. As he gets closer he notices me.

"What are you staring at, Meyer? Get back to work," he snarls.

I continue on to the HR director's office and pop my head in.

"Hey, Jim. Fire who?"

"Can't tell you."

"What did he do?"

"It doesn't matter."

"Jim, I've been here for twenty years. C'mon."

Jim, a colorless, featureless man with no discernible personality, sighs.

"Gomez."

Gomez is one of the facilities guys, a handyman by any other name—doors, lights, plumbing, locks, paint touch-ups, schlepping boxes, that sort of thing. He has been at the company since it started.

"He apparently scratched the Maserati while he was cleaning it."

"How big?"

"The scratch?"

"Yeah."

"Invisible to the naked eye, or thereabouts."

"Figures."

I walk across the parking lot to one of the warehouse buildings where Gomez resides in a small cubicle. His office is the size of a matchbox. His walls are covered with pictures of swarthy, stocky people, like him. They are smiling, sisters, brothers, parents, cousins, friends. Gomez smiles a lot. Not now.

"What's up, Gomie?"

"Hi, Mr. Meyer. Not much."

"Why so glum?"

"I fucked up."

"How?"

"Scratched the boss's car."

"Ah. No big."

"Very big. He called me a dumb spic."

"Lovely. What did you do?"

"Nothing. I walked away."

"Sorry, Gomez."

"He's gonna fire me. I need this job."

I shouldn't have come here. What the fuck can I do? I'm an impotent spectator to blood sport. I have no advice, no counsel, no words of wisdom. No backbone. There are no protections for guys like Gomez. They toil at the base of the pyramid. A thousand replacements await, their breath hot and cloying. He will lose this job, and his chances of finding another are slim. I am not really political these days, my passions for the fight diminished. If I was, I would move smartly left. That's the problem with a good education; you always end up on the fence, with 360-degree vision, always ready to see the other point of view, unable to cleave to principle of any kind. I was in a debating team at high school. I remember coming home after a victory, feeling sullied and dishonest. Like now.

"I'll put in a word if I can." My shame and fraud raise blood to my cheeks.

He says nothing, simply looks at me, haunted. We both know how this is going to end.

I am on my way back to the office, resigned to the inequities, travesties, and the lack of fairness in an uncaring universe.

And then suddenly I am not.

Steal the thing that he loves. Wasn't that what Van said?

CHAPTER 11

STEALING FROM THE company turned out to be ridiculously easy. I know every nook and cranny of our IT landscape. I have such seniority that I have what is known in computer parlance as "administrator access," which is like being the director of the CIA—you can look at and change anything and everything, including things you don't want people to know about. Although you cannot convince the president to invade foreign countries on the flimsiest of evidence.

The scam was simple. There are hundreds of thousands of transactions per month, of various sorts. They are classified and fed into the labyrinthine sets of processes and software that eventually ensure that somebody gets paid. These processes are authorized by various financial and other authorized managers through an arcane process called workflow. The largest of these, transactions worth millions and more, need the personal approval of many people, including the CFO and CEO. But here's the rub. There is a converse to this. The really, really small transactions are barely noticed by anyone, not even the auditors. They are just financial noise, and simply require a passing electronic nod from a generally disinterested low-level manager. How small do they have to be to be ignored by all and sundry? Less than $50. And there may be thousands of these every day.

Given the idiocy with which people choose passwords, plus my access to everything and anything, I can masquerade as almost anyone in the company, dolling out electronic approvals as I choose. Not a good idea when the doppelgänger is liable to notice, but a small invoice from a small office-supply company that I have quietly added to the approved supplier list will not be noticed. Ever.

I do a test run. Enter a company called "Black and Tan Office Supplies" in the approved supplier database. Then I set up the company of the same name in the Cayman Islands (simple, just Google "setting up a company in the Cayman Islands for nefarious purposes"). I open a Cayman bank account (simple, just Google "setting up a bank account in the Caymans for more nefarious purposes"). I set up a trust to own and operate the non-operating entity (simple, just . . .), lowering the chances that anything can be tracked back to me. Then I send an electronic invoice for $32 from Black and Tan to our company for "printer accessory kit." Then I give it the electronic OK, and mark it "Same-day payment." Next day I have an additional $32 in my account.

The question of how to turn $32 into more interesting amounts is next.

"I stole $32 from the company today."

Van is, not surprisingly, unimpressed.

"You really know how to stick it to the man."

"It was a test run. Can multiply at will."

"You don't care that much about money."

"You're right. I intend to give it away."

"To who?"

"I don't know. Charity?"

"You don't care about charity."

"Yes, I do."

"Name one."

I think for a while. I come up with nothing.

"I'll find a cause. There must be a website that lists charitable causes that pull at heartstrings. Maybe I will give it to the Bill and Melinda Gates Foundation. They seem to do good work."

"I'm sure they will be eternally grateful."

"OK. I will send anonymous contributions to worthy individuals who are in need."

"Like who?"

"Like the homeless guy on the corner of Los Feliz and Western, who helped me fix a flat tire once."

"OK."

"So can I ramp up? You're a man with a keen sense of right and wrong, even though you are a gloomy drunk. Am I crossing any moral boundaries here, Van?"

"I'd still rather have him killed. After a light bout of torture. But you have a bigger problem."

"What?"

"He will never know."

"Yeah, but it's the principle."

"The principle is that it should hurt. This won't hurt."

"Shit. You were the one who told me to steal his money."

"Right. Maybe you should steal something else that he loves."

"His Maserati?"

"He'll buy another."

"His girlfriend?"

"He'll buy another."

"Van, you're not helping much here."

"Contract killing plus torture. That's the moral high ground."

He's right. This is a waste of time. I will have to come up with something else.

"Farzad, I want to hurt somebody."

"Later. Do you think she will come by today? I want to see her."

Farzad and I are in Venice again. We don't normally meet at the same place, but Farzad wants to see the rollerblader.

"Why?"

"Watching her last week was an epiphany, bar mitzvah boy. Even Harvard-trained psychologists need epiphanies."

"What was the epiphany?"

"I cannot tell you that. I can only tell my shrink."

"You have a shrink?"

"Of course. All shrinks have shrinks."

"Who's your shrink's shrink?"

"I do not know."

"Won't the shrink community run out of shrinks to shrink them?"

"Nah, it circles back eventually. It is like a Möbius strip."

"Farzad, I want to hurt somebody. How do I do that and still be a good person?"

"Who said you are a good person?"

"You never take me seriously."

"OK. Who do you want to hurt?"

"My CEO."

"Why?"

"He's a terrible person."

"Why?"

"He makes waitresses cry."

"Have him killed."

"That's what Van said."

"Really?"

"Can't have him killed anyway."

"Why?"

"He's a vampire."

"Wooden stake?"

"Worldwide shortage."

"So you want to hurt him?"

"Yes, please."

"Call him fat, to his face."

"He's not fat, and I want to keep my job."

"You want to hurt him *and* keep your job?"

"Yes, please."

Farzad strokes his considerable facial hair. I can tell he is moving into a pedantic attitude, my favorite—at least when I am looking for advice.

"OK, my beloved wandering Hebe, here are my well-considered thoughts on this matter. What we have here is a revenge-and-punishment scenario, a well-traveled road in the annals of psychology, and indeed, in the history of human endeavor. You throw me an interesting curveball, though. It is not you who wants revenge, but you wish righteous punishment on behalf of others, most specifically waitresses. Therefore, it seems as though you wish to serve common justice, the greater good. Which makes you a self-obsessed, narcissistic, attention-seeking ass, trying to play God."

"But I don't necessarily want anyone to know—"

"Shut up, I'm not finished. You feel a need to hurt a man who has hurt others. You feel this need as a sort of mythological vengeance, which will make him feel worse, and make you feel better. The problem with all of this is that it will not make the waitress who cried feel better, because she will never know. Therefore, I can only conclude that you are ashamed of your small penis. You have penis envy, my friend, and the *coup de* psychological *grâce* is that you envy my large Muslim penis. It has nothing to do with the CEO."

"You never take me seriously."

"OK, OK. If you want to hurt somebody, steal something that they love."

"Hey, that's also what Van said."

"Van is a chronic depressive. Therefore, without serious psychological assistance, nothing he says can be trusted."

Farzad stands up and cranes his neck.

"Where is my rollerblader?"

We scan the passing parade for a while. There are multiple interfering currents of walkers, rollerbladers, skateboarders, cyclists, and spectators, all trying, and partially failing, to stay on their designated pieces of territory, some being occasionally—and quite literally—routed off to separate single-purpose arteries, the presumed logic of such expense being the avoidance of lawsuits from injured complainants.

The Venice boardwalk in the height of summer is the stuff of a million dreams. Take a snapshot, from any angle, and it seems like a place of near impossible joy, hope, wonder, happiness. It might strike the disinterested viewer that a perfect society has been built here. There are quaint, trendy, and stolidly honest pedestrian eateries. Shops and stalls catering to every whim, from bangles to bagels to bicycles. Magicians and acrobats and jokers in full throat. By midmorning the babble of the parishioners of this fine church has risen in joyous cacophony, and always, always youth and beauty and sex in immodest display.

But to me, drenched in dread and complication, it feels like an illusion, a trick, legerdemain, sleight of hand. Nothing this good can last. The good cheer of these people, surely, surely will be crushed and deformed as the sky falls on their heads, as it must, for all of us. Particularly me.

I drain my beer. Glare at Farzad for a bit.

"Meyer, I apologize for my flippancy, thoughts of my roller-blader's powerful gluteus maximus has me in a state of mind to consider light matters only. Here is my real answer. You ask me if you can hurt somebody and still be a good person. There are many questions that underlie the main one. The first is whether we even know what a good person is. Do we compare to some objective yardstick? The Ten Commandments, perhaps, revered by your tribe and mine? And that other religion. Clearly not, given that we all covet our neighbors' wives. What then? If someone transgresses the voluminous legal codes of his country, perhaps? Again, this suggestion fails under the weight of its conceit. If one compared the laws of Christian Uganda and our fair Christian land on the subject of gay people, you would struggle to believe that these laws were based on the same concepts of empathy and goodness. What else? Common sense, perhaps? Perhaps the concept of goodness is simply one of those 'you-know-it-when-you-see-it' things. A slippery slope that, my little yarmulke. And I'm sure I don't have to outline the paucity of that argument. Maybe it is purely a personal judgment call, made at the moment. Inherent in your question is also the fact that you consider yourself to be a better person than the CEO. I would suspect that he would differ, and in fact I would hazard that, with the assistance of smart lawyers of your religious persuasion, he could construct a compelling argument that he employs, and thus supports with his personal largesse, tens of thousands of people. Indeed, for all you know, he might well be donating his entire personal fortune to AIDS research."

"Farzad, I assure you—"

"Shut up, I'm not finished. As a beautiful symmetry to the foregoing argument is how we judge *you* to be good, and whether in fact you can damage this self-proclaimed goodness by inflicting hurt on another. If he had selfsame Jewish lawyers turn on you, they would, without doubt, dredge up the whole child-growing-up-without-a-father crime. There are at least two of those in your life, yes? A father so solipsistic that he leaves the responsibility of the rearing of his innocent children to bereft and struggling mothers, while he wanders off, oblivious to the damage caused, to play saxophone and do drugs. Your self-appointed goodness can easily be shredded."

"That's not fair, that's—"

"Shut up, I'm not finished. We now move on to the definition of 'hurt.' Hurting a person is a premeditated vicious act. A consequence of our most base instincts. An anathema to all that we hope . . . there she is, there she is!"

He jumps up, runs down onto the boardwalk, stomach and beard jiggling in sync, just in time for his goddess to whoosh past him, a blur of gold.

Farzad. Fucking pedant. I love him.

CHAPTER 12

IT'S FRIDAY NIGHT, my weekend with Isobel. Krystal and I have been doing well of late. She has laughed at a few of my jokes. We exchanged a few orgasms this week, reversing a worrying throttling of desire and action. Krystal works as a copywriter in a brand-name ad agency, with a bizarrely architectured building near the beach, shaped like a TV set. The building was designed in the '80s, when TV reigned supreme. When *All in the Family* signified the great diversification of the body populi, when cables and satellite broadcast were gleaming promises, inchoate experiments foreseeing a brave new world. Then the sparkling explosion of digital, its many shards rendering the stolid cathode-ray TV set a comical ode to clunk. The building, housing one of the most recognizable names in advertising, embarrasses passersby and inmates alike. Krystal used to talk about the building a lot, how it overwhelmed her, how its kitsch excess poisoned her day, how architecture framed its citizens. I used to find that smart. She was full of surprising observations once. Or perhaps one day she simply stopped seeing the need to surprise me.

We settle down for dinner at a restaurant on Melrose, the avenue stretching out its TV series celebrity well beyond its sell-by date. The place is teeming with people, entertainment-industry workers ranging from the unemployed and hopeful to the employed and cynical. You can feel the new and old hopes and dreams bouncing and colliding arbitrarily off the sharp and asymmetrical architectural fittings of the bar, where we now perch, awaiting our table.

"So, Isobel, how's your friend Cheryl?"

"She's fine. Got a boyfriend now."

She exchanges a glance with Krystal. They keep secrets from me. My good mood finds a small puncture. I can almost hear the hiss.

"What kind of boyfriend?"

Isobel rolls her eyes, an eye roll perfectly evolved across millennia of teenagers.

"How many kinds are there, Dad?"

"Serious boyfriend. iPhone boyfriend. Steady boyfriend. Aspirant boyfriend. Imaginary boyfriend. Older boyfriend. No boyfriend."

She is not as amused as I had hoped.

"Older boyfriend."

Shit. Alarm bells.

"How much older?"

"He's twenty."

"Please tell me you are kidding."

No twenty-year-old is going out with anyone unless he is getting some. That means she is putting out. I am going to call Cheryl's parents and ask them to commit her to a convent.

"Nope, not kidding."

"And you, any boys in your life?"

"Nah. The only boys I know are still teenagers. Not interested in teenagers, anymore, Dad."

Fuck, fuck, fuck.

Krystal is watching this interaction, clearly amused between sips of wine spritzer. Being a copywriter has armed her with a quick wit, which was what attracted me to her in the first place. When your profession demands that something smart and memorable is said in thirty seconds, you become unable to communicate without resorting to your secret stash of riposte, pun, euphemism, or one-liners. Being in secret estrogen-driven cahoots with your lover's teenage daughter makes for a lethal combination.

Krystal is very tall, angular. Sharp bones, long aquiline nose, wide and thin lips, sharply edged jawline, prominent cheekbones, wide eyes. Not classically beautiful, but more striking, perhaps even a little shocking. In addition to a sharp literate tongue, her tallness appealed to me, perhaps as a palliative for my own failings in the vertical department. I considered it a mark of her general excellence and good taste that she would allow herself to be wooed by someone over whom she towered. In the drawn-out fading of our relationship, her height now seems like an optical illusion.

"Krystal, any thoughts on this matter?"

"What matter is that, Meyer?"

"Fourteen-year-olds either dating twenty-year-olds or wanting to?"

"I dated a thirty-year-old when I was sixteen. He was sweet."

"Thanks, Krystal, you're not helping."

Isobel giggles. I decide to back off. These two females will flay the skin off my body. I will have a word with Bunny, appeal to her sense of, I don't know, gender protection? Daughter protection? I also recommit to not trying to save a dying love affair with a tone-deaf person, particularly if she is not going to support the chastity requirements I require for my daughter.

There is a small voice in my ear reminding me of the tender age of my own loss of innocence. But it was the '80s then. The world was in no danger of imminent collapse. Sex was fun. You got a bit drunk, smoked a doobie, groped incompetently in the dark, and then it was over. Nobody got hurt. The girls were as experimentally playful as the boys, or so it seemed. Dread was still an infant. It seems to me that it is now mandatory that kids eschew the temptations of the flesh in favor of saving the planet from the idiocies of their parents. I mean, if they are going to go around fucking each other, who is going to save the whales?

Fathers and daughters. This incarnation of a family relationship is fraught with bizarre irrationality, particularly on the father's side. No, actually completely on the father's side. Doting doesn't even begin to describe it. Our daughters somehow take the place of our mothers, not in an Oedipal sense, but as the embodiment of hope and kindness and softness and warmth. They make us feel strong, responsible, caring. We guard their well-being jealously, we are proud of them, we will kill anyone who looks at them inappropriately. They make us anxious, they steamroll our other priorities.

* * *

"Meyer, you are full of crap, you know that?"

Bunny also does not seem to share my view. I call her when I get home.

"The guy is twenty, Bunny. It's just a matter of time before he asks Cheryl if she hasn't got a nice friend for his drinking buddy, Biff."

"You're projecting. Not all twenty-year-olds are the same as you were when you were twenty."

"How was I?"

"I wasn't there, remember? But I assume you were a prick."

"All twenty-year-olds are pricks."

"No, they aren't."

"Yes, they are. Have you ever been a twenty-year-old male?"

"Meyer, you are annoying me. Let this go. Isobel is a responsible young lady, and I trust her to make the right decisions."

"Please have a chat with her. I am begging you."

"OK. I will tell her that her father thinks she is vulnerable and immature."

"She is vulnerable. And immature."

"No more than any other fourteen-year-old girl. Leave the mothering to me. Let it go, Meyer."

Bunny, unlike Krystal, is not tall. She is short and a bit plump. Zaftig, in the mother tongue of my shtetl ancestors. But she is classically beautiful. Large, dark, impenetrable eyes, blue-black-dyed straight hair, skin one click below albino, and plush, wet, tumescent lips, somewhere between vermillion and ruby. The full thighs and soft belly and generous breasts were endlessly fascinating for me. I wallowed in them. Going against the grain of popular fashion, I must insist that plump makes for better sex.

"How's Daniel?"

The tone of her voice changes to cautious.

"Why?"

"I think I may have seen him in Hollywood the other night. I think he was trolling for whores."

"Goodbye, Meyer."

CHAPTER 13

I AM AT my desk, trying to hack into websites of autocratic regimes. This is a new hobby of mine. I have gotten into a few, and then retreated, as visions surface of having my fingernails pulled out by irritated third world intelligence operatives. Perhaps I will give some thought to hacking in with no back-trace, using dynamically redirected IP addresses from anonymous server hosts in lawless places. Then, when I am in, I will do something mature like replace North Korea's landing page with "HEY KIM—YOUR MOTHER SUCKS DONKEY DICK." Should be entertaining for a minute or two.

"Meyer, the CEO wants you up in his office as soon as possible. Are you free now?"

This call, direct to my desk phone, is from Jim, the HR director. He never calls me. Ever. Then I consider the construction of the request. The CEO did not phrase it that way. He likely said, "GET MEYER HERE, NOW!" Then there is the wistful "Are you free now?" asked politely by the HR director, remembering his psychology courses as he unknowingly trained for a career that would have him being yelled at by the CEO until his retirement.

No, I am not free. I am busy hacking.

"Yes, sure, I can come now. What's this all about?"

"Electronic fraud. I will come by your office and pick you up."

If I refuse to shower in jail, or not wipe my butt properly, and smell really bad, do you think it would lower my chances of being raped? And how do I tell Grace? Innocent? Does Robin Hood still have any resonance? And does Daniel become Grace's new Dad, exchanging looks with Bunny every time Isobel mentions my name? "Some people just go bad, darling, even those we think we know best. I wouldn't get too upset. Would you like to go to Hawaii over the summer?"

Innocent would probably get it. He is studying film at college. He would immediately recognize the dramatic possibilities here. Good man, undone by hubris and incaution. Emerges transformed, gentler, contrite. With AIDS.

We are in the elevator, I can literally feel the blood draining from my face. There is a small twitch in my lip; it feels like I'm going to cry. I turn to the HR director.

"So, what's the story?"

It comes out strangled, dripping with guilt.

"Don't really know. Guess we are about to find out."

Please God, I promise to be good and believe in you forever if you let me scrape by here.

"Meyer, sit down. Would you like something to drink?"

The CEO's face is a mask. Why is he offering me something to drink? Is it like a last cigarette? The CFO, CIO, and security officer are already there.

"No thank you, sir."

This time my voice is no more than a hoarse whisper. I can feel my legs buckling. I get to the chair just in time.

"MONEY HAS BEEN STOLEN FROM THIS COMPANY!" he roars, his face now transformed into a purple mass of throbbing veins, looking at me intently.

"Yes, sir." This is all I can manage. My mouth is a desert.

He turns to the security officer. "I WANT THIS GUY FOUND AND THROWN IN JAIL FOREVER!"

Oh God, oh God, oh God.

Hang on. Wait a minute. He said, "I want this guy found . . ."

They haven't found me yet! Handel's *Messiah* roars in my ears. I breathe deeply.

The CEO turns to me. "Meyer, you know your way around the computer systems. If you wanted to steal money, how would you do it?"

My brain moves into overdrive. Idiotically, I am about to explain the methodology behind my little scam to him, when I realize that this would be a trifle foolish.

"How much?"

"What do you mean how much, Meyer?"

"Uh . . . the method would depend on how much was being stolen."

"About 10 million has disappeared."

Handel's *Messiah* morphs into Queen's "We Are the Champions." My eyes fill with tears of relief.

"What's the matter with you, Meyer. Are you crying?"

"It's just so, so shocking, sir. . . ."

He nods, looking at each one of us in turn.

"Yes. Shocking, indeed." He wheels around and glares at the CFO and the CIO. "Meyer here, not even one of the senior members of this organization, seems to understand the gravity of this. It makes him weep. Do you two fools understand the gravity of this?"

They both nod quickly. I can tell that the CFO is trying to make his eyes water.

"So, Meyer?"

"Sir, there are many ways to do it, but as you know, amounts that large have to be approved by you and the CFO personally, and sometimes by senior management or even the board, online and by signature and by resolution. I can only imagine someone has stolen your identities. I will need time to look into it. Aren't you going to call the police?"

"MY FUCKING IDENTITY? HOW DOES SOMEBODY DO THAT?" Having used up all of his purple, he is now looking gray. Clearly, the theft of the CFO's identity is of no consequence to him.

"I am not sure yet, sir. It is more complex than just knowing your password. There are both paper and electronic trails and fail-safes. I will need dig around, speak to the banks. I don't have that sort of authority."

"You do now."

I am so happy I just want to shit. Not about the bank authority, but about escaping gang rape at San Quentin.

I root around in the banking and Accounts Payable modules. Pore over transactions. Something is wrong, because nothing is wrong; there are no suspicious trails, and the internal electronic books check out. This takes me about an hour of work to uncover. There are no crooks at the company. Besides me, of course. It has to be on the other side, the bank.

I speak to the bank, and they insist that the amounts reflecting in our accounts are correct. I present my new authority by yelling a little. They go back and recheck their transactions and their balances. Something is wrong, they demur. They will call right back. An hour later I get a call. An internal error, it seems. Impossible, I say, it's all electronic, been working perfectly for years. No, they say. Some of their systems crashed the previous week, and some of the redundancies and checks failed, some data was corrupted. They had to re-input certain data by hand, only about three minutes' worth of transactions during that period.

BY HAND? ARE YOU FUCKING SHITTING ME?

Apparently not. This is a big-brand bank. I am extremely pleased that I am not the CIO of this bank, who is soon going to be in hip-deep shit. This is why they have awful words like *governance* and *business continuity.* Governance and business continuity are good and upstanding and righteous things, designed and policed by salarymen with discipline and good intent and focus. Not really people like me. Somebody breached governance at the bank. And now they have made a $10-million administrative error.

Of course, this is all fixable at the push of a button. The quivering wreck at the end of the line is telling me that that it will be reversed immediately. But this is too good an opportunity to pass up.

"Hang on, please don't do anything just yet, I have to make some changes at my end. I will let you know when I need the reversal. I will call you later."

I call the CEO. He has, this once, allowed me to call his cell.

"Hello, sir."

"HAVE YOU FOUND THE FUCKING CROOK YET?"

"It is complex, sir. Millions of transactions to go through. You know how technology is."

"HOW LONG?"

"Give me a few days, sir. I promise you I will get to the bottom of this."

I let him stew for two days, imagining the sweat gathering behind his neck when he has to explain the loss of $10 million to shareholders. Then I call the bank. They reverse the transaction immediately.

I have ruined his sleep for three days. Life is good.

CHAPTER 14

LOS ANGELES IS a collection of communities, like most large cities where the metaphorical boundaries cannot contain but one point of view. LA has to deal with its multiple personalities, a schizophrenia of sort, and is particularly disabled by its veneer, the piercing shine that blinds the rest of the planet: that of celebrity and boundless opportunity. But, as always, the truth is more mundane. The city is widely spread over its coastal desert geography—but go almost anywhere and you will find normal people living normal lives, their friends and schools and shopping and recreation restricted to manageable proximity, excepting work, in which inconvenience often takes a back seat to necessity.

But there is one extended swath of city that exists in its own space-time continuum. It extends from the Hollywood sign in the hills above Los Angeles and along a thin strip all the way through Hollywood, West Hollywood, West Los Angeles, Beverly Hills, and Santa Monica and their adjacents. It is here where the glisten is at its most sparkling, the smell at its most intoxicating. It is where wealth, celebrity, notoriety, youth, and beauty often collide with the clamor of less fortunate aspirants, whose proximity to the anointed few feed a rabid hunger and, often, a ruination of balance.

Krystal and I live within this terrain of dreams. I am silhouetted against the feted Hollywood sign, my small, precariously tilted and cheaply constructed stilt house grasping the canyon side with aging shafts of concrete. Grace is at the other horizon, a few blocks from the sea, but a world apart from the opulence nestling within whispering distance. Hers is an apartment in an old and modest building, built in the 1950s, functional and without conceit. Given the constraints of her teacher's income, this is about as far as she can stretch.

I had insisted on taking Grace to lunch, undeterred by her lack of enthusiasm. The late Saturday morning journey takes nearly forty minutes, even in the absence of drive-time traffic. I spent this time ruminating on her and the mistakes of my youth. She was not a mistake, but my leaving her certainly was. Of this I am sure because the threadbare memories of our few years together are tinged with pale sunset melancholy.

She opens the door immediately when I ring, stepping out into the corridor and closing the door behind her, preventing my intrusive curiosity from taking stock.

She wears no makeup. No heels. Jeans and a nondescript T-shirt. Her hair is short and unkempt. She looks dazzling. One cannot look much younger than one's chronological age—no amount of makeup or surgery or paint or sunscreen can deceive by more than a few years. The trick is to have beaten the odds, to have been graced with those genes that render you attractive, that keep you looking that way long past time's ravage. The beauty industry never got that. It is not looking young that is important. It is simply being lucky enough to be well constructed. Like a great building. Ageless. Grace is that and more.

Her face, I surmise, has been built with mathematical precision, with pi and epsilon ratios dividing and intersecting distances and relationships between ears, eyes, nose, mouth, and chin, triggering some deep universal truth—science personified as beauty.

I lean in awkwardly and kiss her on a quickly offered cheek.

"So, Grace. You look, well . . ."

I cannot find the right words.

"Thank you. That was an articulate compliment."

"It's a pleasure. Perhaps I can finish the sentence after a few drinks."

"And you, Meyer. How are you?" she asks as we make our way down to the car.

"I am good. Mostly."

"Sounds complicated."

"Not really. Or it is, but I intend to sparkle today. I intend not to bore you."

"OK. I'll eat. You sparkle."

We drive to Main Street in Santa Monica. Sit down in the first restaurant we can find, of which there are many, all displaying their modernity and jangling uniqueness and self-conscious design innovations without either modesty or irony.

"So, Grace, when did you last speak to Innocent?"

"Today. He was surprised we were having lunch. It worried him."

"Why?"

"The only reason he could imagine is that you have bad news, like you're dying or something. Are you dying, Meyer?"

"Yeah, a little bit every day. But no faster than anyone else."

"So why are we having lunch?"

"I thought perhaps if we spent an hour or two together, I could remember why we broke up. Why did we break up?"

She picks up the menu and runs her finger down the list of options. She doesn't answer my question at first. This is a small peccadillo of hers, I remember it well. She won't be rushed into a response. She will busy herself silently with something until she has turned over the question, felt its weight, located its core. I wait. She has her head down as she scans the menu, and I marvel at the crown of her head, the impertinent whorl of bristles in the center. I want to run my tongue through it.

"Marriage was very constraining for you, I think. I suspect that you found its demands unreasonable."

"What do you mean by 'demands'?"

"Oh, I don't know. Fealty, responsibility, shared labor, emotional honesty, tenderness, early nights. That sort of thing."

"Right. I've forgotten. That was a daunting list for me."

"For me too, Meyer."

"Nice of you to say, but I think you were better at it."

"Yes, well breastfeeding a child with colic will do that to a girl."

"What's new with Innocent?"

This is our terra cognito. We have spent over twenty years fretting and worrying about whether he was happy, smart, sick, fulfilled, drunk, disappointed, thriving. All of which he has been, at times, like any other kid. There was a time, at the beginning, when Grace and I talked not only about Innocent, but about everything. The life we would build and how we would get old and what movie to see and whether to buy the more expensive lamp for the bedside. This is one of the things that they don't tell you about divorce, the throttling of subjects of common interest. First the split of the assets, of which there were pitifully few in our case, and then the life and times of Innocent, intricately tied to us, then, now, and onward.

"College boy. Sex, drugs, and the rest. Maybe a bit of studying when guilt catches up with him. You remember that, Meyer?"

"Yes, I do. With mean-spirited envy."

We are sharing a single seafood salad. It is a brash affair bristling with rocket and watercress and red peppers and red onion and dwarfish carrots and avocado, garnished with slices of pear and grapefruit and guava segments and incongruous crumbles of feta, spread among shreds of cold crab, tiny blushing shrimp, and calamari rings. I stare at it with some bemusement. Its multihued Dadaist attitude alone is worth the price, which is considerable. It tastes, well, like seafood, vegetables, fruit, and feta. Which is a bit of a disappointment, considering the presentation.

"Anyway, I'm driving up to the Bay Area next weekend to see him."

I stop chewing. A small stab of jealousy intrudes.

"Really? With whom?"

"Stop fishing, Meyer. Alone, as it so happens. I haven't seen Berkeley in ages, and I miss my boy."

"Where are you going to stay?"

"I was hoping Innocent would put me up, but he lives in digs with a bunch of other students and I am not sure I wouldn't embarrass him. So I booked a B&B called Berkeley and Bay. B&B B&B. Get it?"

UC Berkeley was Innocent's first choice. His SATs were up in the impressive percentile and admission was smooth. Money from me, I am pleased as punch. We had an earnest discussion about studying toward a set of skills that would find him an employment window in a declining America. This is the sort of discussion that parents have had with their kids forever and Innocent's reaction was predictable.

"I'm not interested in money, Dad. I am interested in learning about the world."

"You will be. Interested in money, I mean. One day."

"Maybe, but not now."

"So what are you going to take?"

"I don't know. Anthropology. Psychology. Sociology. Philosophy."

"In my day, they were called the fuck subjects."

Eyebrows shoot up, interested.

"Lots of girls in those classes. Lots of fucking."

"Really." Not a question.

"Yeah, but you knew that, didn't you?"

"I suppose."

"So the whole learning-about-the-world-thing has a caveat, doesn't it?"

"Dad, learning about girls is also learning about the world."

Learning about girls is the hardest subject of all, but I would let him find that out without my help.

I look at Grace's excellent face, now delightfully distorted by thoughtful chewing. I decide on a small social engineering project.

I excuse myself and go to the bathroom. Dial San Francisco information on my cell phone. Book a room at the Berkeley and Bay B&B. Then I call Innocent.

"Dad. What's up? Heard you were having lunch with Mom today."

"Yep, she is sitting across the table from me right now. She says I should also come up and visit you next weekend. Thought I should check with you."

"Dad, that'd be great. Can I have a word with Mom?"

"Uh . . . she's just on her phone. I'll get her to call you."

I head back to the table.

"I just spoke to Innocent. He asked me to visit next week-end too."

She looks at me suspiciously.

"Uh huh."

"Really, he did. He wants you to call him, by the way."

"Uh huh."

"So, should we drive up together?"

"This is a gate-crash, Meyer."

"No, really, he wants me to come too."

"Do not think you will be sharing a room with me."

"I wouldn't think of it."

But I would.

Constantly.

CHAPTER 15

FARZAD ONCE USED the term "the threaded life." I was deeply intrigued, but because he was at the time deeply engaged in insulting me and my tribe—quite creatively, if I remember correctly—I had no chance of interrogating the underlying etymology. Today I try again.

"Farzad, what did you mean when you used the phrase 'the threaded life'?"

"I would never use such a phrase."

"You did."

"I pride myself on clarity and essentialism. This is not a phrase used by a person of my breeding. Besides . . ."

"Besides what?"

"Besides, I have decided to stop making fun of your Jewish heritage."

"OK. Why?"

"It no longer bothers you."

"No, it doesn't. Can I start making fun of your Muslim heritage?"

"No."

"Why not?"

"We tend to put people who make fun of us to the sword. It's in the Qur'an somewhere, I think."

"Ah, OK. What's this got to do with the threaded life?"

"I do not know. What is the threaded life? What are you talking about?"

We are walking in Griffith Park in the Hollywood Hills, between the Hollywood sign and the observatory, a beautiful public space of brave small desert flora and sharp canyonesque hillsides and soaring views, somewhat tainted by a reputation for rutting men behind rocks, where apparently anonymous gay sex is the order of the day. We have never come across anyone, but we will keep trying. Farzad's dog, a scrawny nervous creature of indeterminate origin, is straining on the lead.

"So . . . I engineered a road trip with Grace."

Farzad nods sagely.

"This is good. Where are you going?"

"To Berkeley to see Innocent."

"Ah. And is some part of you still attracted to Grace? Besides your microscopic penis."

"Yes, most of me. And my dick is not small, by the way. Bet it's bigger than yours."

"There are no penises bigger than mine outside of Tehran. How do you think I got to marry the blonde American cheerleader? I have already told you, you suffer from penis envy. Trust me, I am a psychologist. How did you engineer this trip?"

"I lied a little."

"And why would you be attracted to Grace now, nearly twenty years after you left her?"

"I think I may have made a mistake."

"Meyer, you know what your problem is?"

"What?"

"You live a poorly composed threaded life."

I say nothing, not wanting to break the spell. His dog, improbably named Great Satan, gives a short bark and stops.

"Ah—there must be two rutting men behind that rock. Perhaps you should go and show them your little penis, Meyer."

I remain silent. I am getting quite good at extracting free wisdom from Farzad. The key is an infuriating lack of response from me. He cannot bear that; he has to play the pedant.

"There are some people who live lives constructed like wondrous tapestries. They integrate their many relationships, their work, their hobbies, their internal lives, and their family—all different colored threads. And among them there are those who can be guided to step back, raise themselves up, and gaze down on this piece of art they have woven. An ability to do this requires a sort of objectivity that most people do not have. The ability to separate the external from the internal, the real from the illusory. To grasp the integrated whole, rather than to fret and worry about one or two misplaced tiny threads that disappear into the grand composition of a life. These people are mentally healthy, they require no guidance. You, of course, are not one of these people."

"I'll have you know I have an excellent ability to—"

"Shut up, I'm not finished. Your threads are, in no particular order of importance: Grace, Innocent, Bunny, Isobel, Krystal, your music, Van, your job, the CEO, your band members, and . . ."

"And you."

"Shut up, I'm not finished. I do not qualify as a thread. That is because I am the omniscient narrator of your life and well above being a mere thread. Now, where was I? Right. So these threads, of which I have mentioned just a few of many, including your shameful private parts, have coalesced into a tapestry that you are unable to see. I, however, can see it clearly. It is spectacularly unattractive, could not adorn a wall even in the most modest dwelling. I strongly suggest that you unravel the threads and reweave it into a composition with balance, structure, and beauty. Then you will become self-actualized and happy. And your penis will grow."

Yes, this is what I wanted to hear. I will reweave.

The conversation with Krystal unravels faster than a poorly woven tapestry.

"You're driving with Grace?"

"Yes, she was going anyway. Innocent invited her too."

"Are you still attracted to Grace?"

"For goodness sake, Krystal. We've been divorced nearly twenty years. I am ride-sharing. We are going to visit our son."

"Where are you sleeping?"

"I booked a room at a B&B."

"Where is Grace sleeping?"

"I don't know. Maybe she booked a B&B too."

"Where?"

"I didn't ask."

"You're a liar, Meyer."

"I don't know where she is staying. What are you implying?"

"I am implying that you want to fuck your ex-wife."

"Oh, please, Krystal."

"You see Grace maybe once a year. Now you're driving together. Sleeping in the same bed."

"For fuck's sake. I have my own room, she has hers."

"Oh, so now you *are* staying in the same B&B."

"I don't know. Maybe. She may have mentioned it."

"Why are you lying to me?"

"Am not. Not intentionally."

"This relationship is fucked, Meyer. Fucked."

"That's a different discussion."

Like most red-blooded American males, I shy away from confrontations with girlfriends. I am not a temper-losing sort of guy and, in the absence of that, there is simply no way to negotiate a relationship argument to a firm conclusion with a smart modern woman. What happens, generally, is that the male is requested to change his behavior and to share his feelings more. That's it. The sum total of gender politics in the new millennium. Change your behavior, and share your feelings more.

Clearly, Krystal is soon going to be an ex-girlfriend. I would rather she waits until I have rewoven the threads of my life.

CHAPTER 16

"I AM GOING to visit my son this weekend. I need to take Friday off. Maybe Monday too."

The CIO strokes his ugly goatee, which I have always wanted to rip off with a pair of pliers. He is my manager, so I need his approval.

"Meyer, this is very short notice. I don't know."

His name is Bryn. The name alone should have ensured that he was banished to the edges of society, there to be subjected to eternal ridicule. But somehow, presumably through pure ass-lickery, he has risen to CIO. Chief information officer. This is a title that came to prominence in the 1980s, when CEOs realized that they knew nothing about computers and needed somebody to pretend that they did, so that they could hide behind deniability. Like most CIOs, Bryn is an idiot who thinks that computers were built to assist accountants.

"Bryn, sign the leave form."

"Meyer, you are on thin ice here. I will sign this leave form if I feel it is justified. I will have to talk to the CEO."

"Listen, you spineless technophobe. Sign the leave form or else I will fuck your wife and put it on YouTube, and release your identity to the Russian cybermafia."

He thinks I am being funny and laughs. A little haltingly.

Being a techno whiz at a large company bestows one with outsized power and reckless courage.

"Bryn, my dick is bigger than yours."

He looks at me nervously. Am I making a pass at him? Being ironic? Making a joke? Presenting a larger metaphor? Talking in riddles?

He folds. "OK, just this once."

Bryn was promoted to be my boss a few years ago. He is somehow connected to the CEO via one of the CEO's ex-wives, mistresses, or girlfriends. I suspect the job was a payoff of some kind, a favor to keep a mistress from opening her mouth, presumably about some unspeakable, disgusting, and probably illegal sexual aberration that the CEO wanted kept under wraps. Bryn had taken a few courses in Computer Science at some community college and had worked as a something or other in a small company, making sure the disks were backed up or something. This apparently qualified him to join our IT department and then to quickly ascend to CIO, where he spends most of his time trying to hide his ignorance, mainly by being a so-called consultative manager, which allows him to remain clueless, delegating important decisions to more knowledgeable underlings. It is not possible to hate Bryn. However, it is possible to gain some pleasure in flaunting his ignorance.

"Hey, Bryn, have you read about this new computer from SAP?"

"SAP makes hardware?"

"Yeah, they do now. It is a tablet about the size of Apple's, has a 20GHz processor, and most impressively, a petabyte of RAM. Resolution of the display is 4K with a holographic option, and it has integrated Bose speakers. And, get this, it is free with the purchase of SAP software."

"God, that's impressive. Where did you see this?"

"I'll send you the report. It's confidential, so don't show anyone. I've signed a nondisclosure."

The CEO calls me an hour later.

"Meyer, I want one of those SAP tablets."

"SAP is a software company, sir."

"Bryn says you have a report on a new tablet of theirs. 4K screen resolution."

"He must be mistaken, sir."

Bryn storms into my office.

"Did you bullshit me about SAP?"

"It's possible that they will make a tablet one day. I was just speculating."

"Jesus, Meyer, I told the CEO."

"Always check your facts, Bryn."

I feel guilty, which always passes, but I decide to take him to lunch, as a peace offering. We head out in Bryn's fancy Acura. He hits the CD button. The speakers spring to life. There are four guitars, no other instruments. It is a version of a classic Hendrix song, the name of which escapes me. It starts off simply, one guitar stating the melody, high on the neck, then joined by another, whispering the chords, a third playing a simple one-five bass, and a fourth sprinkling midrange embellishments, no more than three or four notes at a time. It is haunting.

Then, as the melody comes around again, the song starts to morph, the chords now stepping out of their original clothes and modulating from a major to a minor key, with the melody bending to accommodate itself to its new environment. The bass runs double up, walking the new scales while the fourth guitar changes the short note spicing to long bending leading tones, lifting the melody into a near hymn.

The top comes around again and the fourth guitar moves into a Bach-like counterpoint, arpeggios enveloping the melody, which has changed shape again, now only an echo of the original. The chords too have opened up, their voicings stretched wider than standard form, sometimes across nearly three octaves. The bass has changed personality too, now sustaining bar-long fortissimo root notes, a foundation of deep resonance.

It is astounding. The arrangement reverses, languidly returning to the simplicity of the original Hendrix composition, the guitars slowly returning to the textural fingerprint of the great guitarist, until only one guitar remains, playing the last eight a cappella, the final note ringing out and slowly fading.

"Jesus, Bryn. I didn't know you had taste in music. Who in the hell was that?"

"That was me."

"*What?*"

"I play a bit of guitar. Overlaid a few tracks."

"Bryn, tell me you're kidding."

"No, it was me."

He is grinning shyly.

"WHAT THE FUCK ARE YOU DOING TRYING TO BE A FAKE CIO? WHERE DO YOU PLAY, WHO DO YOU PLAY WITH? ARE YOU FUCKING KIDDING ME?"

"Nowhere. Nobody. I do it for myself."

"Bryn, I play on weekends with my band, which is pretty good. Please come and sit in. Please. We do . . . well, all sorts of stuff. You'll fit right in."

"Nah. Thanks, though. I do it for myself."

I stare at him for a long while.

"Bryn, you are one weird motherfucker."

"Thanks."

You never really know about people. In time, they will always surprise you.

CHAPTER 17

I ARRIVE AT Grace's apartment exuberant, kit bag over my shoulder, like a teenager on spring break. She lets me in this time, handing me a mug of coffee as she retreats into her room to refine some last-minute packing. I wander around the small, tidy living room and kitchen looking for evidence of something. I spy an old, very small photo on the mantle—Grace and me and a tiny bundle of Innocent, bewildered face peering out of a confusion of swaddling. Grace is grinning manically. I look a little worried, which I was and clearly still am. I recognize the photo, but I don't remember the circumstances or photographer. I am gratified that there is some evidence of what used to be us in her daily field of vision.

I circle the room again, drilling one click down to a more sophisticated snoop. Envelopes, books, magazines, tabletops, fridge. No gun magazines, no beers, no books on sports celebrities, no socks, no equity reports, no smell. No evidence of any improprieties that I can divine. Meaning, obviously, any recent tumescent male visitors.

"You looking for signs of recent tumescent male visitors?"

She knows me well. And it appears that she has been watching me for a while.

"Who, me?"

"He left this morning after I told him I simply couldn't bear to have another orgasm."

I stand there like an idiot, hoping she is not only exaggerating, but fabricating completely.

Grace drives a rattling old Honda, most likely purchased for its miserly fuel consumption, which I suspect is no more environmentally friendly than any other car, given the wheezes and rattles that it consumptively emits. We navigate our way onto Route 1, having decided to take the scenic route. It is 8:30 a.m. Grace leans forward and flicks on National Public Radio to catch *Morning Edition*. As Renée Montagne, the authoritative cohost of this eloquent institution, gently intrudes, I lean back in the seat and close my eyes. It is an indication of something, I decide, that a publicly funded entity in a capitalist superpower can be this good. Government supported, further bolstered by grateful listener contributions, this radio station is nonpareil, except perhaps for the heyday of the BBC. Nobody gets rich here. Radio journalists and announcers are paid modest professional salaries; the temptations of great fortunes in stock options and inflated bonuses do not intrude, leaving pure and unsullied reportage, smart and deep, the best of the best. In darker moments, when I consider the certainty of my being blinded one day by some black swan accident involving industrial solvents, I am comforted by the fact that I would always have Ella Fitzgerald, Steely Dan, Stravinsky, and National Public Radio. Life would be bearable.

We listen for a while. It is like old times, the short golden period when all was possible. Me, Grace, the baby. The walls of life were not visible then, obstacles and barriers puny. Any direction we chose to take was clear and infinite. And then doubt crept in, my own inventions, I suspect. That's the problem with youth. It creates so many options that we immediately start comparing them, and that's the end of it. Somebody once mentioned that a study concluded that arranged marriages in, um, "less democratic societies" are more solid, more successful and happier than free choice marriages in the US, beacon of individual liberty. Back then, with Grace, I now wish some stern and rigid and aged elder would have presented me with an arranged life. I simply would have got on with it, built something that mattered, at least to Grace and Innocent. But no, we exploit our freedoms and end up lost in choice.

"What's new with you, Meyer? How are your other families?"

That stung.

"Isobel is a smart, funny, and disobedient teenager, all insurrection and attitude. But fine, thank you. And you, what's new?"

"I'm going back to Zimbabwe next month for a visit. Dad is ill."

"Shit, I'm sorry. Your mom?"

"Old. Broken."

There is a small rent in her voice, like a tearing of silk.

"That's awful, Grace."

"Life didn't turn out the way they expected."

"I'm not sure if it ever turns out the way anyone expects."

"No, it was worse for them. They had a way of life. A little farm that actually produced stuff for sale. Friends. A loyal dog. They were good people."

She falls silent. We were lightweight back then. We never really had concerns of consequence, other than Innocent. We could opine and speculate from a distance. There was no real adversity, no need to test our mettle. Sadly, eventually life submits to its own gravitas. She wants to talk. So I wait for her.

"Then it all dropped away, piece by piece. Mugabe's thugs killed the dog, then took the farm, neglected it into ruin. I left to live in a place halfway around the world. Their savings were simply emaciated by inflation. Friends fled to the gray skies of England. They bought a small apartment in Harare and sat and watched rented videos while their dreams, I don't know, simply withered and died."

"I suppose they could have left."

"They didn't have the money to leave. They just sort of stayed, hoping it would get better, or at least not worse, hoping there was still room for White Africans. There isn't."

"I'm sorry."

"I feel guilty. I should have been there while all of this was happening."

The great regret of all dutiful children in a diasporic world. We say goodbye to our parents, and then move on, like animals in the wild. It is the curse of modernity. We want what is over there, not here. Here is boring. We want to be out of sight of both parental opprobrium and pride as we head out to try our hand.

"How sick is he?"

"Dying."

"Shit. What's your mom going to do? I mean after . . ."

"Then she is going to die too."

I can't think of anything more to say. I am desperate for her, but the more selfish part of me notes grimly that this is not the sort of conversation I was hoping to have with her. I am full of dread; the last thing I need is a conversation about death. The words *dread* and *death* share enough letters, I don't need to add to the load. But it is also not lost on me that I am one of the few people that she would share this with.

"I wish you strength, Grace. It's going to be tough."

She nods grimly, face set. I stare out the window. We are out of the city now, heading toward Santa Barbara, the sea within pebble-throwing distance on our left. This coast is all Beach Boys, Eagles, tanned skin, hazy sky, and soft perfection. The first time I saw it on a college jaunt it held me mute, a cliché made perfect in its skin. Whatever America has become, a set of festering missteps and aging prints of faded grandeur, this stretch of coastline mocks it.

CHAPTER 18

WE HEAD INTO Santa Barbara for breakfast, sliding along the harbor looking for a restaurant until we find something pedestrian, or at least pretending to be.

The waitress brings coffee and then retreats. Grace studies my face intently.

"Why did you lie about Innocent inviting you?"

"Moi?"

"I asked him. You invited yourself."

"Guilty. I haven't spent a weekend with the two of you since we were married."

"Why didn't you just ask me?"

"Would you have said yes?"

"No."

"There you are, then."

"I don't like lies."

"Me neither."

"You lied back then."

"Only a few times."

"Yes, a few times, but about important things."

"Like what?"

"Like when I asked you if you were happy. At Innocent's first birthday party."

"What did I say?"

"You said you were."

"Maybe I was."

"You left me a week later."

"Oh, right. Big mistake that."

"Maybe, maybe not. I was thinking of leaving you."

"Really?"

"Yes."

"Because you weren't happy. That was obvious. And it rubbed off on me."

"How was it obvious?"

"C'mon, Meyer. I knew you pretty well."

I wasn't happy then, that's true. But I wasn't sad. I loved Grace, I loved Innocent. I just wasn't certain. About anything. And if there is one thing you need in a marriage with kids, it is certainty.

There is a commotion a couple of tables down. Some shouting. We stop and listen. A large, corpulent man is dressing down the waitress. The nature of the offense is not clear, but his son, who is about eight, is grinning lopsidedly and his wife is staring at the floor.

My blood rises. Motherfucker. This is my CEO's territory. And I never do anything because he is my boss. The whole restaurant is staring. I fucking hate people who yell at waitresses. I hate them more than anyone else in the world. And this guy does not have my job in his hands.

"I DID NOT ORDER THIS. I ORDERED THE CHICKEN. I AM NOT INTERESTED IN TALKING TO YOU. I WANT TO SEE THE MANAGER. NOW!"

That's it. I jump up. I can see Grace's eyes widen, but in three strides I am there.

"What seems to be the problem, sir? I am the owner of this establishment."

"THIS IDIOT BROUGHT ME TUNA. I ORDERED CHICKEN."

I look at his wife, her pinched and beaten face still staring at the floor. It is evident she hears this tone of voice a lot. And probably worse.

The waitress is staring at me in confusion. I glance down at her name badge.

"Inez, let me see your order ticket, please."

She hesitates, looks back at the kitchen and then back at me. She slowly hands it over. I don't really bother to read it.

"It's says tuna here, sir."

"I ORDERED CHICKEN, DIPSHIT. ARE YOU CALLING ME A LIAR?"

Are you calling me a liar? In any language, this is an invitation to violence. His son has a fat face full of unrestrained glee, his piggy eyes gleaming with the expectation of an ass-whupping handed out by big daddy. He has seen this before and probably knows where it ends. I look at dad more closely. Huge, fat, probably unfit. But then a small flutter of dread intrudes.

Just seconds ago, I envisaged him taking at swing me, followed by a deft sidestep on my part and watching as he crashes to the floor, followed by outsiders rushing in to end the scene. The new dread-fueled scenario now has his punch connecting hard. I fall back, crash to the floor, but not before striking the side of my neck on a table like that woman boxer in the Clint Eastwood movie with Hilary Swank. My spine gets crushed around C3, and I am consigned to a bed as a quadriplegic for the rest of my life, shitting my diapers and speaking unintelligibly through damaged vocal chords. This would be a great victory for dread.

But what the fuck. In for a penny. I lay my cards on the table.

Softly, almost whispering.

"Listen, you fat fuck. You see that sign over the door? It says *Right of admission reserved.* I no longer grant you that right. Or your son. If you are not out of here in twenty seconds, the kitchen staff will shove that tuna sandwich up your ass and put it on YouTube. Have I made myself clear? Your wife, however, may stay and finish her lunch."

He stares at me in shock, mouth opening and closing like a fish. As does his son. His wife, for the first time, lifts her eyes and locks with mine for a brief instant. His breathing escalates. At this point, two stocky Latino busboys step out of the kitchen, presumably to see what all the fuss is about. The moment stretches. My guy looks at the busboys and then back at me. I can see the fight seep out of him.

"We're leaving." The thunder in his tone has receded. He has surrendered. "The food here is terrible anyway. You'll be hearing from my lawyer."

He stands up, glares at his wife and son, who also start to get up. I lean in real close, standing on tiptoes to get near his ear and whisper.

"You mean your lawyer who is fucking your wife?"

He storms out. His wife catches my eye again. I believe I catch a small smile. I turn to the waitress, who is completely wide-eyed.

"Inez, would you mind getting me some ketchup?"

I saunter back to my table and sit down. Grace is looking at me as though I am an alien.

"Good God. What did you say to him?"

"Just reasoned with him is all."

"Who *are* you?"

"You glad I invited myself?"

She smiles.

It is a good smile.

CHAPTER 19

IN OUR EARLY twenties, Van and I once took a road trip across the US. We had in mind some sort of updated Kerouac journey of discovery, and felt self-important and indestructible as we set off, strains of Simon and Garfunkel's "America" bouncing around the car. We had met in New York when I had moved there to try to break into the music scene, after the divorce from Grace, and during a period in Van's life when he was actively looking to flee the wealth of his family. Which contrasts nicely with his current stance, which is to dip in for a top-up when circumstances require, which is not often.

I had seen him playing solo at a bar in SoHo, came back the next week with my sax and sat in with him. We played the Great American Songbook for tips and willing waitresses. It was a fine time. Playing the Great American Songbook, from Cole Porter all the way to Bacharach, will teach a person a thing or two about song structure and chord progression. Moreover, the lyrics—which we didn't sing, but which were sometimes caterwauled by a drunk in high spirits—were a good measure of the history of American culture before lyrical poetic talent ceased to be a requirement of popular music sometime in the '70s.

"Van, let's drive across America."

"OK."

"That's it? OK?"

"Yeah."

Man of few words, Van.

"Don't you want to know why?"

"Not really . . . OK, why?"

"Mandela got released. You see the connection?"

"No."

"Neither do I. But let's do it anyway. We can stop and busk anytime we need spare change."

"I am a trust-fund kid, remember?"

"I thought you hated your trust fund."

"I do. We can busk on the sidewalk if we need change."

"That's what I said."

"Oh, sorry."

"What's up, why are you so distracted?"

"Because I'm depressed."

"That's because you will never have to work for your money. You have no mountains to climb."

"I'm depressed because we have no Mandela in the US. We need a Mandela."

"That's why we're going to drive across America. To find our Mandela."

We didn't find Mandela. But I found talk radio. This, surprisingly, was and still is the heartbeat of America. Forget the *New*

York Times, *USA Today*, CNN, and their new media interactive equivalents and competitors and brave new offshoots. Just listen to talk radio. Rush Limbaugh may not have invented the medium, but he perfected it, gathering disciples around him like a fat, sharp-tongued, smart, abrasive, right-wing Jesus, to the point that he now as near as controls the Republican agenda. You want to know what the evolution-hating, abortion-hating, gay-hating, liberal-hating, Muslim-hating, intellectual-hating rump of conservative middle America thinks? Don't bother with editorials in conservative newspapers, or Newt Gingrich's comical rants about the end of America, or slick blow-dried captains of industry, or wild-eyed Christian fundamentalists. Just listen to the inarticulate and desperate roars of the prescreened Rush callers, blaming everything on everyone. There lies the enemy within.

And the other side, to which I reluctantly belong—the brain-dead, all-tolerant liberal apologists—well, sadly, their talk-show hosts just can't compete, because their stance is defined by why-can't-we-all-just-get-along homilies and infuriating sanctimony. If you are offended enough by Rush, you could always switch to insult radio, burnished long ago by Stern, but that was always a sideshow of sex and celebrity and self-aggrandizement. Leaving the libertarians, a ragtag group of reasonably smart, reasonably interesting, reasonable people who talk loudly, without a hope in hell of controlling any agenda, ever.

Grace smacks my hand.

"Stop fiddling with the radio, Meyer. It's annoying."

"I am looking for Rush Limbaugh."

"Tell me you're kidding."

"No, I love Rush."

"He would have you tarred and feathered."

"This's why I love him. He's a man who knows what he thinks and says it. Unlike me."

"This is my car, and I am not listening to Rush. He makes me want to vomit."

"That's why he's so good. Name me another talk-show host that makes people want to vomit—one who is listened to by, what is it, 20, 30 million people?"

"Meyer, this is not a negotiation. Find something else."

I switch the radio off.

"Wanna fool around?"

She giggles. Which is not an affirmative answer, but it is a signal of some kind. Maybe that she still finds me funny.

Humor. Giggling, snorting, shrieking. That's what I had before dread insinuated itself on my good offices. Grace and I—God, we laughed. Perhaps it was because we were young or simply naive, but I suspect it was something more, a gestalt of some kind. How clichéd does that sound? We would pass a cat on the sidewalk with a strangely shaped head and physically collapse, helpless. Yelp and wheeze at *Seinfeld*. Snigger at bad puns. Laugh quickly and explosively at just about anything.

I look at her handsome profile and wonder. Was there ever a time I was as happy as when I was with her? And why did I choose to sabotage it? Is it possible for life to be truly that funny again?

"You can't recreate the past, Meyer."

She's like a fucking clairvoyant.

"What are you talking about?"

"You know what I'm talking about. Us."

"I thought the expression was—you can't go home again."

She doesn't respond. Looks at me ambiguously and then back at the road ahead. We have joined the 101, and are on the inland stretch, a gentle drive of easy views and small towns.

"How is the PhD going?"

"Well."

"What is your thesis about?"

"The great North American urban intellectual novelists of the second half of the twentieth century, and to what extent their books were great stories for a literate audience or solipsistic rants by arrogant misogynists. The title is a little more restrained than that. It is *Story or Soapbox: Late 20th Century Male North American Novelists—Advertisements for Themselves?*"

"Huh. Who?"

"Roth, Mailer, Heller, Updike, Ford, Bellow, Richler, DeLillo, Pynchon, the usual suspects."

"And?"

"You can read the thesis when I'm done."

"Just a hint?"

"Arrogant narcissists, mostly. But that's why they were so good, I suspect. At least that's what I am going to argue. In order to write books that influential, that perceptive, that incisive, that enthralling, you—through your characters—have to be able to rant without fear or favor. Without the rant, the story loses its color, its import, its weight. *Herzog*, perhaps the best novel to ever come out of the US, was thin on plot and fat on rant. The wonder of some of these novels is how secondary plot is to the characters and their views on, well, everything. Not all, of course, but definitely Roth and Bellow and Updike and Mailer and Heller."

"The only difference between them and the rest of us is that they wrote well enough to have a platform on which to stand and opine."

"No, that's not it. There are great writers who steer clear of personalizing the opinions of their characters, of using them as loudspeakers. And there are plenty of nonwriters who either don't have anything interesting to say about the world or choose not to say it. And I suppose there are plenty of people who use other platforms of opinion effectively—nonfiction writers, bloggers, public speakers, politicians, filmmakers, teachers. But with these novelists there is an earsplitting confluence of art and opinion that is both shining and wondrous. The novel and the narcissistic novelist is a perfect merging of medium and message and Mesmer."

And this is the woman I dumped for superficial pleasures.

"How are you getting by while you do this?"

"I have stepped up my teaching. A few private students of rich foreign parents who wish them to become exceptional Americans. And an ex-husband who helps out."

"Least I can do."

"No, it's enough; you don't have to do anymore."

It is not nearly enough.

CHAPTER 20

RECURRING DREAMS. REPOSITORY of the dread. Farzad assures me that we all have them. He considers these dreams unpleasant, but generally healthy, giving anxieties a platform to kvetch. He gently explained this to me once.

"I didn't say kvetch. That word belongs to your tribe, brought to life in the fetid gutters of Germany before they got nasty with you. I said dreaming gave anxieties a platform to have their complaints aired."

"OK, so what do they mean, exactly? These dreams, I mean."

"Mean? How the hell should I know? I'm a psychologist. Go consult a soothsayer."

"I thought psychologists knew all about dreams."

"You mean because Freud wrote a book about it? He was mistaken about that and a lot of other things."

"The father of psychology? Mistaken?"

"Yes. He may have wanted to fuck his mother. I did not want to fuck mine. You should have seen her. Even for Tehran, she lacked sex appeal. However, I do want to fuck your mother."

"My mother's not around anymore, Farzad."

"Even so."

To enumerate, past and present. Gone are the tumbling-through-the-air-in-the-nude dreams. Gone are the not-prepared-for-the-exam dreams. There is the one where I am called on to play a solo on a song that has chords that I don't know. But this one doesn't count, because I usually end up blowing the audience away anyway. There is the one where I seek drugs, and they're always out of reach, and the police are on every corner. Me and an unnamed young lady looking for an empty room in which to do it, but never finding one. Thereafter the big guns. Cancer. Choking. Car accidents. My dead children, sometimes both children in the same dream. Dead Grace. Dead Bunny. Dead Krystal. Looking in the mirror and seeing an ancient troll. House burning down. Waking up paralyzed. Pursued by Mexican cartel torturers, trying to explain to Isobel that everything will be OK, when I know it won't. Being spilled off a boat into a dark cold sea in the middle of the Atlantic. An error in my code crashing the World Wide Web. Getting stuck in some Israel-hating Arab country and being thrown in prison as an Israeli spy. Forgetting my address, missing planes, losing passports, eating poisoned food, forgetting the punch line of the joke, leaving the stove on, leaving the kettle on, leaving the car on.

The list is endless.

"Do you have bad dreams, Grace? Recurring ones."

"No, I don't think so—not that I can remember anyway. At least not for a long time. Why? Do you?"

We are in the final stretch now after a scenic detour to see Carmel, hoping to see Clint Eastwood sitting in a coffee bar. We're not even sure if he still lives here.

"Farzad says dreams have an important function. Says they are anxiety podiums or something."

"What kind of dreams?"

"Long list."

"Do you wake up screaming?"

"No."

"So they're not really nightmares then . . ."

"I do wake up with a sense of impending doom, though."

"How often?"

"Every day."

"You don't strike me as particularly doom-laden."

"Yes, well, I put on a brave face."

She looks at me. I twist my mouth into a facsimile of clown bravado. She giggles again, like a piccolo flute.

"So let's tell Innocent that we're getting remarried."

"Then again, let's not, Meyer."

"So what are we going to tell him?"

"That you lied to me and gate-crashed."

"Oh, OK."

"He may be in college, but he's a man now. We need to treat him like one."

"Man, schman. I seem to remember that being in college was somewhat like being in preschool. With the added benefit of sex and drugs."

Actually, being in college was everything it promised to be. I remember this through a thick gauze of lightly scented nostalgia. Everything brimmed then, like a near-boiling kettle. Steam and rumble. Learning, fucking, licking, toking, drinking, smoking, discovering, experimenting, studying, braying, baying, arguing, wondering, exploding. Just fucking exploding with the joy of having no shackles. For the first time ever. The onetime viewing of an expanding universe, before the sharp intrusion of responsibility.

"Does he have a girlfriend?"

"None that I know of. I think that they hunt in packs."

"I remember that." And I did. "So, what should we all do this weekend?"

"Well, until you gate-crashed, I was going to spend some quality time with my son, so you decide."

"OK. We'll catch up on a couple of games and do some clubs."

"Funny."

As we turn a gentle bend, a hitchhiker comes into view. It is a woman, with a backpack. She looks young. I turn to Grace.

"Let's give her a ride."

"I don't know."

"C'mon, Grace, it's not safe for her to be hitching. We have room."

We slow down as we pass her. She looks afraid, but perhaps I am projecting. Grace pulls over onto the shoulder. The hitcher runs up to the car.

Dread makes a quiet entrance. Who the hell hitches anymore? Once upon a time it was a form of safe and flexible public transport.

And then, in the '80s, a series of widely publicized incidents of may-hem and rape and dismemberment, fodder for horror movies, and it was over.

The only hitchers left in California are the desperate, reckless, ignorant, or predatory. As I said, I am a student of the odds. Des-perate, reckless, ignorant, or predatory. Lots of potential dread buried in those probabilities, Bayes' theorem not required. What in the world possessed me to make this suggestion? Milk of human kindness? Adventure? As she opens the car door, I have a bad feel-ing in the pit of my stomach.

"Thank you so much."

She is even younger than I thought. She leans in.

"Where are you going?" Grace asks.

"Get the fuck out of the car."

Huh?

That fast?

No preliminaries?

A tiny smidgeon of dread inflates into three sudden Techni-color dimensions. I am staring at an eighteen-year-old girl holding some set-department standard-issue snub-nosed gun. I notice that she's pretty, but her eyes are dead. Fuck, I've drawn a full house. All four—desperate, reckless, ignorant, *and* predatory. I am reasonably pleased, though, considering. Being told to get out of the car is a whole lot better than being driven to a dry river bed and executed.

Except for the fact that Grace has not heard her properly.

"I beg your pardon?"

Grace is now twisted around in the driver's seat, her smile in freeze-frame as she sees the gun.

The problem with most crises, particularly real-time crises, is that the only guide we have is what we have read or seen on a screen somewhere. There are no honest reactions anymore. Only poorly executed copies of old movie dialogue. Scenes flash by. Motive. Motive above all. Why is she doing this? I twist around further, so that I am facing her.

"You don't want to do this."

As the words come out of my mouth it strikes me as the silliest line ever written. Of course she wants to do this. That's why she is doing it. Surprisingly, she slides into the rear seat and closes the door.

"Mister, I do want to do this. What do you see? What you see is a child with a gun. Can there be anything more dangerous than a child with a gun? I like to steal money and do drugs. I have no future at all. So get the fuck out of the car before I shoot you between the eyes."

Grace starts to open her door.

"Hang on, Grace, we're not going anywhere. And what do you see, young lady? You are looking at a techno geek. I am recording you right now; it's going out on the Internet."

Without even a glimmer of hesitation she slams the gun down on my head. I dimly wonder how she avoids crushing her fingers, something I have always wondered in similar movie scenes. It hurts like hell. Grace yelps, bringing her hand up to her mouth.

And then we are standing on the shoulder, the car fishtailing down the road.

"Fuck. FUCK. FUCK! I can't believe that just happened. We could have been killed."

This is Grace swearing. This pleases me. I am holding my head, which is throbbing, but not bleeding, at least as far as I can tell. Then I start giggling, because it seems like the appropriate thing to do.

Grace is appalled. The blood has not returned to her face.

"Why are you laughing?"

"Because I have always dreaded being carjacked; it is one of my recurring dreams. Now it's history."

CHAPTER 21

VICTIM OF VIOLENT crime. I have become this earnest statistic. I am thrilled, as though I've been given some sort of industry award. Avoided serious injury, missed hours of fear, was not humiliated too much, didn't lose anything of importance, can't say I feel too violated.

Grace does not agree. She is trembling, near tears.

"Meyer, what were you thinking? You could've gotten us killed!"

"I was acting on impulse."

"Well, next time act on impulse with somebody else's life. That's why we broke up. You were always acting on impulse."

"But you used to love that about me, used to tell me that you loved my impulsiveness."

"Meyer, we were staring into a barrel, for God's sake. It's not the same thing."

We are sitting on the shoulder of the highway, awaiting the cops, who I have called on my phone. She will be arrested soon, this is certain. Either in the Honda, or the next time, or the next. Nobody who does something this rash can make it for long. She obviously wasn't a student of the odds. I try to capture her face, in case I am ever called on to do a lineup, which is unlikely. Oval face, light skin, a little acne-scarred, deep green eyes with dark lashes, ski-jump nose, pretty dimples, slight cleft chin. Short straight dark brown hair, cut short, dirty.

Even while I am trying to recall her face, I realize that I am making half of this up. If memory is famously fickle, then visual memory is particularly deceitful. I sometimes cannot remember the faces of people I have spent hours talking to. I briefly wonder how many people have been erroneously admitted into our justice system based on somebody's traumatized and untrustworthy recall.

The world is full of people like her. OK, maybe not full, but omnipresent. The overflows and rejects and remainders who live among us. Whose lives have cruel and sad turns, either self-inflicted or by random careen, lives so offtrack and outside the normal protections of common sense and prudence that they eventually power headlong into the stern gaze of protective statute and steel bars. How did this young woman arrive at such a juncture? At a point where murder was contemplated, at least with some level of intent. Whose victims were to be strangers, Good Samaritans even, mere barriers to the temporary freedom of a temporary vehicle.

It gets worse, though, moving out of the realm of the interesting near miss. The cops arrive. We are questioned. Dockets are opened. We are taken to San Francisco. Dropped off at Hertz to rent a car.

Within an hour, we get a call. The car was spotted, a chase ensued, the car is a wreck. Our bags are caught in bureaucracy, but they will be returned at some point. And the driver, I ask. Is she behind bars? Will we have to testify?

There is a moment's silence on the line.

She is dead. Killed instantly.

I find it difficult to formulate an appropriate emotional response. A human being whom I know has died. Suddenly and violently. I am a party to this, perhaps even a cause. Certainly, if one works the chain theory, I was an important link. If I had, for instance, simply acceded, stepped out the car when Grace first tried to, there would have been the matter of a different space-time continuum. Everything would have been delayed by some thirty seconds, the time it took me to resist and the time it took her to react with the pistol. And those thirty seconds were likely, I suspect, to have changed her course of history. Whatever caused her to lose control of the car may not have happened and the ensuing call would simply have been for us to come and collect the undamaged car.

These causal chain arguments, retrospective imaginings, and forward engineering are the root of infinite strands of anxiety. Chains of events are long and complex and a what-if analysis of this and anything else will ruin my sex life forever.

I shake my head and resolve to depersonalize this. Her death was regrettable, I decide, using the icy phrase dredged from stone-faced military spokespersons.

Grace is not so sanguine. She collapses in tears. She is unable to articulate her grief. We sit. I have my arm around her shoulders in the saturated yellow of the Hertz rental agency and I wait for her to stop sobbing.

"She was just a girl, Meyer."

"Yes."

I am going to tread carefully here. This is not a time to enter into philosophical debates about either causality or divine justice, which is another thought that briefly pops into my head before being contemptuously banished.

"She didn't deserve to die."

"Yes."

"Especially in my car."

"Yes."

"She probably has parents, siblings, maybe even children."

"Yes."

Her sobs are subsiding now.

"Don't you have anything to say?"

Yes. No. I try to wriggle out of talking about this.

"I am still in a state of shock."

"You're trying to wriggle out of talking about this."

Fuck's sake. She's like a witch.

"No, I'm not. Really."

"Then tell me how you feel about it."

I know I am under scrutiny here. A wrong answer and it's back to the distant ex-husband for me.

"It's awful, Grace."

This is clearly not going to cut it.

"Meaning what?"

"She seemed lost, even though she smashed a pistol over my head."

"Yes, she did."

Ah. I am on the right track.

I make a few more conciliatory comments that I don't really mean, because now that the initial moment is past, I solidify my position. This was not my fault. It may be true that she didn't deserve to die—at least not in this way—but I must hold my moral high ground here. I even risked life and limb to give her a chance to back out of the transaction.

But Grace stands elsewhere—behind a gender curtain that I will never fully understand. There is a slight stab of guilt as I commit the small deceit of pretending to feel more than I do.

So be it.

We decide to have coffee before driving on to Berkeley. Fisherman's Wharf beckons, notwithstanding its hoarse tourist barking that does little to damage its unashamedly picture-postcard aspect. We find a place at a coffee bar hanging over the harbor and feast on the bay, Alcatraz, the majestically engineered and history-colored bridge, the headlands, Sausalito, Oakland. We are silent for a while, allowing the spectacle to settle into perfection.

Grace is quiet, the trauma of the hijacking affecting her in a way that seems to have eluded me. We react differently to trauma, I suppose. Perhaps it's because I expect it, every moment of every day. I don't know why everybody doesn't.

Farzad is right. The fucking world is collapsing, caught in multiple traumas of every stripe. Capitalism's banner boys, from the US to the civilized countries of old Europe, stagger around drunk and teeter on collapse, while leaders offer platitudes and promises and economists and academics flail. Nobody knows what the fuck is going on. We have statistics pouring out—unemployment, debt, growth, housing starts, markets—looking a lot like those failed states on far-flung continents upon which we have grown used to pouring smug and silent scorn. Economists snipe at each other over failed models and faulty algorithms. Banks twiddle their risk policies, regulators fret about capital requirements and other arcane ratios. But for the rest of us proximity to the euphemistically titled "economic collapse" looms, sending millions into the purgatory of reduced circumstances—unemployment, underemployment, constrained expectations. And at the center of it is the white American male breadwinner and master of his domain, his seat at the table no longer reserved, trying to hold on to any shred of dignity. I am among them, staggering around, center of gravity lost, buffeted by all matters uncertain, which are many and varied.

Grace's face looks haunted. I take her hand, apprehensively. She does not pull it away. Its warmth and softness stir me beyond my expectations.

"You OK?"

"I suppose."

"I am sorry. I hope it doesn't ruin the weekend."

"I'll be OK."

She smiles gamely. Her hand is still in mine.

"So."

"So."

"You glad I came?"

"Besides the fact that we got hijacked and someone got killed?"

"Let's ignore that for the purpose of the question."

She removes her hand.

"When are you going to settle down, Meyer?"

"In what way? I like being unsettled."

"No, you don't."

"How do you know?"

"I know something about you, Meyer. Remember?"

"People change."

"Not in my experience."

I am at a tipping point here. Grace is not going to be interested in the Meyer she remembers. She needs a new one.

"I have changed. In some ways. In the important ways."

"Go ahead. Make my day."

"I don't want to be a famous musician anymore."

"That's not internal change. Lady Luck didn't smile. It was not to be. It took no courage for you to reach that decision. You just had to face facts."

Shit.

"Yeah, but I submitted gracefully. With dignity. Continued to play. No bitterness."

"OK, I'll give you a half-point. What else?"

"I am not promiscuous."

"Define your terms."

"Uh, what do you mean?"

"Do you still look at women with intent?"

Shit again.

"I suppose, but it is appreciation rather than leering."

"But you don't act on it."

"No, not when I'm in a relationship."

"Why?"

"Because I have changed, like I say."

She takes a long sip of her coffee. Eyes stare at me hard. There is a small glint of affection.

"Maybe you're too old to get someone to sleep with you. Maybe your confidence is gone. Maybe you can't get it up anymore."

I feel my male pride squawk in protest.

"Well, I've got news for you. . . ."

"Yeah, yeah, Meyer, I know—you're still a stud."

And then, suddenly, she is kissing me. Her mouth is still partially full of coffee, which decants into mine, while her warm tongue darts in behind, and then retreats. She pulls away. Her eyes are locked on mine. A small flush of red creeps up her neck, a state of fluster I remember well.

"Forget that I did that, Meyer. It means nothing."

It means plenty.

CHAPTER 22

THERE ARE SOME things I understand. Like what kind of altered chord will enhance the emotional underpin of a musical phrase. Like when the flattened 5th or minor 3rd is being overused in a blues solo. Like when I have just played something awful, or good. Like the inner workings of a computer. I mean the deep inner workings. What the microprocessor does, the function of registers, how a transistor works, how a compiler works, how a device driver is written, transport protocols, radio transmission, Shannon limits, Moore's law, Metcalfe's law.

But there is much more that I don't understand. In fact, if you compare the volume of things I know about with things that I don't, I understand almost nothing. Bill Bryson had this problem. So he wrote down all the things he didn't know about and wanted to know about, and then went on an über-search to find out, and then wrote a book about the things he now knows about. This is breathtakingly impressive and well beyond the outer reaches of my disciplines and capabilities. I do not want to meet Bill Bryson. He intimidates me. Even though, when you read his books, you immediately want to be his best friend.

Most of the things I don't know about do not bother me much. It is ignorance well chosen. The absence of these large wedges of knowledge has little effect on me. As long as someone knows about particle physics, or how to pick a lock, or how to tell a person's age from an old skeleton, I can potter about in my little corral of knowledge in peace, safe in the certainty that out there, somewhere, someone knows how to make pesto from pine nuts and basil.

Which leaves the things that I want to know about and don't. This should be a manageably small pile, but it isn't. The pile itself is nebulous and shape-shifts like some imagined and evil alien creature. However, like all mushy things there is some consistency.

What I do not know about most of all is myself and why I always think that the sky is about to fall.

A close second is women. I am an educated, politically aware, liberal, Bill-of-Rights sort of guy, who has supported every NOW issue since I can remember. Viscerally, unconditionally, and with total commitment. So why do I know so little about these people? Who I have revered from about the age of four when I told a girl called Sally at preschool that I wanted to marry her, and she threw sand in my eyes, which only made my heart grow fonder. Or Constance, to whom I wrote a scrawled letter in, get this, second grade, proclaiming that my status as wounded soldier and hers as ballerina foresaw a life of bliss for us. The teacher found the note and gleefully read it out loud to the class. Constance was so embarrassed that she never again talked to me, which, again, made my heart grow fonder. By fourth grade I had kissed a girl with tongue. Not to brag or notch, but because she was so beautiful that kissing her was the only paradise I sought. Nonsexual and profoundly romantic. And the legions of young ladies at high school, pursued with vigor and determination, some requited, some not. Thought about them constantly. Talked to them as often as possible. Hung out with them. Chatted on the phone with them. Masturbated to their images. Had inarticulate but meaningful sex with some. Had my heart broken, mended, remolded, shattered, reanimated, deflated, dirtied, buffed, and shined. Sometimes in the course of a week.

I shared their concerns, their triumphs, and their disappointments. I sought out their company, in massive preference to male friends. Not that I had no male friends, but the mystery of these strange people was like the strong nuclear force: the closer you got, the more the attraction tended toward asymptotic. Not attraction actually, but something more magical, like allure. These people are almost like my gender. They have hands and feet and nostrils and teeth. But a little smaller, a little more slender, with higher voices and more intriguingly, soft, swaying protuberances on the chest that trigger ancient longings and an astonishing set of folds and textures and odors and wetness and open invitations lower down—deep, dark, and overwhelming. Beyond ken. Beyond reason. Beyond reckoning.

"Krystal, I don't understand you."

"What are you talking about, Meyer?"

"What do you want?"

"Again, what are you talking about?"

"What do you want from me?"

"I want you to do what I tell you to."

Well that's settles that. Perhaps she is right. Perhaps I should do what she tells me to.

Bunny was different toward the end.

"Bunny, I don't understand you."

"You're not supposed to understand me. You are supposed to understand yourself. Which you don't. Which is why this marriage is in trouble. Why don't you go into therapy?"

Touché.

"Isobel, I don't understand you."

"Of course you don't understand me, I'm a teenager."

I call Farzad.

"Farzad, I don't understand women."

"Of course you do not. Nobody understands women. Least of all psychologists. Especially male ones."

"Bullshit. Do you understand your wife?"

"Certainly. We have a simple understanding. I tell her what to do. This is built into my history and culture. Patriarchy is the only workable solution to the gender gap."

"Does it work? Does she do what you tell her to?"

"Of course not. She is an American. She does what she wants."

"So what happened to your simple understanding?"

"It gets lost in the implementation."

"So you don't understand your wife?"

"Of course I do. We have a simple understanding."

"Which gets lost in the implementation."

"Exactly."

CHAPTER 23

EXCEPT GRACE.

I always understood Grace. Her heart had been warmed by the Zimbabwe sun and a barefoot youth on a small farm where echoes of British colonialism had grown faint, save for good cheer, early mornings, and benefits of a straight-backed education. The leaden weights of unquestioned physical safety and success-fed isolationism have stunted the natural curiosity of many a US childhood and tainted many of my generation who are now beset by a lamenting apathy. So when Grace arrived here she was lifted above the crowds—good-natured, optimistic, widely read, inquisitive, passionate, enthusiastic, grounded, moral, innocence dented but intact. And the scabrous and violent desecration of her country has left her grateful for the abundance of everything that she finds here. Not the sort of gratitude proclaimed by the wild-eyed my-country-right-or-wrongers, but the gratitude of the thankful immigrant.

We rent a car and a debate ensues as to whether or not we should get the cheapest. I am dead set against it, spewing dire warnings about how easily they crumple on impact. Grace won't let me help with money, so I have to bow to the tiny box into which we squeeze.

We arrive at the B&B B&B with newly purchased emergency items of clothes and toiletries. It is a modest green clapboard house in Berkeley, in a residential part of town not too far from campus. It has two stories. As we sign in I note with a ping of excitement that they have placed us in adjoining rooms on the top floor.

We walk to our rooms and open our doors simultaneously. I look over to Grace just before she enters. I feign disinterest.

"Don't even think about it, Meyer."

"Moi?"

But she is gone.

We pick up Innocent from his place, low-rent stucco student accommodation that looks unfit for human habitation, which makes it perfect for the aspiring Berkeley intellectual. He is a gangling young man, with a tall gene that I can only ascribe to Grace's father rather than my little ancestors. He has a lopsided smile, Grace's perfect proportions, and my propensity to grin a lot. Or maybe an early-twenties Berkeley student's propensity to grin a lot. Film-star looks, thankfully balanced by an early receding hairline.

He slides into the back seat and leans forward to kiss his mother on the cheek.

He looks sideways at me. I raise my eyebrows. I get my kiss too.

"Forgotten how to kiss your dad, now that you're a college boy?"

"Means something different up here," he counters.

My family was loving, but not particularly physically affection-ate. There was a time in my late teens when I became fixated on Italian movies. I remembered a few of the plots—some had none as far as I could tell, but I was deeply struck by all the hugging and kissing. Plotting a direct line from the discovery of heated baths to Michelangelo to Florentine architecture to sleek sports cars to physical warmth, I imbibed the family-should-always-kiss-and-hug ethos, now firmly imprinted on Innocent.

"Like old times, hanging with my mom and dad."

"You were about one year old when we split, Innocent," I remind him.

"I have a good memory."

"How are things, Innocent? You eating properly?" asks Grace. Mothers are the same the world over.

I turn in my seat to look at him. It is a good question. He looks tired. Burning-the-candle-at-both-ends tired.

"Mind if a friend joins us for dinner? She lives just around the corner."

I feel my eyebrows bob up.

"Sure, of course."

Grace is staring at him through the rearview mirror.

"Girl friend? Or girlfriend?"

"Ha ha. Nosy parents. Just a friend. For now."

It is dark by the time we reach the restaurant, a place called The Green Fig, a health-food restaurant priding itself on fair trade, everything-free, union-picked food, which is predictably tasteless, edible only with liberal gobs of soy sauce.

We have picked up Innocent's friend, a rake-thin, pallid-skinned girl named Wanda. She is logorrheic, words tumbling out of her mouth, subjects careening off each other, tangential thoughts exploding from nowhere, inappropriate giggles bursting forth from phrases without humor. It is unnerving. I have seen this many times before.

"Oh my God, I have heard so much about you both I mean Innocent just loves you guys talks about you all the time he is so smart Innocent oh my God look there's Jerry don't let him see me that's such a nice jacket Mrs. M where did you get it and Innocent that is such an awesome name combo which is not to say I don't like the name Meyer too Innocent says everyone calls you by your last name but I should stop talking now you guys need to catch up please excuse me I have to go to the bathroom."

Cocaine. Or meth. But probably coke because she still seems to have all of her teeth.

I glance at Grace. She is smiling at her son. I turn to Innocent.

"My, she's sparky, isn't she?"

I can tell he is a bit embarrassed.

"She was excited about meeting you. She'll calm down."

He picks up the menu and pretends to read. I look at him more intently now. There are dark rings under his eyes. His skin is sallow.

My son is doing drugs. What kind and how often is not the issue. He is doing drugs and he is fucking a cokehead. I have a long history here, both personal and by close witness. This is a fetid breeding ground for dread, a swamp in a humid summer. I know coke. It is a stupid fucking drug. Unlike dope, which is occasionally a very clever drug, which when mixed with the right company or food or music or conversation can make for a great evening with little next-day residue. Alcohol, ditto, a versatile lubricator, if you have an off switch that kicks in just before melancholy, violence, or vomit. Heroin, king of the drugs, not really that stupid because it is a premeditated choice basically to commit suicide slowly and pleasantly, interspersed with moments of sheer panic. Ecstasy, mindless rather than stupid, in a fun/dance/sex kind of way. Meth doesn't even count as stupid because it is just shrieking death.

But coke? The most stupid of drugs. I cannot remember a single interesting thing that I said or did under its dictates. And I have watched more people embarrass and debase themselves under an illusion of fascination and self-importance than I care to remember.

CHAPTER 24

WANDA IS MERCIFULLY long in returning from the bathroom. Grace does not know the world of sparkling substances and altered realities and seems blissfully unaware of this dark cloud gathering over Innocent.

"Innocent, I'm serious, you look thin and pale. I want you to eat more and get into the sun occasionally. Are you studying too hard?"

"I am fine, Mom, really. How's the PhD going?"

"Nearly done. It's been good."

"My mom, the doctor."

He flashes a white-toothed, off-center grin. Even in the circumstances it is hard not for me to feel proud of his pride in his mother.

"And Dad, you?"

"Same as. Playing and programming."

"You playing easy?"

"Easy as pie. Easy as a 2-chord jam. Easy as Norah Jones."

"And Sis?"

"Isobel is in full teenage mode. She is a danger to herself and others. She should be sent to a nunnery. She should be forced to wear a chastity belt and sent to live in a tower. She is fine. Sassy and smart. You won't believe it when you see her."

"Krystal?"

"Krystal who? How are your studies? Anything grab you?"

"Yeah. Genetics."

Grace jumps in.

"Genetics? I didn't know you were doing Genetics?"

"I'm not. I went to a guest lecture by that Venter guy. I'm sold."

I can get behind this. A brave new world indeed. Genetics and its practical cousin, genetic engineering, represent an intersection of hard-ass practical science, molecular biology, chemistry, medicine, evolutionary theory. Among other things. With it man will supplant God, sculpt and mold life in ways that will at first alarm us and then eventually nurture and comfort us.

In my day, which admittedly was not that long ago, a student chose a field and walked down its path, which was reasonably well worn. Medicine or computer science or law or math or engineering or psychology or astronomy. And within those fields, the sum of past knowledge had reached such a volume that even the most determined individuals could only glimpse the whole from the one or two parts in which they labored. But human progress these days is much broader. It requires the melding of many ingredients, multidisciplinary fusions and crossovers and borrowings that blur across vast and cluttered silos of old and new knowledge, bewildering and crushing even the most excellent of intellects, who get lost in sheer bulk. A scientist friend of mine, an old school friend, now an assistant professor and the only real live polymath I know, complains bitterly about this.

"I spent seven years getting my doctorate. Now I find I have to study ten other subjects to gain any new insight. I spend my days and nights reading textbooks and research papers on abstruse subjects that were not part of my original degree, trying to make connections. I have no life."

I am cruelly unsympathetic.

"Hey, you want to win a Nobel, you have to pay the price."

"It has nothing to do with winning prizes. It's about keeping my job."

"You were the one who wanted to be an academic. You thought the vacations were cool, and you thought that you would have an endless supply of women."

"Yeah, well, no time for that now. Maybe I should move into the commercial world. I didn't sign up for this, it's too damn hard. There is no end to it. Is there a job for me where you are?"

"Sure, we can really use someone in neuro-patho-psycho-cosmo-philo-onto-chemo artificial evolutionary intelligence imaging whatever the fuck it is you study."

"Nice to get respect from you, Meyer."

But he was wrong. I am pretty much in awe of him and his ilk, foraging around in the totality of human knowledge to synthesize and codify something gleaming and new and useful, to turn ignorance into algorithm, to push the boundaries of our species, if only by a smidge. As opposed to, oh, I don't know, writing enterprise resource planning code for a big company that makes stuff. If I had the remotest chance of edging the sum total of the universal knowledge forward, I would do it, and effort and sacrifice be damned. That would definitely take care of the dread problem.

Innocent is holding forth, in between anxious glances toward the bathroom.

"So I'm going to drop some subjects and take some of the audacious hairy monsters next year."

"Like what?"

"Like math, biology, chemistry, that sort of thing."

"And what are you dropping?"

"The dumb subjects."

Grace takes offense.

"There are no dumb subjects."

"OK, Mom. The easy subjects. Dad calls them the fuck subjects."

"He does, does he?"

I make a show of studying the menu, my eyes earnestly downcast.

Wanda arrives back from the bathroom. She is wiping her nose in the matter-of-fact way of all cokeheads.

"Sorry, there was such a long line and I ran into Jerry who I was trying to avoid what a douchebag sorry about my language have I missed the waitress I'm not really hungry anyway I had a huge lunch you're soooo pretty Mrs. M I can see where Ino gets his looks."

Wanda sits down, eyes ablaze. I am scared of setting her off again, so I decide to ignore her.

"So, Innocent, who are your friends?"

But alas, there is no stopping her.

"Ino has *such* cool friends they're all so smart *and* they like partying I like partying more than studying I'm *so* jealous of these guys you'll really like them there's Alan and Philip and the Chinese guy and the Arab guy and the guy from Australia what's-his-name and the weird fat one who never goes out and oh my God just reads and reads and reads and I'm so glad Ino can be serious and fun you know what I mean?"

There is a stunned silence as we all stare at her. Innocent's face has gone red. Grace turns around to summon the waitress and I catch a brief transaction under the table between Wanda and Innocent.

"Gonna hit the head. Be back in a moment."

Innocent returns a few minutes later. His eyes are also ablaze. His voice has gapped up a major third in pitch, his rhythm is now allegro. His appetite has disappeared.

My beautiful and talented son has become a cokehead.

Fuck.

CHAPTER 25

WE DROP INNOCENT back at his student digs. He piles out of the car with Wanda. I suspect that for them the night is young. I am about to break the grievous news to Grace—who is totally oblivious, believing him to have only been in high spirits—when my phone chirps.

"Hey, Josh. It's me."

Only one person on the planet calls me Josh. My father, Samuel. He lives in Florida, a late-life widower. He is old now, slow moving, tentative, beset by irritating short-term memory loss, but all there. Still drives to the market once a week, against my advice. And reasonably happy in the old-age community in which he is ensconced, playing canasta and bingo with residents whose names he cannot remember and flirting with Latina nurses and administrative assistants who dislike their jobs as much as their charges. When Mom died, he went into pause mode, staring at the TV in a house too large for him, walking the dog, eating only peanut-butter-and-jelly sandwiches, writing letters.

He never was able to make the leap to electronic communications and, with Mom gone, letter writing became his last opportunity to be heard. He was, in his day, one of the great letter writers. Long rambling outpourings of opinion and news and jokes and concern. A lost art now. And with most friends dead or demented, and only me left in what was always a small extended family, he continued to write. But like a tap drying up, the volume of output diminished year by year. When I suggested the move into the facility he was relieved.

He was a good man, my dad. Is a good man. In every aspect of his life he bathed warmly in mediocrity—he wasn't a genius, he wasn't rich, he wasn't charismatic except for an edgy wit and a command of the art of clever repartee. And an occasionally sparked sense of steely rectitude and moral outrage. At these he excelled. He worked hard. He loved his wife, his son. Paid his taxes. Watched football. Cleaned his car. Cared about the middle, not the edges. He adored me quietly and I him. On shoulders like these America was built.

I visit annually, usually on a long weekend. It is not a burden for me and it is the highlight of the year for him. We eat at a good restaurant or two. See a game. Catch a movie. Go for a drive. I am his last link to the life that he carefully built. When Mom died, he spent a while deciding what to do next. His age, which was seventy at the time, presented a paucity of choice. It was a world of diminished possibilities. He couldn't go back to work—nobody would have him, despite being a qualified pharmacist. It was unlikely that he would find another partner. He admitted to me that he still thought about the physical warmth of another woman, about sex, but was at a loss as to how to pursue it. I might have suggested the Internet, assuming that this electronic market for all tastes may have some small corner bazaar for older, widowed men, but he wouldn't have tried it. He was seventy, and looked seventy, and suffered seventy-year-old ailments, none of which he wished to foist upon someone he was wooing, assuming that was even a possibility. Once, when I was commiserating with him, punting platitudes to try to assuage the sting of aging, he said: "It's not important, son, it's just a life." My eyes stung from the depth of that statement—it's just a life. Anyone who ascribes any more importance to it than that, one life out of billions lived, will surely find death a gloomier embrace. The safe community that we chose for him to live in, with all amenities within close proximity, was surely just a consolation, a place merely to contemplate what was done and what little was left.

And that was then. He is going on eighty now. A little shorter, a little more forgetful, a little balder, but still robust, considering.

"Dad! Nice to hear from you. You OK?"

"Fit as a fiddle. You?"

"All good. What time is it down there? Must be early."

"I'm sort of in jail."

Silence.

"Dad, what do you mean you're *sort of* in jail?"

"Not sort of. I'm in jail."

"What are you talking about? Why?"

"I robbed a department store with a gun."

"YOU DID WHAT?"

"Wait, it gets better. On my way back to the car, a kid tried to mug me. So I shot him."

"Oh, my fuck. Tell me you're kidding."

"Nope. And you swear too much."

"When did this happen?"

"Last night."

"Dad, I have to ask, what did you think you were doing? WAIT, IS THE KID DEAD?"

"Nah, just a flesh wound. He tried to mug me. What kind of a person tries to mug an eighty-year-old man?"

"What kind of eighty-year-old man holds up a department store, Dad? Are you OK?"

"Never better. They are treating me real nice in here."

"Oh, Jesus. Where did you get a gun?"

"I've always had a gun."

"What? Why?"

"In case."

"But not for holding up department stores and shooting people. Dad! Jesus!"

"So how is Innocent? How is Isobel?"

"Dad! Focus. Do you have a lawyer?"

"No. They are assigning me a public defender."

"Whatever got into you? Why? I am speechless."

"I was bored. Not much to do when you're eighty."

"Dad, you could end up in prison."

"So? How is that different than now? It's not like I'm going to get raped or anything. Unless they have some really sick people in there."

"OK, just don't do anything. I'm going to track down a local lawyer for you and I'm flying out on the first flight. FUCK! I CAN'T BELIEVE THAT YOU DID THIS!"

But actually, I can. I can believe it zealously, to the point that I can see myself doing it one day too. Why not? This is not a society that reveres its aged. Kids are not there to muffle the sounds of decrepitude. Every image on every page, on every screen, on every billboard celebrates that which you are not. Drugs keep you alive and ticking, more to wring every last bit of misery out of every day of your synthetically lengthened life. A quiet and good man, deformed into an armed robber and shooter by the boredom and certainty of an end close at hand.

Why not rob a store? Shoot a bad guy?

Why not indeed?

CHAPTER 26

AN AGING FATHER in jail for all manner of felonies and a cokehead son. Dread 2: Meyer 0.

Hyman Meyer is a resident of the GoldLife Jewish Senior Living Center in Palm Beach, Florida. Scratch that, he is currently a resident of a Palm Beach county jail. The first thing I do when I arrive is call the Center and assure them that Dad is with me, thereby diffusing a crisis at the Center regarding a certain missing resident. I fudge the questions and apologize profusely for not informing them that I would be taking Dad on a short vacation.

This vacation, I explain, will be a "few days," an answer designed to be fuzzy. My thinking here is that, with luck, I'll be able to find a lawyer, convince the prosecutor that Hyman Meyer is only a confused old man, and pay the medical bills for the flesh wound, plus a little extra for the trouble.

I am quite certain that should the word get out about his little aberration, Dad would be banished from community games and relegated to a life of isolation in the shadows of the old-age community. Dad will be released, I will return him to the Center, and all will be well.

Dad has other ideas.

"I want to go to trial."

We are sitting in a room at the county jail with a prosecutor and our hastily arranged attorney, a pretty young woman from a well-known criminal law firm. I start to object, she shushes me.

"Mr. Meyer . . ."

"Please call me Hyman, young lady."

"Hyman, you do not want to go to trial. The prosecutor here is prepared to accept that you were, let's say 'confused,' The department store owners have agreed to drop charges if you write an apology and sign various other paperwork, including a psychiatric report. The young man has apparently disappeared and if he does not file charges then we should be able to get this all behind us. Nobody wants to sentence an eighty-year-old man. OK?"

My father nods for a long time. For a moment, I think he is going to sleep.

"I want to go to trial. Please charge me with armed robbery and attempted murder."

"Dad, what are you doing? If you go to trial you will end up in prison."

"No, I won't. I'll win."

"You're guilty, Dad. What do you mean you'll win?"

"I am going to plead not guilty by reason of sanity."

The lawyer and the prosecutor exchange looks.

"Dad, there is no such thing."

"Of course, there is no such thing. I am going to create one. Muggers should be shot. Price-gouging department stores should be robbed. These are the actions of a sane man. The jury will love it."

The prosecutor, a tired and beaten man who is certainly younger than he looks, speaks gently.

"Mr. Meyer, I am happy to recommend to a judge that the State has no objection to bail or even to dropping charges, conditional on certain matters. But I want you to realize the gravity of what we are dealing with here."

"Mr. Prosecutor, I may be old and forgetful, but I absolutely understand the gravity and the meaning of 'conditional on certain matters.'"

"You are extremely fortunate that the young man was not seriously injured or worse, and even more fortunate that he seems to have skipped town. He has a bit of a history with the system. You are fortunate that the owners of the department store are part of the Jewish community and are prepared to forgive and forget based on your, um, heritage. I would suggest that you not try to derail your string of good fortune."

"Mr. Prosecutor, the owners of the department store are a bunch of *gunnifs* who deserve to be robbed. Get a taste of their own medicine. As for the young man, he had a knife. I acted in self-defense. I want to go to trial."

Both the prosecutor and lawyer look at me.

"I'd like a few words alone with my dad."

They nod and step out.

"Dad, Dad, Dad . . . What are you up to?"

But I already know.

"Josh, you've never known me to do anything particularly irrational, have you?"

"Nope."

"So do you imagine that I have suddenly been afflicted with an age-related, personality-warping condition?"

"Nope."

"So here's the deal. I am sitting in this old-age home, surrounded by the dying and the sick. I know you offered me a room in your home in California, but I said no, absolutely not, and I meant it. Parents should never be a burden to their children. The Center is warm and safe and the food is reasonable. There are activities to keep us alert and the grounds are nice and there are drugs for pain and sleeplessness and constipation, and I should be grateful. But it is an awful way to die. There are no *good* ways to die, I suppose, but to slip away under the crushing weight of this daily monotony among the decrepit and infirm seems a crime against life."

I start to talk, but he lifts his hand.

"I know that my life was not exceptional. But it was good. I had middle-class freedoms, some of which I took advantage of, some of which I ignored, to my regret. This is surely true of most people. And the process of aging is grievous, which is presumably true of all people, particularly if your partner is gone before you. This doesn't mean that I have to accept it."

"There are other alternatives besides running around shooting guns, Dad."

"Yes, I'm sure that there are many, but that was the one that came to mind at that moment. I'm eighty, for God's sake, I am not capable of that much planning. We were playing cards and out of the corner of my eye I was watching an old woman, Sophie, I think her name is. She is infirm and suffering from extreme dementia. Every day they wheel her to the sun room and put her in front of the TV. Her head lolls to one side. She drools. She certainly does not watch the TV. She has no idea where she is. She does not recognize her one and only visitor, a daughter, I think, quite old herself. There is nothing to signify that she is a sentient human being. Except one thing. Every few days I see her start to cry. Her bottom lip trembles, the tears drop, and she sobs. For a few minutes only. But it is the saddest thing I have ever seen. She is crying for what she has become. She is begging tearfully for death. I am sure of this."

He stops. I wait.

"So yesterday—while we were playing a card game in which I had no interest, and never will—she starts crying again, this time accompanied by a whimper, which I have never heard. And then she says, 'Isaac.' She says it twice. Whimpers more. And then stops. I do not know who Isaac is or, more probably, was. A husband? A child? A brother? But I do know this. Isaac was the person she wanted, right then, at that moment. If Isaac had appeared, she would have been whole again. If your mother were with me, I would be whole again. I am not whole, I realized. I will never be whole again. I am just disappearing while I play canasta. So I stood up, got my gun, and climbed into my car. And I robbed a store of $20. And I shot a mugger. And I am in jail, which is infinitely more interesting than the sun room. And I may go to prison. And I am a little more whole than I was yesterday. And everyone wants me to go back and play canasta so that one day I can end up like Sophie."

I am unable to respond.

CHAPTER 27

BAD THINGS HAPPEN. I know this.

My twin sister died when I was eleven. She looked nothing like me. She was tall and blonde and athletic and quiet, a contrast to my short, dark, noisy self. I adored her.

I like to imagine that we spent nine months chattering and cackling and musing comfortably in the darkness and warmth of the womb, formulating our views on the world to come, hatching strategies, proclaiming fealty and mutual protection.

And when we emerged, me mewling and bewildered a few seconds after her silence and surety, we kept our pact. Sleeping in the same bed, chest to back, our childhood smells and breathing in perfect sync. Wearing the same clothes even, until she drifted into the mandates of her gender. But we were as one, a telepathic wonder of simultaneity. Hungry, angry, sad, good humored, and wild at the same time. Finishing sentences. Laughing before a joke was finished. Finding endless comfort and constructing an impenetrable bulwark against loneliness.

Her name was Rebecca. My dad called her Rebbe, cleaving to the Hebrew name for teacher, notwithstanding its insult to ancient

Jewish patriarchy (at which my father scoffed anyway). She was smarter than me. She was better looking than me. She was taller than me. And she was my sister. My pride was immeasurable.

It is hard now to imagine the impact of this slight and willowy girl at my side while I struggled to navigate the exigencies of childhood. Most children want to please their parents. I wanted to please my sister. Most children are selfish, as any parent can attest. I was too, with the caveat that my selfishness included Rebbe. The world owed us. I could not even contemplate a me without her.

She was good at sports; I was klutzy. So she often remained after school to run or swim or toss, hit and slam balls of various sizes while I headed home to my books, looking out of the window every so often, imagining the sound of the bus that was soon to come. And when I heard that diesel purr I would stop what I was doing and run down to the gate, open it wide, and step onto the sidewalk, where she would turn the corner and see me, the smile planted on my face launching her own. Perhaps at this remove my memory is romanticized. I surely forget petty jealousies, territorial scraps, short tempers. But this is what remains now, the chaff shed from wheat. This is what I choose to retain.

An incident at school. I am walking to the bus at the end of the day, which is a short hop from the front gate. I am eight years old. My path is suddenly blocked by three older boys. Even an eight-year-old knows things. I am going to get my ass kicked and my stuff stolen, not that I have much.

"Joshua Meyer fuckshitcuntface. You dissing me?"

I stop. Consider a run. But I'm too slow. I stay silent. My heart starts to hammer. I'm scared. Their faces are twisted with cruelty. I am in a phase of my young life where I have discovered war stories. Books and graphic novels, left over from some parent or cousin. I devour them. The heroism knotted into the stories only occasionally causes me to wonder—weren't they scared? All the time? Of dying? Of capture and torture? Of horrible injuries? How awful it must be to be scared all of the time.

My young life had taught me that fear was temporary. An injection. A noise in the night. A spider. A lie carelessly told and due to be uncovered. They had short lifespans, these moments of fright, of anxiety. The fear either disappeared (its half-life depleted) or was banished by my bemused mother, my smiling father, or was mitigated by a lecture, a warning, a wake-up. Everything always turned out OK.

My well-being was threatened in short sharp jabs, but I always knew that soon, real soon, it would pass. Not so in the war stories. How awful to feel that cold hammering for days, for weeks, for years, forever. I was barely even able to articulate this thought. Could one live with fear forever?

And now, with my chest tight and my persecutors dripping with leering anticipation I was aware in a moment beyond my years—looking down at myself from some other existential plane—that this boy is scared. This boy is not having fun. Please make it stop.

*   *   *

Much later in my life, long after Rebbe's memory had slowly seeped its energy inanimate, like color leaching from a water-color painting in the rain, after my loss and grief were camouflaged by the long journey to adulthood, and in a wild moment of spontaneity, Grace and I went to Zimbabwe for ten days to announce our marriage plans to her parents. This was followed by a trip to a game farm, a rite of passage for a young American city boy visiting this unspoiled place. Accommodation was sumptuous and exotic and in the early morning and late afternoon we were driven around in an open vehicle, along with about ten other tourists—Russians, Indians, Germans.

The calm and earnest black driver-ranger had a weapon, a large-bore rifle, holstered and racked against the dashboard. His neck and cheek were shockingly scarred. He saw me staring. "Leopard," was all he said, and all he needed to say. On the second day, he spotted a herd of elephants on the horizon and with a curt, "Let's track," he raced off at an angle, parking at the bottom of a rise under a tree, awaiting their arrival.

And arrive they did. Some thirty or forty of them. Gray, mountainous, and, to my eyes, disturbed and irritated. Mostly because there were calves sheltering near their mothers' legs. They stopped at the top of the rise, sensing the vehicle below, perhaps a hundred yards' distance between us. The babies backed up into the shadows of their mothers' gigantic bellies. And then the ears, those massive wrinkled evolutionary throwbacks, first twitching and then flapping in alarm. Trunks, awful and serpentine and alien, starting a series of warlike sinusoidal dances. Front feet, massive and unforgiving, pawing the ground.

I saw the driver's hand move slowly toward the rifle rack. The tourists were snapping shots, exclaiming, praising, awash with noisy awe. Only I noticed the unblinking stillness of the driver.

"Please. We must be quiet." A harsh whisper, like a lash.

The effect was instantaneous. Looks of wonder morphed into quiet discomfort, which increased markedly as the ranger very quietly unholstered the rifle. One of the cows suddenly bolted forward with shocking momentum and barreled toward us, an unearthly sound roaring from some deep and practiced place. The ranger lifted his rifle with his left hand, but dropped the right outside the door, banging loudly against the solid metal, and yelling, "STOP! STOP!"

As I envisaged the inevitable carnage, tipped vehicle, tourists stomped to death, all I could think of was how the ranger could assume that the elephant understood English. I heard screaming as bodies leaped to the far side of the vehicle and Grace buried her head in my shoulder. The elephant stopped a few yards from the truck. I could see the oily excretions from its eyes. I could smell it, mud and musk and dung and sunrise. It backed slowly away. The silence in the truck thundered and the smell of fear rose fetid, the sort that only can come from humans faced with a situation in which their self-proclaimed evolutionary advantages—reason and rationale and sentience and language—mean shit.

A mock charge, it was called. A shot across the bow.

"OK, let's go, let's leave."

This from a shaking Indian woman whose country's reverence for elephants was clearly limited by current events. But we couldn't leave. Because the old truck on which we sat couldn't outrun elephants and a retreat would be a red flag. And so we sat frozen in whimpering terror as we were repeatedly mock charged, for about forty-five excruciatingly unpleasant minutes, after which the herd simply got bored and moved off.

My throat dried up. I could hear the insistent pounding of my heart, which had become an ugly and painful presence. My pores leaked sweat. It was unbearable. Grace turned to me at one point early, her eyes leached of color, and whispered—I don't want to be here, I don't want to be here.

Which is how I felt when the three schoolboys removed their belts and started tapping them across their thighs. They were going to whip me raw, for no other reason than the cruelty of children, cruelty that required little forethought to animate. This was a raw fear, blasphemous and unrelenting. I had the wisdom to understand that nothing I could do was going to save me. Not crying, not running, not pleading.

And then, on the periphery of my sight, I saw Rebbe striding toward us, behind the boys, who had their backs to her. She had a tennis racket in her hand. She had seen and understood what was transpiring from the tennis courts far away where she was playing. She had to know from the belt display and cringing body language of her brother what was going down. The largest of the boys noticed that I was staring over his shoulder. He turned and was greeted with an eight-year-old girl's junior tennis champion's full-bore forehand to the tip of his nose, which exploded in a fountain of blood. Within the same graceful stroke, she pivoted and reversed into a backhand, the racket now tipped off the vertical so that the wooden edge caught the second boy in the throat, from which he dropped to the floor with a terrible gurgling squeal. The third boy stared for an instant and then turned and ran.

My sister Rebbe was, quite simply, my protection against all things dreadful. It seemed to me that I could never offer her the same, never provide the sort of fear-shattering protection she offered me. But perhaps I did, in other ways, as we chatted long beyond our bedtime into the night, our company each other's sustenance.

And so came the day when I sat in the kitchen one afternoon waiting, as always, for Rebbe's return. And then a phone call and my mother's quiet "Oh, oh," and the terror on her face as she turned to me, her eyes wide and filling, contemplating not only the loss of her firstborn, but the burden of watching her young son lose his childhood, starting now.

The accident was barely page-three news. No reason. No explanation, physical or metaphysical. A car hit Rebbe outside school as she was crossing the road. She died instantly and the soft pillow of my life was ripped open.

It is difficult for me to imagine, even at this remove, how I managed. What damage was done. I cannot remember the edges of my grief. Those days, months, years afterward are grainy and difficult to shape in my adult mind. My mother and father did their best, but they too soon decided that perhaps the best memory was studied forgetting, and clothes, toys, photos, and reminiscences were quickly swept away.

A really bad thing happened to me. Over years I have pushed it away, locked it up, averted my gaze. And now, beset by dread I do not understand, it takes little introspection to smell its roots.

Charging elephants and a twin sister taken. Some things pass by, some don't.

CHAPTER 28

WHILE I AM on the plane flying back to LA from Miami there is an accident. I am not there, but I could have been—or should have been.

I imagine it this way. It is dusk, the driver has been on the road for about four hours and is now anxious to get home. She leans forward to change a radio station. She has been listening to a music station dedicated to singer-songwriters. It is a station that steers clear of transient fashion, delivering compositions over the last fifty years, their commonalities being that the artist must have written and performed the songs. A Carole King number has just finished, written around the time she was born, its trajectory having landed it firmly in the iconography of US pop music. It is called "(You Make Me Feel Like) A Natural Woman." She knows all the words, and has sung along. Now she thinks about her son and his erratic behavior over the weekend, and her ex-husband, away on a family emergency. She wishes he was with her and then banishes the thought as childish and inappropriate.

And so she leans forward to change the station, looking for something smart and verbal to keep her alert because she is tired.

In the instant between looking down, pressing the requisite buttons on the radio face and looking up again the car has started to drift left. It is a rental car, she is not familiar with its handling, and so when she registers minor alarm and twists the steering wheel to reverse the drift, she overcorrects. She twists in the other direction, causing a second overcorrection, and now the back wheels lose their traction and within seconds she has lost control. The car hits the shoulder barrier and its center of gravity is now in an adversarial relationship with the new obstruction, setting in motion a chain of Newtonian mechanics that causes the lefthand side of the car to become airborne. The car leaves the road and begins to fly. She is aware of the sudden silence as the car begins to turn over, all four wheels now spinning against air rather than asphalt and the odd vertiginous sensation of being briefly upside down as the car begins a series of somersaults. She does not feel the second or third or fourth turn because she is now unconscious.

When the emergency vehicles arrive, she is still alive and still unconscious. She has to be cut out of the car, a cheap rented vehicle, now twisted and crushed. She is airlifted to Cedars-Sinai Hospital. She is still unconscious when I arrive the next day.

"What do the doctors say?"

Innocent's voice is strangled by grief and fear. I am on my phone, from the hospital room where Grace lies, tethered to all manner of high-technology equipment like a medical Medusa.

"They're hedging their bets, Innocent. There are fairly extensive head injuries. But they haven't used the word *coma* yet."

"I'm catching a flight this afternoon."

"I'll pick you up at the airport."

"No, stay with Mom. I'll catch a cab."

I have not been home yet, having come straight from the airport, and Krystal is not answering her phone. I arrange a ride to Grace's place to fetch my car and head home.

There is a note on the dining table.

Dear Meyer,

The time has eventually come. I need to move on. This is not working for me and, I suspect, not for you. I wish you had been who I wanted you to be. For a while there, you were. And then you just meandered off to do what you do. Which is a pity because it was nearly perfect. I have taken most of my stuff. I will come back and collect anything that I have left at another time. Please do not call me. I have nothing more to say.

Goodbye,
Krystal

Dread 4: Meyer 0.

A funny thing happens when multiple crises arrive simultaneously. A calmness sets in, even a sort of peace, akin to sitting down to a long exam. Time takes on a new and pure texture, thick and lush. Peripheral distractions are batted away. I get a beer from the fridge and toast dread.

"Game on," I say aloud.

I sit down at the dining room table and reread the letter, marveling at its solipsism. There is a pile of mail on the table by the front door, which I idly scan. Included is a stern-looking letter from the IRS, smelling acridly of opprobrium. I don't open it. There is a message on the home phone. It is from Jim, the HR director, insisting that I phone him urgently. I seem to have left my favorite jacket in the cab. The trash has not been taken out, leaving a faint rancid odor in the kitchen and I notice a water stain on the ceiling. I look at the sky outside the window. It is a perfect blue.

And it is falling.

CHAPTER 29

THE DOCTOR MAY not have used the word *coma*, but the word settles like concrete in my head as I awake. I get up and do a bit of light Googling. By some measures at least, being unconscious for more than six hours means coma. It's been a lot longer than that. The better part of me is thankful that she is not dead, but it is a tattered consolation.

I struggle for emotional traction. I run the scenarios. Four options.

She will wake up, and everything will be fine.

She will wake up, and she will be damaged.

She will not wake up and will remain vegetative forever.

She will not wake up and will die soon.

A student of the odds, I mumble. One in four. Only one option not to dread.

The other crises and looming catastrophes are pushed aside for the moment. Innocent and drugs, Dad and prison, Krystal's exit. Grace consumes the greater part of me. If only I had bought her a plane ticket. If only Dad had waited a day or two before crossing his Rubicon. If only, if only, if only.

I debate calling Van, asking for support. Of what sort, I am not sure. I am not looking for brows furrowed in concern. I am also not looking for the faint odor of schadenfreude from a gloomy depressive. I am looking for escape. Which used to mean drugs and drink. Which I consider for a while, deciding on sobriety by a hairbreadth.

Instead I call Farzad and lay it out.

"This is a storm of bad news, my friend. How you holding up?"

"Um . . . Not sure."

"I can either counsel you or we could get drunk. In which case I can also counsel you, except you will not remember it later."

"I thought drinking was a poor idea in a crisis."

"Who says that?"

"Everyone. Particularly psychologists, I should imagine."

"There are psychologists and psychologists. And Iranian Muslim psychologists. Who happen to like drinking with their friends."

"OK. You win. I'm going back to the hospital first. Six p.m?"

Innocent is at Grace's bedside when I get there. His eyes are red. I give him the benefit of the doubt and assume it is from crying.

"How you doing, son?"

"Not great. I just spoke to the doctor."

"And?"

"There is not a lot to be done here. The injuries cause swelling around the lining of the brain and, because of the skull, the swelling has nowhere to go, so the brain is pushed down toward the brain stem. That shuts down the reticular activation system, which is like an on/off switch. Until it switches on again she'll be in a coma."

"How do they know it'll switch on?"

"They don't, Dad."

"I'm so sorry, Innocent."

"It was great to see you two together Friday night. I was sort of hoping—"

He gasps, cannot complete the sentence.

There is nothing like seeing your child in pain. It is metaphysically primal, and eclipses all else. It causes a deafening and blinding anxiety. There is no priority other than to try to comfort. I sit down and take his large hand in mine. I try to think of something to say that might offer succor rather than cliché. I can't. So we just look at her. Her face is slack, skin gray, hair lank, contusions and bruises an insult to her beauty. The electronic monitors behind her chirp and bleep disinterestedly, oblivious. Grace looks like a corpse.

I am suffering from a numbing despair, the sort that envelops rather than confronts. If it would only confront, I could defend, rationalize, argue, object. For the moment, I am in a fog, directionless. And it is compounded by the acrid smell of guilt as I consider my impotent and heedless attempts to convince her to rent a safer car.

This should be simpler. I try to separate the desperation I feel for Innocent from the more complicated fear of losing Grace, who has once again, after nearly two decades, burrowed under my skin in ways I do not understand. We sit for a while, saying nothing.

*   *   *

"Meyer, come to me."

Farzad wraps me in a bear hug at the front door and I sink into his ample chest that smells repellently of Old Spice. He has never done this before. He kisses my head, like a father. I fight back tears.

"And so, my little friend, an uncaring universe has turned on you, proving of course that there are forces outside of your control, and your well-being will be determined by your reactions. We will discuss tonight, over vast quantities of vodka, what these reactions should be."

"The whole uncaring universe thing is something I never doubted."

We are at Farzad's apartment, a glorious affair in Santa Monica with 270-degree views overlooking the Pacific. We move to the deck. His wife, Cherry, comes out from the kitchen and pops a kiss on my cheek.

"Meyer, I'm so sorry about Grace. How is she?"

"No change. They say we will just have to wait."

The whole Cherry-Farzad hookup still bewilders me. Farzad is a poster boy for the ethnic autre. And even within that context, he can hardly be called handsome, with close-set black eyes, a single long thick eyebrow spanning both orbs, a titanic nose, and all manner of jowls and double chins. If he were to insert himself into a photo of one of those all-male, unsmiling revolutionary fundamentalist governmental committees in some hot desert land over there, mustachioed, overfed and austere, he would fit right in. Cherry defines perky and homegrown—the corn-fed white teeth, the insolent breasts, the tan and gold, the laughing blue eyes.

They met at an academic conference, the theme of which had something to do with the role of psychology and developing nations. Farzad was a minor star, the book of Iranian Muslim psychologists being thin. Cherry was employed by the event organizer, seeing to name tags and programs and dinner seating and the like. The details of their courtship are hazy. It is my considered belief that Farzad hypnotized her or gave her psychoactive drugs. Whereupon she spilled her darkest secrets, at which point she was beholden. After which he certainly sodomized her, shaming her into a life of servitude.

Her family is from Alabama, Dixie people, steeped in generations of class hierarchy and privilege, dating back to plantation ownership. Her mother has still not recovered from the shock of seeing her daughter ravished by al-Qaeda. For her father, it was a minor irritation between golf, horse breeding, cigars, port, and high-class strippers.

Their apartment is another mystery. This is at the top end of the market, and would have cost many millions. Not on a psychologist's and academic's income, this is certain. Two scenarios spring to mind. Either Farzad's family siphoned off some of the Shah's excesses or, more likely, Cherry's mother quietly bought it for them on condition that Farzad never show his oily face at family gatherings.

I like Cherry. She is smart. She is a great cook. She is generous. One day I will ask her why she married Farzad. It strikes me obliquely that perhaps she fell in love with his wisdom and generous spirit and humanity and courage, but I perish the thought.

She brings ice-chilled Stolichnaya, guacamole, and chips onto the deck.

"Cherry, I've been meaning to ask you this for years. How could you, a Mayflower girl, marry this, this, this . . . you know?"

She smiles at me.

"He is really well endowed."

Being distracted by my multiple calamities, I do have not have any fast comeback, so she grins and retreats into the apartment, leaving us alone.

Farzad eyeballs me severely.

"You are making light. This is not the time to be making light."

"I suppose."

"I want to start with Krystal."

"OK."

"Irredeemable?"

"Yes."

"Why?"

"I don't love her. She doesn't love me."

"Why have you stayed together this long?"

"Sex."

"I have to terminate this line of questioning because the thought of you having sex with anybody makes me nauseous."

He downs his vodka. I wait.

"Anybody angry?"

"Pissed off is more accurate."

"Why?"

"I need to have company. I don't like being alone. I'm a coward."

"Her?"

"She is pissed off because I wouldn't change."

"Ah, OK. Let's leave Krystal for a moment. Your father."

"My father?"

"Yes, how do you feel about your father."

"Great guy."

"Did you want to fuck your father?"

"*What?*"

"Only kidding. Just keeping you on your toes. How do you feel about what he did, what may happen?"

"I'm OK with what he did."

"How so?"

"He explained it well. It seems like a rational and appropriate choice."

"And are you fearful for him?"

"A little. I'm scared that they will send him back to the Center. I think he'd be happier in prison, at least that's what he's implied. Who would have thought that? Do you think there are other Jews of his age in prison? He likes the high holy days."

"Do you feel guilty?"

"About what?"

"Not doing more for your father as he got older?"

"Yes. Doesn't everybody?"

"Not me. My father was a torturer for the Shah."

"Ah. No wonder you are so fucked up."

"Let's talk about you."

We have downed a few more shots. The vodka is taking hold. I feel loose, pleasantly melancholy, more a witness to than a participant in my crumbling life. I feel like abandoning myself to bacchanalian impulses.

"Yes, let's talk about me."

"Grace."

"Grace."

"Tell me about your weekend with her."

"It was going well until it was truncated by the trip to Florida. So it consisted of the drive up to Berkeley and one dinner."

"Go on."

"I should never have left Grace. I was hoping to get her to believe that."

"I do not understand, Meyer. You have seen little of her since you divorced. Barely mentioned her. And now she is the woman of your dreams? Something doesn't compute."

I pour another shot and ponder what Farzad has just said. A life is made up of an agglomeration of decisions. Billions of them, from the trivial ones, up the chain of impact, to the weighty ones. Our current reality is a branch at the end of a giant decision tree. Walk backward in time and make other choices and you end up elsewhere. Of course, there is the great debate about our ability to make choices at all, but let's assume for the moment, for reasons of common sense alone, that our free will is just that. Statistics (there I go again) ensure that we will make the wrong choices often. Right choices require perfect information and, as bumbling, impulsive, and imperfect humans, we rarely have that luxury. So I conclude that our lives end up in pretty much a statistical coin toss, with our chances of ending up on the juiciest branches of the tree about the same as ending up on the rotten ones. I am falling in love with Grace again because I took the wrong branch last time. I am correcting errors.

"I may have missed something the first time around."

Farzad is gentle in expressing his opposing viewpoint.

"Rubbish. Balderdash. Poppycock. Horseshit. Childish nonsense. What's your *point*?"

"I was acting on imperfect information when I left Grace. It was the wrong decision. And if I had made the right decision, she wouldn't be in a coma, Innocent would not be fucking around with drugs, and I wouldn't be stuck under dread's boot."

Farzad knocks back another shot.

"You are a naive and silly man, my little friend. What you need is a good whack upside the head. This is true too of many of my patients, but the code of conduct of the American Psychological Association frowns upon physical violence—a great failing of vision on their part, in my opinion. So let me educate you. Firstly, we have already determined, and agreed, that the universe does not give a fuck about you. Secondly, you have posited that our lives are nothing more than a series of decisions, made largely on imperfect information by imperfect humans. Of course, this leads to the bizarre conclusion that we all stumble through life like a bunch of clowns, in which viscera and impulse are our only guide. This is clearly the reasoning of a man who wishes to escape judgment."

"I never said that I wanted to escape—"

"Shut up, I'm not finished. The entire edifice of humanity across all cultures is based on judgment. That is how we live. That is how we govern. That is how we teach. That is how we learn. That is how we love. The concept of blame is inimical to healthy societies. We do it every day, in greater or smaller ways. And what is this judgment? It is simply a comparison of other people's behaviors to our own. We scold our children when they don't live up, reward them when they do. Choose our friends and partners based on values that are measurable against our yardsticks. The whole human endeavor is based on the ability to judge others. So when I hear your little deceit, a faux philosophy based on some pseudo-intellectual premise of blamelessness, I want to hit you upside the head."

"I wasn't really—"

"Shut up, I'm not finished. Some of these calamities that have beset you are in the realm of the arbitrary, others you must take some blame for. But as I said when you walked in the door all trembly and pathetic, it is our reaction to crisis that defines us, not the self-indulgent application of probability theories to past human events. And so, my little victim, how are you going to react to all of this? What are you going to do?"

"What should I do?"

"How the hell should I know?"

"Because you're a psychologist. You see this all the time."

"A good psychologist assists patients to gain insight, to understand themselves and then to make their own decisions."

"Ah. So you are not going to tell me what to do."

"No."

But he already has. We define ourselves on how we react, wasn't
that what he said? He has told me to man up. He has told me to
stare dread in the face and not to blink until she backs down.

CHAPTER 30

I ARRIVE HOME a bit drunk. Innocent is asleep in the spare room. I log in to the company servers from my desktop. Within seconds I am rifling through the CEO's mail, documents, browsing history. Even his personal Gmail, for which he predictably uses the same username and password as his company mail.

I hit pay dirt immediately:

- Sexually explicit messages and photos (himself, exhibiting himself, both erect and flaccid) to numerous women, one of whom is fifteen years old, as I uncover after a little additional sleuthing

- A request to a respondent named Carlos about procuring "Bolivian marching powder"

- A discussion with another well-known CEO about plans to implement illegal offshore tax-avoidance strategies

- Spectacularly vitriolic opinions about powerful captains of industry, many of them supposedly his friends

I print out the incriminating documents and images, put them in a file, and slide them into my briefcase.

I have no strategy at all, no plan of action, not even an eagerly imagined scenario. I just know that my entire fucking miserable life hinges upon being able to stand up to him, balancing the scales of Farzad's judgment and reaction. I may never use this stuff. I simply know that on the off chance that you may confront an adversary, you need to be armed. At least in theory. I am happy to allow the CEO to be an imagined foe. Imagined foes are sometimes more powerful. Real ones tend to disappoint with their human foibles.

I go to Innocent's room. He is asleep. A soft light from the passage drapes itself across his face. I sit down gently on the bed. As I watch his quiet breathing I catch a glimpse of the tiny baby who used to fall asleep in my arms. That's the trouble with being a parent. Your child is always, in some small but profound measure, a tiny baby. And now his mommy is in a coma. My heart just breaks.

And then I am weeping.

But it hasn't ended.

Bunny calls.

"Isobel's sick, and I'm worried."

"Please don't tell me that."

"She had a very high temperature on Friday. By Sunday she was burning up and delirious. I took her to the doctor this morning. He clearly doesn't have a clue. Made vague noises about waiting a day or two."

"Please don't tell me that."

"The temperature is down a bit now, but it keeps spiking. There don't seem to be any other symptoms. Her throat and lungs and nose and tummy are fine."

"PLEASE DONT TELL ME THAT."

"Meyer, is that all you have to say? Are you OK?"

"Not really, but this is more important. I'm coming over."

I call Farzad.

"Isobel is sick. I need a really, really good doctor. Do you have a recommendation? And I am not making light."

"How sick?"

"High temperature for three days. Spiking."

"What else?"

"Too weak to get out of bed. Occasionally confused. Splitting headaches."

"Take her to the hospital—now."

"You are not a medical doctor, Farzad. I need a doctor."

"I am in the healing business. TAKE HER TO THE HOSPITAL. NOW!"

As always, I do what he says, especially when he shouts. Which I have never heard him do before. When I arrive at Bunny's, Isobel is too weak to walk. I carry her to the car. It strikes me that one has a finite set of arrows for coping with stress. My quiver is empty. A part of me, I mean a real and urgently complaining part of me, suggests that I should drive to Tijuana, get drunk for a week, and then come back, when all will be well.

Man up. That's what Farzad said.

"We are going to run some tests."

The doctor at Kaiser, to which Bunny is bound by Byzantine health-care regulations, looks to be about seventeen years old. Isobel is now in the hospital room, asleep, mysterious clear fluid dripping into her arm.

"Meaning you don't know what's wrong."

"Well, we can eliminate some things at this point, but no, we don't know what's wrong."

"What can you eliminate?"

"Well, there are no swollen glands and she has no respiratory or gastric distress."

"So what could it be?"

"I wouldn't want to hazard a guess at this point, Mr. Meyer."

"MY DAUGHTER HAS A FUCKING TUBE IN HER FUCK-ING ARM AND I WANT YOU TO HAZARD A FUCKING GUESS."

The blood drains from his face. He is about to get beaten up by a half-crazed maniac father. Bunny grabs my arm.

"MEYER! Let's walk. Excuse us, doctor."

She hustles me down the hall. I feel the fight leave me. Actually, I feel everything leave me. I sink down onto my butt in the hall-way. The floor is cool. It feels good.

"Meyer, get a grip."

"Yes, I would like to do that."

"She will be fine. She is in professional hands. It is probably just a bug. She'll be OK, I promise. Now please stand up."

"No, I like it here."

"Meyer, what's going on? You're freaking me out."

"Grace is in a coma. Dad is in jail. Innocent is on drugs. Krystal is gone. Isobel has the *Ebola* virus. I am never going to play sax like Cannonball Adderley."

She is suitably speechless.

CHAPTER 31

VAN CALLS.

"They want us to play tonight. The other band canceled."

"Can't."

"Why?"

"The sky has fallen on my head."

"How so?"

"I'll tell you later. What time?"

"So you're in?"

"Sure, how much worse can it get?"

"Huh?"

"Later." I hang up.

I call Jim back at the company.

"Jim, you called."

"You didn't come in today. I thought you were due back."

"Yeah, sorry, personal problems. Will be in tomorrow. Why did you call me instead of Bryn?"

"He quit."

"The heck you say. Why?"

"Told me he didn't think he was very good at his job. Told me he was going to try to do something that he loved."

Hallelujah. Score one for truth and justice.

"I want to have a chat to you about Bryn's job. It's an opportunity."

"No thanks."

"Why not?"

"Because then I have to spend more time with the nexus of evil and his fat fuck COO."

"Please don't talk that way, Meyer. It puts me in a conflict situation."

"Would you like me to rephrase that?"

"Yes."

"Because then I have to spend more time with the nexus of evil and his fat fuck COO."

"I like you, Meyer, but this is not a way to get ahead."

"What makes you think I want to get ahead? I am already ahead. I like you too, Jim. I'll see you tomorrow." I hang up.

I call Bunny. Isobel's temperature is still spiking. The blood tests are inconclusive. The doctors have said that she is not in any immediate danger, but they are keeping her for observation.

I call the lawyer in Florida. Dad is holding firm. He doesn't want a deal.

"What do you want me to do, Mr. Meyer?"

"Nothing. He is a man in full. He is old, but not crazy, notwithstanding guns and bullets. He is going to do what he wants to do. Can you get him to call me?"

I drop Innocent at the hospital on the way to the gig. I have not told him about Isobel. I don't see the point.

It is a warm night in Los Angeles. The Santa Ana winds are scuffing and whining menacingly, giving voice to the seared descriptions tackled by writers and songwriters and playwrights and sidewalk maniacs as they slouch toward Bethlehem. People are up and about, in bars and clubs, wanting to share the otherworldly hot breath of this desert wind with strangers in crowded rooms. Early punters are already here; it feels like a big night is brewing. Women with barely legal exposed skin for the warm air to caress, men looking tough and casual, save for furtive glances at opportunities and threats. A few regulars are already drunk, in that alcoholic one-sip sort of way, where there is a subtle change in the musculature of the eyes, both pupils off-tilt from center.

One of the minor conveniences of playing sax is the short setup time. There are no multiple items in misshapen containers, no electronics, no plugs. I sit at the bar and order a Coke while the others set up.

Gordon, the wily young proprietor, who I suspect is getting quietly rich off this little bar, comes over. He is a quintessentially Los Angeles character. He is of indeterminate Midwestern origin, threadbare education, and almost complete lack of charisma other than a certain deadpan handsomeness. He arrived friendless and almost broke a few years ago, searching for his few nuggets of the shiny little things, like so many others. It is a familiar story and most end up with the saddest of conclusions, disappointment etched deep for the rest of their lives, in which nothing they ever aspire to again will compare to the promise of fame in Los Angeles, every day of their broken lives a day of fossilized locusts. But Gordon spotted a tiny window, a run-down bar in a seedy Hollywood side street, scraped together a month's rent, painted it black, scrounged a few posters, bought a few cheap beers and set out to find unusual bands. We were his first and he named us El Tango Sexuales. Not strictly accurate, but hey.

"That Coca-Cola?"

"Yep."

"You on the wagon?"

"Nope."

"OK."

"Expecting a big night, Gordon?"

"Santa Anas. You know how it is."

"You owe us."

"What do I owe you?"

"Your life."

"How so?"

"If we didn't come and play here for door money a couple of years ago you would be back in Arkansas smoking meth."

"And if I didn't spot you, you would be playing 'Hava Nagila' at bar mitzvahs."

"Right. So we're even, then?"

"Yup."

I smile. He moves on.

I call Innocent.

"Dad, it's fine. I'll call if there's any change, I promise."

I call Bunny.

"Meyer, you called an hour ago. I promise I'll call you if there's any news. Go play. It will take your mind off things."

We tune up. Not too long ago guitarists tuned by ear. They referenced a keyboard or tuning fork for their initial string and then opened their ears and tuned each additional string off the previous one. Those days are gone. Everybody now tunes using an iPhone, which listens to the note and guides the tuning in like a tug boat. As a techno geek this, surprisingly, annoys me. It is slothful. As a bare minimum for entry into the cloistered club of musicianship, one should be able to hear pitch. Of course, cloistered is now a relative term. All one really needs for entry these days are two chords and the balls to stand onstage. Musicianship has little to do with it. Few people realize that there is a standard piece of real-time technology now that keeps a vocalist on key in live performances. You are not hearing the songstress. You are hearing the songstress, corrected. I find myself getting grumpier and grumpier at the intrusion of clever new technologies into the composing and performing of music, turning the whole enterprise over to software engineering. I am in a definite minority here. I am starting to sound like my dad, who insisted that electronic keyboards were the work of the devil. He may well have been right.

The thought of my dad creates a stab of anxiety. I am looking for escape and have been courageous enough to lay off the sauce, so give me a fucking break. I need to play.

By the time we are ready to start, the room is beginning to heave. It is packed. People have escaped their homes where the wind will be whipping through open windows and complaining noisily against obdurate wood. There is little ventilation in this hole in the wall. There is a slightly rancid sweat smell, mixed with deodorant, which will slowly tip toward pungent as the night progresses. People are talking loudly, jockeying for a position at the bar, sitting two to a chair, holding up walls. A sibilance of sex and aggression careens off the walls as odd disembodied words of flirt and challenge float past the stage. People are watching us impatiently, waiting for us to start, as though the beginning of the music will give them a cause, a catalyst for something that they can't quite articulate.

We launch into the playlist and I am feeling loose. We start with a couple of gypsy jazz numbers, written by the legendary three-fingered guitarist Django Reinhardt. He was a gypsy from the Manouche region of France so this entire genre is sometimes dubbed *Manouche*. It is fast-moving swing, all AABA in structure with a sizzling rhythm guitar punching out chords on the second and fourth beat of the bar and the bass walking the scales. Nice chord movements, all well within popular progressions of the time but smart and sassy even within that framework. Scary fast heads and the expectation of even faster solos, over which I sometimes acquit myself with dignity, and others over which I sound like I am running to catch a speeding train—all huff and puff and obvious desperation. Tonight, I am flying, though, on both soprano and alto, swapping solos with Tim on accordion and violin, speaking each other's language, trading 4-bar phrases, just dovetailing on everything—tone, texture, quotes, playful plagiarism, clever variations, argumentative musical conversations, driving each other into new territory. He is smiling as he plays and he never smiles. We are simply cooking. My mood has lifted. It is all about this, life's looming misfortunes and responsibilities now just shadows at the edge of my consciousness.

Usually, there are not a lot of people actually listening that hard. People are at places like these for reasons other than musical fulfillment; this is the sad truth realized by a working bar musician. But occasionally, when circumstances conspire, when there is a serendipitous convergence of mood and generosity and spirit, the claps and cheers will rise above the merely polite and there will be genuine and joyful appreciation. Tonight is turning out to be such a night. It must be the Santa Anas. There is foot stomping and whistling and whooping, and a few people are even moved to jive on the few square feet in front of the stage. It is nights like these that renew the fire that got us to pick up instruments in the first place, a few moments of perfect match between appetite and nourishment, when we are elevated a small step above the average human, dispensers of chimera and wonder.

We finish the set. I head over to the bar and order a double vodka, losing the will to maintain sobriety. Why, I ask myself? To whose benefit? I check my phone. There are no messages.

Gordon comes over.

"You are on fire, my brother. Crowd is loving it."

"It happens, sometimes."

"Keep it up, the booze is flowing."

"So are you going to pay us more tonight?"

"Only if I can pay you less when you sound like shit. Can get you laid, though. Anyone you fancy?"

"Gordon, you are a generous human being. I'll take money instead."

"No can do, hombre. Too valuable."

I head into the alleyway. Mike is bathed in sweat and smoking furiously, laughing with Tim, their previous altercation clearly long forgotten. They are discussing a singer who sat in with us a few weeks ago who was so off-key that we suspected she was deaf. Van is sitting on a trash can, rolling a joint intently. Billy the monosyllabic bass player is not around, most likely trawling for sex somewhere, which is his primary motive for playing music in the first place. He is very good at it.

"Good gig tonight, guys."

There are various grunts and disinterested nods. When you have been playing together for a long time, everyone knows that sometimes you flame and sometimes you flame out. It is just part of the territory. No need for great analysis.

Van calls me over.

"Want a hit?"

"Nah. Driving tonight. Makes me crash into poles."

"What's with the sky falling and all?"

"Ah shit. Another time. I'm having fun."

The second set begins with a mash-up, which has become something of a signature for us. We mash Nancy Sinatra's "These Boots Are Made for Walkin'" with Ravel's "Bolero" with the theme from *Glee*. It sounds smart, funny, and bizarrely right, but the arrangement nearly broke us when it was suggested by a drunk Van one night a few months ago. Tim is our resident genius in the mash-up department, his arrangements coming from a place of deep musical perversity.

I am having such a good time that I am starting to forget the audience, concentrating largely on the singular and rare perfection of our ensemble performances, where everyone seems to be suddenly telepathically connected, a blue moon occurrence. We end the set with the Piazzolla tango called "Oblivion." It is played slowly, majestically. The alto plays the melody, which starts on a low concert G and jumps tragically up a single octave for the second note, as the band nails the traditional tango rhythm to the stage. It is an unbearably beautiful melody, full of unrequited love, intimations of anger, blind hope and broken dreams. As I move into the solo I sail over the accordion arpeggios, eyes tightly shut, transporting myself to dark halls in the working-class *favelas* of Buenos Aires in the early part of the last century where strangers came to dance and to drink and to love and to regret and to forget the world in which they toiled. I am above the chords now, composing, not improvising, sliding from harmonic underpin to emotional intent, above algorithms, above structure, singing the body fucking electric, surfing the tsunami, seeing God, inventing myself again and again and again.

The song ends quietly. I open my eyes. As always, most of the audience has heard nothing. This was not dance music—the audience had returned to more immediate concerns of the evening's chase. I catch a few nods and smiles here and there, but it doesn't matter. When I play that good, it doesn't matter.

I make my way to the bar, order another double. Check my phone. Nothing. A large hand comes down gently on my shoulder.

"Damn, that was pretty."

It is Innocent. It is not Sanborn, not Brecker, not Parker. It is Innocent.

And I cannot imagine anyone else making me feel as good.

CHAPTER 32

AFTER TALKING TO his nonresponsive mother for an hour, and holding her slack hand, Innocent has taken a cab from the hospital to the bar.

The gig is over; we are heading to Cantor's for a late-night snack.

"So, what did you say to her?"

"Why do you want to know?"

"I just do."

"It's private."

"Do you think she heard you?"

"No, I don't. But I heard me."

We are silent for a while. I negotiate traffic along Santa Monica and swing onto Fairfax and park. Cantor's is a Jewish deli of such Hollywood iconography that you can smell the echoes of dreams and hopes ranging over fifty years. The restaurant is quiet. We get a table by the window, ordering the comfort food of our ancestry—borscht with boiled potatoes and sour cream.

"There is something we need to talk about, Innocent."

"Besides Mom?"

"Yes."

"You mean my coke-addled friend, Wanda?"

He is not looking at me as he says this; he knows what is coming. It reminds me of the rare occasions when I was called in by Grace to inflict a small measure of patriarchal displeasure after he had committed some misdemeanor or other. I hated it. He hated it. But we walked through the charade together.

"You're getting warmer."

"You mean me?"

"Warmer."

"You mean me and drugs?" We are here now. The rub is upon us, and I want to differentiate this from our historical "talks." This is much more serious shit. This is hard drugs. This is the fork leading to one life or another.

"Bingo."

He nods a while, says nothing. I wait.

"Yeah, I partake occasionally."

"What does 'occasionally' mean?"

"I'm not sure this is a conversation I want to have with you. I'm an adult who makes his own decisions now."

"Not really. You're on my payroll. That gives me employer oversight."

"I don't need your money, Dad, I can get a part-time job. If you're going to pay for my education, the only way I will take the money is on a no-strings basis."

He has me, of course. But he knows he is lost here. This is not an academic debate. I am tired, emptied out, want to sleep. But I have to be heard. This is my child. You do anything to protect him from harm.

"OK, I retract. But I want to talk about it."

"Not sure I want to."

"Innocent, I'm an old hand here. I have done almost every drug you can think of and some of them I have overdone. Consider me a wise elder in these matters."

"I know, Dad. I would watch you when you took me to gigs when I was growing up. It was pretty obvious. I was kind of proud—my dad was the kind of guy who would take risks, he was out there, experimenting, on the edge. It was impressive to me. So if you want to know why I partake, it's because I had a role model."

Shit.

"Yeah, well, I wasn't always a good role model. And the drugs were mainly a great big nonsense."

"Yes, that's the point of drugs, Dad."

Shit again.

"OK. Let me try this, without trying to mimic your average drug counselor. The problem with drugs is that, firstly, they're worth less money than you pay for them. You wouldn't spend $100 on a film, so why would you spend that money on a gram of coke, which is never as valuable and usually not as long-lasting as a good film? Secondly, the experience itself, while perhaps fun under the influence, is never fun in retrospect. What you are when you are flying, in everyone's eyes except your own, is an asshole who talks too fast about himself and nothing else. Thirdly—and I do sound like a counselor here—is that it is truly addictive. As in, I-can't-leave-home-without-it addictive. Which eventually makes it more important than anything else in your life, and that's just a sad blues. Fourthly, nobody ever did anything useful on drugs."

"Uh huh. I know all this, Dad. And you're sounding like a counselor because you're not being honest."

"How so?"

"Plenty of people did useful things on drugs."

"Who?"

"Charlie Parker on heroin."

"Heroin killed him."

"Yeah, but he did something useful. Sigmund Freud on coke."

"Perhaps, but he also wanted to fuck his mother. And he stopped doing it."

"Even so."

"OK, I retract objection number four."

"You're also generalizing, Dad." This is the problem with a smart kid. He has seen you traffic in the gray areas of moral dialectic for years. He has learned the tricks of debate, he can find the loopholes. He can justify anything. "If you are going to have this conversation with me you really, really, really have to have your arguments ready."

"How am I generalizing?"

"All drugs are not the same. Do you object to my getting drunk occasionally?"

"Yes. No, not really."

"Do you object to me having the occasional joint?"

"Uh, no."

"Crack a tab of E and go dancing?"

"OK, I get your point."

"Well, then, define your terms."

My fatigue totters toward parental irritation. At an empty Hollywood deli in the dead of night, with a son who may or not be falling off the edge.

"Don't be a wise guy, Innocent. This is serious shit and I am your father. I don't want you to do coke. You're too smart to do anything stronger, but I definitely draw a line at coke. It's a vampire squid that will suck you dry. It nearly did me."

"Really?"

"Long story, not important now. It is an evil succubus cunt. I can't put it more strongly than that."

"That's pretty strong."

"How much are you doing?"

"Every couple of nights. When we party."

"You know the golden rule about drug confessions, Innocent?"

"What?"

"Multiply by five. That means you are doing it every day."

"I'm not."

There is a particular incident from a certain period in my life that stands out. I was living with Tamara, a sweet and trusting soul. An artist, who spent long days drinking tea and singing softly to herself while she painted gentle landscape vistas festooned with otherworldly flora. I was all over the place at the time. I had recently graduated and had not yet started my career. I was playing a lot, gigging, partying, rehearsing, seeing bands. And starting to slip grindingly into cocaine dependency. A bump before playing. Then a line during the breaks. A line to wake up. A line when I felt good. A line when I felt bad. Then a friendship with a friendly dealer, then a come-rain-come-shine stash in my back pocket, then an experiment with smoking it. Then more of an experiment. And finally, a pustulent lifestyle, shrouded in secrecy and deceit, with Tamara an unsuspecting backdrop. A classical study in drug advancement.

During this period, I took a job as a programmer, speeding cocaine-fueled through complex programming tasks, sometimes not sleeping for days. One day, a Saturday, I told Tamara that I had to go to work, when in fact I was looking to flame the soldier. I headed into Hollywood, made my score, and sat in the car in a darkened side street smoking, until paranoia took hold, as it always eventually did. I drove around, scored again and then again, until my bank card would no longer function, shut down by some auto-fraud-detection software at my bank, which assumed that more than three withdrawals in an hour meant trouble. I had told Tamara I would be home not-too-late. It was no longer that. I called her from my cell phone, panicked at the come down, panicked at my inability to score, panicked that she would divine the truth and the whole edifice would collapse.

"Honey, sorry I'm late, it's going to be a while. I have had a flat tire. I have to do the whole jack-and-change thing."

"How long will you be?"

"I don't know. An hour maybe." Padding it a bit, in case I found a spare twenty in my pocket.

And then I find a pen knife in the glove compartment. Get out of the car. Plunge it into the rear tire. Change the tire. Crawl under the car. Run my hands under the undercarriage, till they are black with oil and whatever the hell else congeals under there. Wipe it on my face, my clothes. Make a small cut on my hand to attract the sympathy vote. And then drive back to Tamara, in my costume of duplicity. She bought it and I disappeared into the bathroom to throw up from guilt and shame.

Innocent won't hold my gaze.

"You're doing it every day. This conversation is over. Tell me you've heard me."

"I've heard you."

"Tell me again."

"I've heard you."

I kiss him on the head. I can do no more.

"Let's go see Grace before we head home."

He is quiet as we leave the restaurant. He has heard me.

CHAPTER 33

WE ARE ONLY a few blocks from the hospital and as I turn into Beverly there is the familiar heart-stopping whoop from a siren behind me. It is LAPD.

Shit.

Saying *shit* is standard fare for being stopped for a possible traffic offense. If you are stopped in London, you say *damnation*. If you are stopped in Paris, you say *merde*. If you are stopped in Congo, presumably the same sort of word comes to mind, perhaps with a tad more astringency. I am a mostly law-abiding citizen. I pay my tickets, don't do drugs anymore, only think about killing people, my license and registration are current, and I had, what, two drinks at the bar? Three maybe? The barkeep and I are friends. Did he double me up? I am vaguely aware that blood alcohol levels in California require little more than a half-glass of slightly turned milk to trigger Breathalyzers. And I am also aware of, and am indeed supportive of, the medieval edicts of torture and evisceration for drunk drivers.

But, hey, the corrupt and brutal cops of *L.A. Confidential* are ancient history. These guys are now the pinnacle of civility and professionalism. The last time there was a corruption or brutality case was, well, a long time ago. These guys are so perky and bursting with rectitude, you almost look forward to an encounter with them. A dark shape appears at my window, a torch sweeping the inside of my car.

"Evening, officer. Did I do something wrong?"

"Good evening, sir. May I see your license and registration please." Not really a question, more of a command.

I glance over at Innocent. He is grinning. I am not sure why. Maybe he wants to see how his hero handles the cops. I hand over the documents.

"Please remain in the car, sir." I like the whole *sir* thing. I believe every word of it. The man clearly has a great deal of respect for me.

He heads back to his vehicle and busies himself with his dashboard. There is now evidently all sorts of fancy communication going on between the vehicle and disembodied servers over encrypted radio networks, matching my ID and car to fabulously articulated databases, all seeking transgressions and misbehavior of any kind. I am amused and pleased by our police procedure, our technology, our adherence to law and order, our modernity and fairness.

Mr. Nice Policeman is now standing ten feet from my window, gun drawn.

"PUT YOUR HANDS ON THE STEERING WHEEL!"

"What?"

"PUT YOUR HANDS ON THE STEERING WHEEL—NOW!"

There is a second cop, next to Innocent's window. His gun is also drawn.

"PASSENGER! LET ME SEE YOUR HANDS!"

The word *shit* is no longer appropriate. The word *fuck* similarly milquetoast. Even *cunt* is pabulum.

However, the word *dread* does come to mind.

The next few minutes blur by. I am on the asphalt. There is a painful handcuffing, a Miranda recital, and something about being arrested for something felonious. I can't be sure, but I think the word assault-with-something-or-other is mentioned. Innocent is standing ashen-faced with both hands on the car, obviously not a suspect in whatever terrible thing I have done. I tell him to call my cousin Mendel, a low-life, ambulance-chasing, immoral schmuck, but a criminal lawyer nevertheless. The last time I saw Mendel was at his son's bar mitzvah about five years ago. I had to leave after getting into an argument with Mendel about certain earnest matters relating to truth and justice, and then calling him a low-life, ambulance-chasing, immoral schmuck. In addition, his son was utterly tone deaf, screeching his dissonant way through a long haftarah piece about Elijah, I think.

I am working on the assumption here that blood is thicker than water and that Mendel has forgiven me and will arrive to get me out of jail before the gang rape, which is no doubt currently being planned, whereupon Mendel will present me with a startling bill to cover his humiliation at the bar mitzvah, under the guise of legal services rendered. It will be capitalism at its finest.

The cops do the nice gentle don't-bump-your-head maneuver and put me in the car. We drive off, leaving a bewildered

Innocent on the sidewalk, trying to use his cell phone with shaking hands.

The black-and-white travels nice and slow along Beverly, the cops chatting amiably about sports. They are casting aspersions on my favorite quarterback and this irritates me, but I am too distracted by other matters to mount a spirited defense. I am in the back, hands secured, running through rape avoidance scenarios. A tiny but pertinent thought fights its way through a particular scene I am now wrestling with, which involves a toothless gangster trying to force a broken beer bottle up my rectum. And this little thought is that I have never actually assaulted anyone. In my life. Except for that guy who vomited in my sax while I was playing it. But that was very long ago and my attempt to gouge his eyes out was comically inept, and surely our stolid justice system would see the justification in that.

"Excuse me, officer?"

My voice is small, respectful, modulated.

The cop who is driving glances in his rearview mirror, seemingly surprised to see me there.

"Yeah?"

"I think there has been some mistake."

"Uh huh."

"I have never assaulted anyone in my life."

He goes back to sports, now onto golf. He presents an interesting thesis about professional golf having lost its soul, with a series of identically stenciled players and no one who misbehaves, which in his view, is the point of watching sports. I consider countering with a philosophical view that golf is not really a sport, but more of a craft, and that when observing a craft well executed, personalities become less important. But the little thought still nags at me.

"Officer?"

He casts an irritated eye into his rearview mirror.

"Yeah."

"You've got the wrong guy. I don't assault people because they tend to hit back. I'm telling the truth here, officer."

"Shut the fuck up or else I will pull into an alleyway and beat you with a rubber hose."

I consider this for a while and whether this sort of thing still goes on in our fair country. I decide that it does not and that he is just kidding me.

"Officer . . ."

His partner swivels around in one smooth motion and brings the flat of his hand down on the top of my head, somewhat like swatting a fly. It makes a very loud noise and hurts like a motherfucker. The loud noise is more alarming than the pain. It sounds somewhat like a cymbal.

"SHUT THE FUCK UP, YOU PIECE OF SHIT!"

I make a mental note to discuss Iranian law enforcement with Farzad next time I see him, to interrogate him as to whether any similarities exist between our two countries, given my fresh new understanding of the subject. It would go a long way to support the liberal cliché that our similarities are more important than our differences.

We reach the station. I am led from the car, and my handcuffs are removed, to be replaced by a meaty hand gripping my forearm. My pockets are emptied, my belt is removed (I find out later this is to prevent a suicide attempt), and various paperwork is filled in. As I am being led to lockup by the cop who whacked my head, I suddenly, in a moment of crystal clear stupidity, twist out of my handler's grip and swing my open hand down upon his head, figuring misguidedly that payback will be understood and accepted. Not only do I miss by a mile, but the cop, being an old hand in placating violent arrestees, proceeds to plant a practiced fist into my solar plexus. I drop to the corridor floor, gasping.

"I thought you said you never assaulted anyone?" He says this while looming over me as I try to catch my breath.

I am tossed into a holding cell. As the pain of the punch subsides and my breath returns, I look around. There are about fifteen people with me in a small, windowless room. There are no chairs, everyone is sort of slumped in degrees of unhappiness and agitation on the floor. Most people are silent, looking at the floor. A few eye me malevolently. I am the oldest person in there. There is one conversation in process, between two youngsters dressed in gang threads, low pants, hoodies, tattoo identifiers of some sort on ears, cheeks, necks, back of hands.

"I love her man, but I had to cut her. Understand?"

"Yeah."

"I can't be dissed like that."

"Yeah."

"I was pretty high when I cut her. Not sure what went down. She was bleeding like a cunt."

"Yeah."

"Man's got to do, you know?"

"Yeah."

He turns, catches my eye.

"What you looking at, bitch?"

I look down. This is perfect.

"I'll hurt you, mothafucka."

I continue looking at my feet, which suddenly look remarkably small, almost girlish. Out of the corner of my eye I see the gangster stand up and start walking toward me. My fight-or-flight or play-dead instinct kicks in, contrasting with the instinct to wail and cry like a little mama's boy. Two feet appear in the center of my vision, outfitted in clean Nikes.

"Stand up, mothafucka."

I look up. He is glaring down at me. One of the tattoos appears to be a set of teardrops dripping down from the corner of his left eye. I seem to remember that this signifies something very, very bad. Like a predilection to stomp forty-year-old software engineers to death. I am briefly consoled by the thought that death by stomping is slightly preferable to death by gang rape.

"I think I'll stay here if it's all the same to you."

He sets his foot on my shoulder and pushes hard. I fall back from a sitting position to a pathetic, sniveling rat position.

"You don't stand up I am gonna take your eyes."

I search his face for signs of irony or perhaps even the beginning of a humorous anecdote. There are none. This whole eye thing opens up a whole new vista, so to speak. The vista is rather dark and featureless given that I am soon to be blind. I consider this for a second. I would still be able to play sax, this is good. And there are all sorts of technologies to enable the blind to be excellent software engineers. This is good. On the minus side, I will never see Isobel, Innocent, Grace, or indeed anyone else again. I will never be able to drive again. I will walk into walls and fall down stairs. If there is a piece of schmutz on my face, I will not see it in the mirror. No, having my eyes plucked out by a Central American gangster does not seem to have many advantages. I stand. Pretend to look tough, hoping he will ignore the fact that there is no blood in my face, and that there may or may not be a small wet stain beginning to spread on my trousers.

Another shape intrudes at the periphery of my vision. It is very large. It is another gangster—although I am not up on gangster culture, so perhaps it is just another mean-looking young man. He is black and pissed off and his neck is as thick as my head. I am about to get stomped to death by the rainbow-colored team of the historically marginalized. Perhaps there is some greater social retribution served by this and I will go down as a martyr to racial harmony.

The big black guy talks.

"Back off, hombre." He is not talking to me.

"What the fuck . . ." the Latino gangster equivocates. He looks back at his buddy, who is studiously examining his fingernails.

"Back off now. I've had a bad night and I don't feel like this shit."

"Look, man, this is not your stuff, you know what I mean?"

"BACK THE FUCK OFF!" His voice is majestic. James Earl Jones. I wonder if I should invite him to sing with us.

The gangster looks at me, spits on the ground.

"I will catch up with you later." He slinks back.

I look at the black guy, but he is already walking away to his spot in the corner. He sits and doesn't look at me.

A cop arrives and unlocks the gate.

"Meyer?"

I stand up on unsteady legs. I look at my lord and savior as I leave, but he doesn't look at me. I flick gangster man the bird, a foolish move, I am sure. His eyes bug out satisfyingly.

Mendel and Innocent are waiting for me in the front of the station.

"Mendel, my blood and tribe. Thanks for coming."

"Don't even talk to me, you piece of shit. My wife told me not to help you. You're lucky I'm here."

"Mendel, about the bar mitzvah . . ."

"Don't want to talk about it. Have you lost your wallet recently?"

"Huh?"

"You lost your wallet recently?"

"Uh . . . wait, yes, I lost it at the bar where I play a couple of weeks ago. Got turned in at the end of the evening. Nothing was missing. Why?"

Mendel is holding my driver's license. The one taken by the cop. The one used to interrogate willing databases all over the nation. The photo looks a great deal like me. Except that it is not. It is not my name, not my address. It is, in fact, someone else's. Presumably Mr. Assault-with-something-or-other. He does, however, look remarkably like me. Especially if you are a cop at night comparing face to photo by torchlight.

"Fuck." This is all I can muster.

"You swear too much, Meyer. Someone swapped his driver's license for yours. Nice crowd at that bar you play at. Now we are going to sue the LAPD for a king's ransom for wrongful arrest."

"Where is the cop who brought me in?"

"Outside, as it so happens."

"I want to talk to him."

I find him at the entrance.

"Officer. A word please?"

Mendel is not happy. "Meyer, there is nothing to say. We have them by the short and curlies."

I wave Mendel away. The cop and I walk a few steps so that we are out of earshot.

"It was an honest mistake, sir. The photo looked just like you."

"My lawyer wants blood."

He says nothing.

"Specifically, he wants your blood."

He still says nothing.

"I will walk away from this if you do two things."

"I followed procedure, sir. The ID photo is easily mistaken for you."

"Two simple things."

He says nothing.

"You whacked me on the head. It was pretty sore. Undignified, really. Also unnecessary. And my neck is really hurting. Not sure whether it will heal."

He says nothing.

"I want you to apologize for that."

"And the other thing?"

"Huge black guy in lockup. Saved me from an ass-kicking. You know the one I mean?"

"Yeah."

"What's he in for?"

"Drunk and disorderly."

"Let him go."

"Can't."

"Why?"

"Procedure."

"OK, see you in court."

He looks around nervously. The last thing he needs is a bulldog lawyer on his ass with a wrongful-arrest incentive.

"Wait here."

"Hang on. Where is my apology?"

"I apologize." Voice throttled with aggravation.

He disappears inside. Innocent and Mendel are peering at us from behind the glass window. I motion for them to wait.

About five minutes later the cop appears with my protector.

"OK, officer. Have a good night. Go catch some bad guys."

The cop shakes his head and disappears inside. I look at the big guy. He is looking bewildered.

"Name is Meyer. Thanks for stepping in."

He nods, says nothing. His face is inscrutable.

"Come by The Beast Belly on Vine Saturday night. I'll buy you a drink."

He says nothing. Then he just walks away into the night.

I am feeling good for the first time in a while.

CHAPTER 34

I PHONE JIM, the HR director, the next morning.

"Jim, I've got some family stuff going on. I need a few more days."

"What kind of stuff?"

"Bad stuff, trust me."

"You know that you are out of leave days and personal days and sick days?"

"So?"

"We have policies, Meyer."

"Jim, fuck the policies."

"I'll see what I can do."

Innocent and I go to see Grace. No change. Doctors inscrutable. We sit in the room, silently, for an hour staring at what is, for all intents and purposes, a non-sentient mass of tissue and bone. I leave Innocent and head down to Kaiser to see Isobel. She is still spiking. The doctors don't seem to have a clue, mumble obfuscations. Isobel looks terrible, feeble and tiny as though some regression has taken place, from teenager to scared little girl.

I sit with her for a while, holding her hand. I try not to cry. I try not to punch walls. I try not to think *why me?* I try, and fail, not to think *why her?* She sleeps for most of it.

As I get ready to leave she opens her eyes.

"Daddy, what's wrong with me?"

"Some bug or other, honey. We just have to wait it out."

"Am I going to be OK?"

"Of course, honey." But this is just dissimulation, verbal salves to kid her and me.

My ability to process the past few days has disappeared completely, such is the scale of my undoing. I suppose there comes a point after repeated calamity and random acts of shadowed fate when one simply become unmoored, adrift in an unknown sea waiting for the next storm.

Farzad is nonplussed.

"Job."

We are having a drink later that afternoon at the Formosa Cafe, a West Hollywood landmark on Santa Monica Boulevard. It is a bar and restaurant dating back to the Cambrian period of the great days of film, all dark wood and burgundy red, carrying the ancient fragrances of too many whiskeys and cigars and vaulting ambition, cozy too-small booths and tables and signed photos of greatly or barely remembered stars adorning the walls. The place and its history are fabulously and unapologetically authentic. The drinkers, by and large, are not—most of them are utterly unimpressed by the brightly lit characters in the faded photos and the short melancholy walks of fame foretold by their anxious smiles.

The venue is Farzad's choice. He thinks he might be mistaken for Francis Ford Coppola, who once had a film studio nearby and to whom he bears utterly no resemblance other than a fecund beard. He also mentions the additional sweetener of the occasional passing hooker outside, whom he likes to rate for gender, this neighborhood being a smorgasbord of sexual oddities. It is also a place where one can, without irony, order a Singapore Sling from a remarkably hair-gelled and sculpted bartender who likely does not know that Singapore is a place.

"Huh?"

"Job, Meyer, Job. Think."

"Mmm. No fucking idea what you're talking about."

"Did you not ever read the Bible?"

"Not more than absolutely required by my family rituals, no."

"You are a deeply ignorant man, Meyer."

"More to the point, why have you read the Bible? I thought your people were more Qur'an sort of people."

"Ah, Meyer, Meyer, Meyer. Anyone with any interest in the world around him reads all of it: Qur'an, Old Testament, New Testament, Talmud, Kabbalah, Bhagavad Gita, Tripitaka, Tao Te Ching, Avesta, Evangelion. It is these books that form the basis for all good. And evil. Please do not tell me you have not read these books."

"No. Sorry."

"Why am I not surprised? You are barely literate, my friend. It is a wonder you can even find employment."

"So what about this job?"

"The Book of Job, you brainless Semite."

"Ah. The Book of Job. What about it?"

"One of the great tracts of literature in the Old Testament. You are a modern-day Job."

"How so?"

"God is smiting you."

"Great. Why?"

"Testing your loyalty."

"What did he do to the real Job, of Old Testament fame?"

"Oh, nothing much. Job was a righteous man. So God sort of had a bet with Satan that suffering would not change Job. So he killed his ten children, had his livestock stolen or burned to death, conjured away all his wealth, and gave him terrible boils. That sort of thing."

"All this for a fucking *bet*?"

"Yup. You Hebrews and your deity have a pretty weird legacy."

"And did he remain loyal? Job, I mean."

"Yup. As a reward, God gave Job a new family and restored his wealth."

"Great. I'm sure that made up for the loss of his firstborn children."

"It did. He rationalized it. God giveth and taketh away and all that. It addresses the question of why good people suffer."

"Why do good people suffer?"

"How the hell should I know? It is your holy book, not mine."

"So I'm a modern-day Job."

"Yes, you have it."

"All this shit that's happening to me is a smite? A splatter of smites? A storm of smites? A swarm of smites? A smittering?"

"Indeed."

"Firstly, a Bible parable doesn't interest me because it was written when people believed that the earth was flat, so what the fuck did they know? Secondly, I was never a really righteous person. I was kind of middling in the righteous stakes, perhaps even in the lower fiftieth percentile. Thirdly, I am a little dismissive of what and who is testing me for what purpose, since I am not much of a God believer in the first place."

"You are an embarrassingly literal person, Jew. I feel like I am speaking to a child. Try, just this once, to think laterally. The Job story is interpretive. It has resonance for your life. Adapt it. Mold it. Learn some lessons from it."

"I want another Singapore Sling, how about—"

"Shut up, I'm not finished. The last time we talked about your little problem I told you to toughen up. This was, I see now, a mistake, because you and toughness are oxymoronic, as are you and the concept of a decent-sized penis. You are, as you endlessly boast, a student of statistics. You have then, of course, studied not only classical statistical theory, but also the interesting extrapolations of Nicholas Taleb, of Black Swan fame, and who is, I think, vaguely related to my tribe. In any event, you are simply experiencing a set of circumstances somewhere near the tail end of the Bell Curve, as we all must, in all of our endeavor. The title of this particular Bell Curve is called 'Smiting Meyer.' Are you getting warmer now?"

"Well, I—"

"Shut up, I'm not finished. Your god is science and the deterministic unrolling of a disinterested universe marching to the beat of an immutable set of laws. This universe has taken a bet with you, my friend, although you do not realize it. And that bet is that you will whine tremulously *why me*, which will be a terrible surrender to the forces of superstition, and will taint you forever. If you are truly to remain loyal to yourself, you must conclude Black Swan and rejoice in the supremacy of science and logic, whose mandate will be certain to return you to the middle of the 'Smiting Meyer' Bell Curve soon."

"Ah. So, what you are saying is that—"

"Shut up. I am not finished."

But he is. He suddenly brightens.

"I am just popping outside to see if there are any interesting-looking hookers. Want to come?"

"I'm good."

He wriggles his way out of the booth and waddles out the front door.

There is, if course, a terrible flaw in his analysis. Taleb's proposition extends well beyond events at the tail end of a normal distribution. What he talked about was the consequences of an unusual event far exceeding its statistical rarity. Yes, I am reasonably sure, maybe, perhaps, possibly that the sky will stop falling on my head soon. But the residue might linger—dark foul-smelling ectoplasm dripping down from the crown of my head. A dead ex-wife. A dead daughter, struck down by an unknown disease. A son stealing to feed a drug habit. A beloved father in the Florida prison system until he dies. There is no return from these consequences. There is no reversion to the mean.

Farzad comes back, slides in.

"There is a wildly attractive creature down the block who is, I suspect, a man with breasts and a vagina, masquerading as a male homosexual with transsexual tendencies. I am excited. Purely academically, you understand. Would you like to have a look?"

"That's the problem with you Arabs or Persians or whatever the fuck you are. You see one man with a twat or woman with a dick and you get all overwrought. You were brought up in a dark, repressed society where you masturbated to American lingerie ads. You are a sick man, Farzad."

"Yes, well, little friend of misfortune, at least I had a dick to wank. Yours was like an adolescent pimple. Only worth a quick disgusting squeeze between two index fingers. I tremble with revulsion at the thought. Another Sling?"

"I thought you'd never ask."

CHAPTER 35

JIM CALLS THE next morning.

"CEO wants you back at work. He says that unless you can produce a doctor's certificate, you must come back now—you've had enough time."

"Uh huh. Did you tell him I have some serious family issues that I am dealing with?"

"Yes."

"Did you tell him that I can shut his company down with a couple of lines of well-placed code?"

"No. And don't even joke about things like that."

"Tell him I will come in now."

"He also wants to see an audit trail of the SAP transfers to the bank because he intends to sue them for negligence."

"Of course he does."

I go to the bathroom and stare dully at myself in the mirror. I think to myself: this man has a business to run, I am a small but important cog in his wheel, why shouldn't he want me back? Why should my personal problems, manifest though they are, interest him? Why should I feel volcanic rage against a man who, by all accounts, has climbed the capitalist mountain, has supplied where there was demand, has been the catalyst for thousands of jobs and aspirations?

I go into the kitchen and drink two bottles of water. I get dressed in some of my less-favored threads and head out. I stop at the 7-11 to buy a large bottle of water and drink it in the car.

I pop my head into Jim's office. "Back at my station, Jim."

"Thanks, Meyer. It avoids a possibly awkward situation."

"Yes, it does. We wouldn't want that, would we? Is he in?"

"Yes, I think so."

I head up to his inner sanctum on the tenth floor, a self-contained private suite of offices, with two personal assistants, a private bathroom, and possibly other hidden recesses in which secret handshakes and virgin sacrifices are offered. I poke my head into the reception area, which is sumptuously decorated with fine art and finer furniture (dark and heavy, smelling of expensive wood and oil), their splendor and excellence testament to his ability to hire the best art buyers and interior decorators that money can buy. A stern-looking older woman, with severe facelift syndrome and hair so tightly pulled back that she looks like an onion, is peering earnestly into her oversized flatscreen monitor.

"Hello, Gretchen."

"Hello, Mr. Meyer."

"What's happening, Gretch?"

She stares at me with open contempt.

"Can I help you, Mr. Meyer?"

"You know that you are the only person who calls me Mr. Meyer? I mean the only person in the world. The known world, that is. Everyone else calls me Meyer. Even your boss. It signals lack of formality, amicability, trust, friendship even. Yo, Meyer, how ya doin'. That sort of thing. Don't you prefer it when I call you Gretch? Doesn't it make you feel warmly toward me, like perhaps, if the circumstances were just right, we might, perhaps, well, you know, exchange phone numbers? A great and ultimately tragic love affair between the knowing older woman who knows what she wants, has been there, has the experience and maturity, and the flighty, hard-bodied, irresponsible but lovable devil-may-care young programmer."

She stares at me, expressionless.

"Can I help you, Mr. Meyer?"

I give up. But I will crack her open one day, I swear. Like an oyster. And there I will find a pearl.

"Is the boss in?"

She stares at me hard. I wonder suddenly whether she has wild secret vices. Dominatrix comes to mind. Or even an alter ego, a submissive, dressed in diapers, mewling for mercy. Perhaps, in a less extreme vein, she does archery or tango on weekends, or, God, yes, maybe she roars the blues with whiskey-stained vocal chords.

"He is on the phone to Dubai. I will make an appointment for you, Mr. Meyer, but he is very busy. Perhaps at the end of next week? What is it regarding?"

I take a long swig of my fourth bottle of water in an hour and place the bottle down on her desk and smile. I turn and walk up to his door.

"MR. MEYER!" Her voice leaps up an octave.

I open the door and walk into the CEO's office. I close it softly behind me, lock it from the inside, and turn to face the CEO who is sitting at his outsized desk, but with his chair swiveled around, so that his back is to me. He is yelling into his handset.

"FUCK HIM. CHOKE OFF THEIR AIR SUPPLY. TODAY! GOT IT?"

I have little idea what this is all about, but surmise with a great degree of confidence that he is talking to an underling, and that someone, somewhere, is due to lose his livelihood soon, home and family. I assume that this is the normal consequence of the lack of an air supply.

He slams down the handset and swivels around, seemingly surprised to see me standing there.

My bladder is close to bursting.

"MEYER! WHO THE HELL DO YOU THINK YOU ARE? YOU MAKE AN APPOINTMENT BEFORE YOU COME IN HERE! NOW GET OUT OF MY OFFICE!"

"I need to go to the bathroom."

"WHAT?" His face is rage and confusion.

"My bladder is really full. I drank too much water. I need to go to the bathroom. Can I use your bathroom?"

I motion to a door off his gargantuan office.

"THAT IS FOR THE CEO ONLY. WHAT THE FUCK ARE YOU TALKING ABOUT?"

There is just the slightest hint of bewilderment in his voice. A tiny crack in his armor as he tries to understand the color of the insubordination standing at his door.

"Please can I use your bathroom?"

He stares at me uncertainly. There is large blood vessel pumping furiously at his temple. He reverts to type.

"GET THE FUCK OUT OF HERE BEFORE I FIRE YOU."

In one fast movement, my zip is down and my dick is out. I walk quickly to his desk, holding my dick in one hand, and my phone in the other, video camera rolling. His eyes grow large. His mouth is open, but no voice comes out. Clearly, they don't teach this in asshole school.

And then I let loose. A long yellow massively powered stream arcs forward, driven by a distended bladder and righteous fury. He tries to jump up, but not fast enough to escape a direct hit on his expensive shirt. I jump onto the desk now, the stream painfully halted by the exertion. I turn, feet planted wide and shoulders thrown back, and aim again and manage a direct blow to the side of his head as he tries to get to the door.

And even as I am doing this, I am imagining more, much more—exquisite tortures and humiliations for which this, an arguably masterful performance in its own right, is merely the prelude. The leaden events that now surround and threaten me are rendered silent, their eyes downcast and vanquished in the face of my comic Zeus, as I mete out justice and balance against my tormentors, of which the CEO stands proxy. Given time and money and determination this would be a pallid beginning of many splendid plagues upon his head and all others who choose to cross my lines in sand, even in their windswept disguise.

"FUCK! WHAT ARE YOU DOING? STOP IT. GRETCHEN!"

From my perch on the desk I am now able to leap toward him as he reaches the door. He tries to open it and, finding it locked, whips around, face white. I am on him again, close enough to soak his pants as he stumbles toward his bathroom. My urine is now wetting carpets, walls, books, photos (I am thrilled to see a picture of the CEO and Donald Rumsfeld, taken at some ass-licking corporate-government contribution fest, become artistically splattered). Great parabolic waves of piss, like an Olympic sport involving ribbons and the mathematics of gravity, rise and fall in terrible retribution.

As he reaches the bathroom and flings opens the door, a final heroic surge catches him square on the ass, creating a serendipitous Zorro-like zigzag.

The bathroom door slams shut. I finish up my load on his desk and chair. I turn to the bathroom door. I can hear shocked silence behind it.

"Jeez. Sorry, boss. I'll use the employee bathroom, shall I? Oh, and I quit. Keep the severance pay—use it to buy a new suit. Oh, and I may post this on YouTube. We'll see how it goes."

I unlock the door, walk out. Gretchen, who has been trying to get in from the other side, stares at me, eyes wide.

"I always liked you, Gretch. Too bad, we could have made beautiful music together."

And then I am out of there, my load lightened, metaphorically and physically.

CHAPTER 36

THE UNIVERSE APPLAUDS.

Isobel's temperature stabilizes, the doctors start to pack up their gear and move on to more pressing problems.

My father agrees to the dictates of the justice system and moves back into the facility, car keys and gun now firmly behind lock and key.

"Great news, Dad. You came to your senses then?"

"Pah."

"What do you mean, 'Pah'?"

"I got irritated in there. Everybody's very angry with everybody else. You'd think with three square meals, a TV room, and access to books they would lighten up a little. But no, everybody wants to stab everyone else. Plus there are no women."

"So what now?"

"Back to the same old."

"C'mon, Dad, it's not that bad."

"I'm gonna break out of here and take a cruise to Jamaica, meet a girl, fall in love, get married, have some kids."

"Ha."

"How are you doing there on the coast?"

"Good, Dad. I pissed on my boss yesterday."

"Ah, that's good. How?"

"By pissing on him."

"Really?"

"Really."

"Why?"

"He pissed me off. See the pun?"

"You really, really pissed on him?"

"Yup."

"What did he do?"

"He hid in the bathroom."

"I assume you no longer have a job."

"Correct."

"Won't he press charges?"

"For what? Urine assault? Besides, I videotaped it—I'm pretty sure he doesn't want it on the Internet."

"Such pride I feel for my son. What a little puissant. See the pun?"

"Better than shooting at people."

"No, it's not. Well, maybe it is."

"You really want to go on a cruise? I'll take you."

"Not really. Besides, you're now unemployed."

"I'm fine. I'm a pretty smart guy."

"You are. That's why you're my son."

"I am glad you're not in lockup, Dad. Promise me you won't pull a stunt like that again."

"No can do, kiddo. I have plans."

"I love you, Dad."

"I love you too, my boy."

I put down the phone. I am weeping.

CHAPTER 37

THE UNIVERSE STOPS applauding.

Grace dies.

Things just shut down, I am told. They don't fully understand—some people wake up. Some vegetate. Some die. This seems to me to be a massive failing of science, civilization, the cosmos, some-fuckingthing. Why don't they know? Why can't they fix this? Why do good people die? Why is it necessary to devastate my beautiful son, who is now catatonic with grief on a sofa in my house on the hill, dully watching reality shows with veined eyes. Who's in charge here, for fuck's sake? Don't they understand the concept of fair play? Rules? Balance? Justice? You don't just snuff out people for no good fucking reason. Especially if I am about to fall in love with them again. Especially when I should never have left them in the first place. My grief and anger battle for dominance, and I oscillate between the two, finding myself alternatively raging and crying, sometimes both.

There are many things to be done. Grace has no relatives here, other than Innocent, and the extent of his competence now is to move from bed to living room and back. So I brace myself. I call the attorney we used when we were married. A small break—he has remained on her payroll, and there is a current will, which mandates that all effects go to Innocent, which is good, even in the face of her relative penury. I try to get Innocent to help me go through her things, but he is near autistic with shock.

I gain access to her apartment using Innocent's key and I gingerly open cupboards and drawers and cabinets. I rifle through physical files (neat, labeled, symmetrical) and computer files (a complete shambles of digital disorder). The apartment is riven with her smell, the perfumes and oils of a lifetime of personal pride and private grooming. I open her underwear drawer, stare, close it again before my thoughts stray, sick with longing. There are old photo albums under the bed and I cannot bear to open them, but I put them in my briefcase, their melancholy secrets unexamined.

After six hours' intruding on a life now absent, the final tally is barely legible, with few possessions of material value—a car (now a heap without function, like Grace's body in the morgue), clothes, old furniture, books, $15,000 in savings, no insurance, a small dildo (carefully and sadly entombed in a paper bag and disposed of in a far-off trash can) and a treasure trove of echoes and ghosts. And then there is the codicil to the will, which is that Grace should be buried in Zimbabwe, under the heated sun that nurtured her youth and strength.

My dread is gone and I want it back. Its promise is now born and animated, fulfilled and writ large and black with loss and grieving. It makes me wish for the good old days, when disquiet and anxiety were my companions with whom I could argue and bicker, parry and thrust.

But there is no arguing with this.

The whole Zimbabwe thing, while pregnant (or freighted) with metaphysical gravitas on some level, is a pain in the ass. I have never cleaved to notions of final resting place. I have never visited my mother's grave. It is sand, mud, and long-decomposed flesh. Her memories, although faded, are much more fertile ground for me. With this request of Grace there are now official documents and coffins and air tickets and bureaucracies and health certificates, and the prospect of sharing intimacies and paperwork with representatives of an awful, incompetent, brutal buffoon-ridden regime. And worst of all, a sad and worn mother, and a lonely and dying father whose last handhold to life and laughter has now crumbled.

And me? Fuck, if I were a stumbling, clueless, lost, bewildered, and bemused fool before, I am the same, without the bemused bit. There is nothing to be bemused about. Amused about. Replace bemused with poleaxed. Numbed with all manner of heavyweight blows. Uncomprehending and sad, so very, very sad. There is death in my face. There is a shattered son, now reverted to a little child. Sobbing. Asking himself why. Asking his daddy why.

Oh, and I am also possibly facing assault charges, although Van disagrees.

"Meyer, you know my family was very rich, right?"

"You think?"

"And my dad was a big cheese and had powerful friends?"

"Indeed."

"My father would have ripped his tongue out before facing public humiliation. Even if he could, after the fact, have exacted exquisite revenge."

"I see where you're going."

"Mr. CEO doesn't want to be on YouTube drinking your piss. So you are in the clear as far as assault charges are concerned."

"I concur. You affirm me, Van. This is the meaning of friendship."

"However, he is also likely to be arranging to have you quietly killed."

"Shit. Can he do that?"

"Polonium. All the most fashionable intelligence agencies use it these days."

"Fuck. You think?"

"No, not really. Having you beaten to within an inch of your miserable life is more likely."

"Fuck again."

"How are you?"

"Sad, Van. Very sad."

"Want to get stoned?"

"No."

"Want to get drunk?"

"Maybe. Actually, no."

"Want to hear some crush-your-testicles Bulgarian lesbian close-harmony choir?"

"Yes. Definitely."

*   *   *

Farzad has another view, as always. We are ensconced on his deck, watching the sun plunge bruised and bloody into the Pacific.

"Loss."

"Huh?"

"You are dealing with a terrible loss."

"Thanks, Farzad, that's very perceptive."

"You think this is a problem?"

"Are you fucking kidding me?"

"You think you're the first person to deal with loss?"

"OF COURSE I AM NOT THE FIRST PERSON. YOU THINK THAT MAKES IT EASIER?"

"Why are you shouting at me?"

"Because it's your fault."

"Grace's death is my fault?"

"No, your inability to make me feel better is your fault."

"I am a psychologist. We love loss. It is 62 percent of our revenue."

"I am going to hit you."

"You are not going to hit me."

"Of course I'm not, but the fact that I want to should give you pause."

"You want my advice?"

"Not if you are going to—"

"Shut up, I'm not finished. Again, I can tell you stories of Iran. Stories of loss and pain and grief that would make even your Holocaust stories nod in empathy. Just what happens when we live upon this earth and deal with randomness, unpredictability, arbitrariness." There's a nanosecond of silence, a silence I choose not to break for I know now how it will end. "Take earthquakes. Do you know how many earthquakes we have in Iran? Many. Poor areas and mud structures mean that there's death everywhere. And dead kids—especially, dead kids. I was sent to one of these places to help once. Dead children, grieving and maimed parents, siblings—just an awful, writhing, keening maelstrom of loss. And for what? Why? We cannot understand these things. Some people know how to do a trick, passing on responsibility to God and then thanking him for his wise plan, but I suspect that that's not your bag. So what do we, the human race, do? We nod our collective heads in empathy. As I nod mine toward you, my little friend.

"You have lost an ex-wife, the mother of your child, perhaps somebody in whom you placed expectations of your own salvation. So I tell you this, my friend. You must grieve. You must not listen to people who tell you that time will heal all. You must grieve with titanic energy, with explosive anger. You must punch walls, you must rail against the universe, you must be impolite to strangers, you must kick the dog, you must abuse drink, drugs. And then one day when you think it cannot get any worse, you must think of this. You must think of the small child I found in the village where I went, spine crushed, limbs useless forever. She was perhaps two. Crying incomprehensibly for her mother, who was dead—along with her father, eleven siblings and all of her known cousins. She was also horribly burned, her face a melted monstrosity.

"And when that time comes, when you wake up hungover, wishing you were dead, consider her. She is now fifteen years old and begging on the street. She would swap her life for yours in a heartbeat. In a heartbeat."

"But—"

"Not finished. Loss is measured on a spectrum. All loss brings pain, also on its own spectrum. Measure yours on that spectrum and feel grateful. Now we shall get drunk and talk about women."

I stare at him.

"You done?"

"Yes."

"That's it?"

"Yes."

"Someone else has it worse, so I should feel better?"

"Indeed."

"And how long did you study for?"

"Sorry, that is all I have got."

"We will get drunk but we won't talk about women. You will tell me every fucking detail about every loss in that earthquake. In graphic detail. Spare me naught."

But at the end of the night, drunk and numbed, I am left with this. It simply cannot be, under any reasonable statistical analysis, that these blows keep coming. Surely it must end now and allow me to grieve in peace.

CHAPTER 38

AH, REBBE, YOU come back to me now, features clear, force strong. Those pale eyes into which I used to gaze, always seeing the better part of me reflected in brighter hue. Color me now, I plead you.

How would you protect me now as I crouch from the brutal nonchalance of happenstance? What would you say? What would you do? Against whom would you yield a child's tennis racket with such terrible vengeance?

Do you remember a conversation we had, on the school bus? We were what, seven? You looked at me strangely for a long while and then spoke.

"If only we could marry each other."

I was appalled. I knew it to be a shocking thing, even then. You went on.

"I mean, not for real. I know we can't marry each other. But if we could pretend we were, so that we could always be together. Even if we were married to other people."

I knew what you meant then. You learn the lessons of affection and safety at home. Mom and Dad fussed and coddled and enthused and encouraged each other and us. And through frictionless osmosis, this was how we related to each other.

Then you left, Rebbe. You left me alone, without farewell, without pomp. I was left gaping, eyes wide, confounded, uncomprehending. Life was one thing and then it was another. It was good and rich, and then colorless and impoverished. Can you imagine the damage, Rebbe? Can you imagine that certain part of me that lost its center, leaving me insect-like, on my back, pathetic limbs pivoting and grasping for traction and finding only the cold, odorless air.

So, Rebbe, you know I do not cleave to optimistic visions of afterlives, and in which one of those you may have found your peace (we talked about heaven and hell, even as little children, and found the whole idea silly). But the texture of what life should be, should have been, is imprinted on my memory, which is painted with my memory of us. Our early experiences, they tell us, are everything. The man becomes the simulacrum of his first few years. Violence, smarts, trust, kindness, rage, discipline, calm— all wired concrete and impenetrable early on. We wired each other, with Mom and Dad as a soft-lit backdrop, gazing at the strength of our interplay, the certainty of our gestalt.

So you see, Rebbe, I was set adrift, and in the tumult of recent events I feel that since that awful phone call I have forever lost sight of the shore.

I have learned to cope, I suppose. Our circumstances were a long shot. Separated by biology, joined in time, we were a rare breed. Not quite joined by the mandates of a single strand of DNA, but thrown together by the odds into a life of welcome proximity, causing me to escape the certainty of aloneness we are all supposed to feel, the isolation of identity as a necessary step to becoming an adult.

I buried you deep when you left, Rebbe. You surfaced occasionally, first every minute, then every hour, then every day, then at longer intervals. And as I grew into a bewildered adult you hardly surfaced at all. I could have maintained our severed relationship forever, Rebbe.

But not under these circumstances. Come back, Rebbe. I need your guidance, your fealty, and your protection.

CHAPTER 39

INNOCENT WILL ACCOMPANY his mother's body to Zimbabwe. I am profoundly anxious about him. He is frail and silent, either about to implode or explode. I don't know whether he is using—I suspect not, because he does not go out. But half my life has been spent around musos who stick shit up their noses, in their mouths, in their veins, in their lungs, and they are a wily bunch, able to score under even the most constrained of conditions. But he is consumed with grief, dulled, hooded. One line of coke will open up someone like that, start the engines, open the valves between consciousness and mouth. There is no sign of that.

"Let's go for a drive."

Innocent is sitting in front of my TV set, the Hollywood sign rearing up behind him in the plate-glass window.

"Why?" He doesn't bother to look at me.

"To see your sister. She's been sick."

He whips around to look at me.

"What d'you mean, sick?"

"It was nothing, she's fine."

Innocent and Isobel. He took to her like a big brother when she was nothing more than a gurgle with little feet and brown eyes. The age gap was too big for them to be playmates, but Innocent, even as a seven-year-old, was imbued with protective big-brotherness, attending to her every need on the occasions where family arrangements overlapped. Both being only children, they lapped each other up, celebrating their stepsiblingness, clinging to the half-blood that they shared. Spoke on the phone and, later, a secret life shared on Facebook and other recesses of the new world. I never pried, so relieved was I at the bonding of this relationship. It somehow seemed to absolve me of the guilt of two failed marriages. They shone a light on my genes and let me hide from the stern gaze of wasted time and poor judgment.

Bunny has held the news of Grace's death from Isobel. Although she is now out of danger, and improving fast, Bunny has decided, rightly, that the Grace tragedy is a step too far. We will tell her soon.

Innocent and I head out in my battered Prius, my sop to environmental concerns, notwithstanding my skepticism about the sucking of electricity out of sockets being all that superior to sucking petroleum out of hoses. Just five minutes on the Internet will disabuse one of any easy answers in that department.

"So, how you doing?"

Innocent doesn't answer. He stares out of the window as we head down the steep slope of Beachwood Drive, houses on either side of the road giving way to cheaper apartment blocks lower down, erected in the fading shadow of the great sign, and housing residents scrabbling in the alleyways of the entertainment industry, hopeful that the sun will emerge from those shadows and shine on them. The road is bordered by palm trees, a foreign import to LA, semiotic in their mocking symbolism.

I thread my way through the commercial district of Hollywood, at once run down and renewed, depending on which side road one chooses to avoid the tourists and buses and grand old buildings on Hollywood Boulevard and Highland Avenue and Vine, all still bearing witness to dreams.

As we turn right onto Santa Monica Boulevard, my chosen artery for this journey, which along with its equally well-traveled neighbors, Sunset and Beverly and Olympic and Venice boulevards, will carry us for forty-five minutes to Bunny's place nearer the coast.

Innocent is mute, so I turn on the radio and scan for distraction. There are hundreds of stations, none tuned to my mood, so I turn it off.

I try again. "So, how are you doing?"

Innocent looks at me. His handsome face is drawn and still.

"Dad, what happened with you and Mom?"

"Now or then?"

"Both."

"I didn't appreciate her when I had the chance. Twenty years on I began to realize that. That is why I gate-crashed San Francisco."

"Did she know?"

"I think so."

"Was she going to take you back?"

"Maybe. I would have had to work at it. But maybe."

"I'm sorry, Dad."

"Yeah. But I'll get over it because I can convince myself it was just a fool's errand. How are you doing?"

"She was too young to die. She was my mom. I am not old enough to lose my mom."

His voice cracks as he says this.

"Innocent, she did good with you and with herself. And you still have me."

"Yes, I do. But you know what they say?"

"What?"

"Nobody will ever love you as much as your mother."

I don't answer because I am trying to hold it together. Beverly Hills flashes by on the left, streets and stores of impossible ostentation. Even the police station dazzles.

"So what d'you think about going to Zimbabwe?"

"Would prefer it if I wasn't going to a funeral."

Innocent has always been curious about his mother's homeland. Pestering questions about Africa. Why is it at the bottom of everything, he asked. Poverty, corruption, brutality, discrimination against gays and refugees and albinos and every l'autre. I demurred. Pointed to other countries in other continents where it is worse to be gay, female, different, outspoken. But he hammered on. Colonialism. Exploitation. Slavery. Racial stereotypes inbred for hundreds of years. Resource stripping. Is this why, he asked. I tread lightly here, trying to be a useful liberal and a wise pragmatist. Jazz, I argue. Botswana. Mandela. Democracy sprouting everywhere. Ellen Johnson Sirleaf. Joyce Banda. Writers and artists. Wole Soyinka, Wally Serote. Landscapes, mountains, Serengeti. Kenyan long-distance runners. The diaspora. Usain Bolt. James Baldwin. Obama, for Christ's sake. Mobile cash technologies in Kenya, Square Kilometer Array.

Bodies down the Congo River, he counters. Starvation. *Heart of Darkness.* Muti murders.

No, I counter. Institutional rape and torture in Iran, Iraq, Libya, Saudi Arabia. Forced starvation in North Korea. Rape camps in Serbia. Buffoonery in Venezuela. Kleptocracy in Eastern Europe. Autocracy in Russia. Nefarious Haliburtons right here.

No, he counters. Africa, a special case of awfulness, no-hopers. Why?

I have no answer. These sorts of discussions tread on the quicksand of culture and race and blame and victimhood and oppression, and these days I steer clear. Besides, the fire in the belly has flickered of late, so I am thankful this looming debate has become buried under the tragedy of the moment.

We arrive at Bunny's house; she answers that door and throws herself into Innocent's arms, sobbing. I move past them trying to avoiding the contagion of grief and head into Isobel's room. She is propped up, reading.

"Hello, kiddo."

"Hi, Daddy."

I do a little kiss smother on her head. She smells like baked apples.

"What are you reading?"

"*Catcher in the Rye.*"

"Of course you are. Rite of passage for burgeoning young intellectuals." But my pride knows no bounds. A book. A great book. A real book. No power supply in sight. Hundreds of white pages covered in black ink. There is hope yet for our blighted youth.

"Don't patronize me, Daddy."

"OK. You feeling better?"

"Yup."

She puts down her book as her smartphone vibrates, grabbing it and glancing at the screen. Actually, there is no hope for our blighted youth at all.

"When are you going back to school?"

"Doctor says soon."

"That narrows it down then."

She is looking perky given that vengeful and unknown micro-organisms have had their way with her. Ah, the resilience of youth.

"Where's my brother?"

On cue, Innocent walks in. He beams when he sees her, the first smile since Grace died. She bounds out of bed and throws herself around him, coltish limbs enveloping his torso. My DNA step into the spotlight and do a merry jig.

"Big brother. I've missed you." She has her head burrowed in his neck. The words come out muffled and warm.

"Someone said you were sick. I don't believe them."

"Only a little. How's Berkeley? Do you have a girlfriend yet?"

His eye catches mine for a nanosecond.

"Hundreds of girlfriends. Waves of girlfriends. Can't study for all the girlfriends. How about you? Got a boyfriend?"

"I'll tell you when Dad's not around."

I pout exaggeratedly. "Innocent will report back to me."

"No, I won't."

"No, he won't."

Isobel slithers back into bed and her brother slumps down next to her. Bunny is at the door and I motion for her to follow me into the living room.

"She doesn't know, right?"

She shakes her head.

"We have to tell her sometime."

"Maybe Innocent can tell her? It'll be better coming from him."

This strikes me as an odd concept. Does the information change shape depending from whence it comes? Are facts not objective entities? Perhaps not. That's another problem with death. You have to tell people. It is like a viral expansion of sadness, upsetting all sorts of people in a widening ripple, at least until the fading amplitude robs it of power. I am done telling people. It has emptied me out. Let Innocent tell her; I will be a secondary comfort. Which suits me because I am a fragile thing now, holding on for all I'm worth, fingernails torn and bleeding from the downward slide from dread to this. Grasping for straws, I find myself arguing that there is an upside. Innocent smiled. Isobel has emerged intact from dread's maw. My father won't join an Aryan gang in prison. My boss is not only not my boss anymore, but has been vanquished by my mighty sword.

Farzad was off the mark this time. He asked me to imagine someone else, worse off, and in comparison, to rejoice in my good fortune. But this was asking for an etiolation of empathy beyond my skills. But to imagine *myself* worse off, that I can do. Things could be much worse and they are not.

Right?

CHAPTER 40

UP NEAR THE Hollywood sign, obscured from view until you have threaded your way along some skinny and snaky canyon streets, is a well-hidden geographic treasure: a lake. Actually, a large reservoir, given that my city is in a coastal desert, but it appears so unexpectedly as the last corner is turned that it seems to be a massive special-effects trick, with shimmering water, dam wall and the entire city dropping down below it. I know longtime LA residents who have never heard of it, let alone seen it. I have never found out who built it and where along the great chain of water engineering it nestles, but those residents in the know quietly revel in strolling, dog walking, and jogging opportunities along its perimeter. It fosters an elite camaraderie among its admirers, who nod at each other like Freemasons as they pass.

Innocent and I are on one of its trails as the day wears down. He is due to leave in the morning, boarding a series of aircraft that will ferry a coffin in their holds until touching down in Zimbabwe. It will be an exhausting and macabre trip, with Innocent bouncing from airport to airport, across the longest of journeys, knowing that his dead mother is on a similar trajectory, in a dark and cooled recess among other biodegradable goods, most of which are being kept fresh for human consumption, while his mother is being preserved for consumption of another sort.

Innocent is ill prepared for this. As would anyone be, I suppose, but I suspect that his dance with drugs indicates an incompatibility between life's sterner demands and the abilities of what is, to be fair, a very young man just beyond adolescence. Still, perhaps this sad experience will add some mortar to his young life. Then again, it may collapse it completely.

"Think I'm going to take some time off school. Go back next year."

"You sure? Where are you going to live?"

"You got a spare room?"

My heart does a little skip. A roommate. A second chance at being a father. We can watch *Seinfeld* reruns. Go to ball games. Repaint the house. He can stitch his broken heart together, internalize the lessons of sudden loss, learn to be a man. I can teach him things, things I never did before. We could listen to complex and inspired music, tease apart the harmonies, shine a light on the composer's intent. I could buy a pair of motorcycles and we could head into the great California deserts, sniffing out histories and dashed hopes. We could cook, rifling through celebrity cookbooks, fine-tuning recipes, switching coriander for basil, carrots for radishes. We could go clothes shopping, like giggly teenage girls. And women. We could talk about them. Watch them. Dissect their curves. Go to clubs. Seek them out. Go girl-hunting together. Me, a dissolute forty-year-old and my handsome, robust, and youth-advantaged son.

Shit.

"You can't sleep with any girl I date. And I get first dibs."

"Eew, that's gross, Dad. I can't believe you just said that."

"What are you going to do?"

"I can play keyboards in your band."

He could, of course. He was always good enough.

"Nope."

"Why?"

"Late nights. People who drink and do drugs."

"Girls. Music."

"Pitiful little money. Brawls."

"The roar of the crowds."

"No. Dads playing with sons is a no-no. Besides, it's tacky. Like that awful family TV pop band from the '60s. The Partridge Family. The blond, healthy-looking ones. Who probably indulged in cat sacrifice and incest."

"Can I sit in with you occasionally?"

"Yes. Definitely."

He nods. We walk for a while.

"I think Mom would have liked to see us play together in public."

Innocent has no experience with grief. Back then, twenty years ago, when I slipped off into the night to do drugs and fuck strangers and find myself, he was too young for the grief of abandonment, I believe, somewhat hopefully. Certainly disadvantaged, even damaged by a fatherless upbringing. But that is a different matter than grieving—it is more dispersed, diluted by time. Grief is sharp and unyielding, like a dentist's drill. Like now, where even as we dream up a new future for him, for us, the small furrow of sadness in his handsome brow remains obdurate.

Grief. Third cousin of dread. Once or twice removed. Same ancestral line harking back to the Last Universal Common Ancestor, which is Shit Happens. And now, a mere week from Grace's death I find myself on equal footing with grief. We are standing toe to toe, I smell its fetid breath, its short sharp breathing, but I am still standing. I am Jake LaMotta—you can't knock me down, you motherfucker, you can beat me, but you can't knock me down. Against the ropes is as far as I am prepared to fall, at least this time. I used to love Grace, perhaps I would have again, you hurt my son, you took her away, you piece of shit, but this will pass. This will pass.

At least for me. Innocent is another story. He is without ballast. Perhaps there are reserves within him that are hidden. Losing a parent is hard, no matter what the circumstances. But Grace wasn't a mom. She was his entire support system. Someone to whom he said I love you at the conclusion of every phone call. I am a mere Shakespearean walking shadow, strutting and fretting. It is time for me to step up and be a model for this broken boy.

"Innocent, remember Grandma?"

"A little."

"You were ten when she died. She was a good woman, a fine mother. A protector, like Grace. Although not as pretty. She died slow and awful. We watched it creep over her like a rash. Starting with small things, a name forgotten, a key mislaid, an overflowing bath. And then accelerating to car accidents and burnt meals and confusion and bewilderment as her brain tangled all of its routes, leaving her in a strange and terrifying world. She cried all of the time, Dad tells me. And when I visited she mistook me for her father, an old boyfriend, an old boss. And then, bit by bit, her body sort of crumpled, physically. Her hands balled up, her neck disappeared, her spine bowed until, at the end, she just lay like a brittle and curled shell in the bed, unknowing."

"Why you telling me this?"

"Death took my mother's dignity. Grace had dignity until the end. It's not much, but it's something."

He nods.

"Yes, it's something."

And it is.

CHAPTER 41

I DRIVE INNOCENT to the airport, the coffin bearing his mother being transported separately via cargo, courtesy of a lawyer we found on the Internet. The guy specializes in transporting bodies around the world. The rate card has the price directly linked to the awfulness of the destination country. A body to North Korea is apparently a bank-hemorrhaging exercise. Zimbabwe falls somewhere in the middle. I wonder whether the lawyer is proud of his specialty, in the same way an undertaker might be. His office, in a Beverly Hills building of impressive ostentation, was sumptuously decorated. I asked him how he got involved in this little sliver of commerce.

"I was assigned body-shipping duties when I was in Kuwait and Iraq."

"How did that happen?"

"Previous body postman got killed. I stepped up."

"Body postman?"

"Yeah, I made that up. Not bad, huh?"

"How did he get killed?"

"Coffin fell on him. Go figure."

"So why you?"

"The other guys thought the job was cursed. I figured that I'd prefer to do the paperwork than get shot at."

The chair on which I am sitting costs more than my car.

"So business is good?"

"Yes. Not everyone has the stomach for it. You get to be around bereavement a lot."

"Did they teach this in law school?"

"If memory serves, they taught nothing in law school. At least not at the one I went to."

"Huh. What can I say? Well done on finding a zero-competition niche."

"Yeah, thanks. Zimbabwe, huh?"

"Yeah. My ex-wife's family is from there."

"Piece of cake. We route through Johannesburg, which is pretty First World. Then on South African Airways to Harare. Paperwork is not too bad, but your son may be asked to pay a little bribe to the guy who releases the body. I have arranged with a local undertaker to accompany him to the holding area, so the coffin can be transported from the airport."

"So does he pay the bribe?"

"I would advise that he does. You don't want to get all politically correct about bribes over there."

"How much?"

"No more than fifty bucks, I guess. That goes a long way in Zimbabwe. Probably as much as he gets paid in a month."

So here's a guy who goes to law school and watches *L.A. Law* and dreams of defending the innocent or slaying the guilty, or becoming an acquisition king, or a congressman, or a professor. And then the quirks and peculiarities of fate deposit him happily in the rare atmosphere of the body postman business.

I wonder how many of us end up with the life we construct for ourselves in the fervid imaginings of our youth.

Not this lawyer and certainly not me.

I walk Innocent to International Departures.

"How you feeling?"

"Better, Dad."

"Good."

"You going to say anything at the funeral?"

"I think so. Not sure what, though. It'll be as much for my grand-parents as for anyone. I want them to know how great she was."

"OK. You call me or email if you need anything at all."

"Dad? We should spend more time together. We missed out before."

"My fault. I wasn't ready for you. I'm sorry."

"It's OK. You can make it up to me when I get back."

"Yes. Careful over there. It's full of people who hate Americans."

"Nonsense, Dad. Love you, see you in a few weeks."

I hug him, his large and frail young frame filling my arms. It is difficult to let go.

Innocent reaches Zimbabwe in one piece. He is not taken into cus-tody for being young, white, and American. The coffin is unloaded without incident. His grandfather and grandmother meet him and they embrace. Their tears run unrestrained. I know this because even in that blighted dictatorship they have the Internet and Innocent emails me daily. Sometimes twice or three times. He pours it out. The language is pure, his voice sure, his internal monologues surprising and mature, his emotions uncensored. I am taken aback by his command of narrative, obviously nurtured by a lifelong diet of rich literature from his mother.

He emails me of his tightening relationship with his numbed and dying grandfather, who he has started to call Gramps. He observes his surroundings minutely, with affection and care. He gently describes the few remaining sad and weathered family acquaintances who cluster around the grave as his mother is put to rest under the soothing and thickly accented oratory of a black minister, who comforts Innocent in ways in which I could not. He writes to me mercilessly and endlessly, his commentary rich and profound. He writes to me of the eulogy he delivers. It is bold, confident, respectful, and uplifting. He writes to me as though his entire life has led him to this point, in a distant African land, surrounded by menacing politics and breathtaking vistas and poverty and the kindness of strangers, a place in his mind where everything he was, and is, and will be suddenly fits, makes sense.

And then I get this.

Dad,

I have been here only a short time, under warm skies and among strangers who are becoming friends. I find Gramps staring at me often, not because I am his newly met grandson, but more because I seem to be a totem of sorts, a way for him to gather his strength before he dies. He is not really all that ill—just old, and tired of the many battles of life, which in this country are numerous and frequent. He is a kind man, but Mom's death has emptied him, and I suspect he will go quickly now. His few remaining friends tell me of heroic and charitable acts quietly carried out over decades. I like him. I like Gran too, but she is just lost. I see her confusion when she looks at me. I think that she has started the slide toward dementia, but she definitely knows that he is dying, and she won't let him out of her sight. I am something new for her. I don't think she wants to deal with the new. Gramps talks often of Mom, a tomboy growing in the safety of another time in the heartland of this country. Wild, barefoot, guileless, curious. I wish I knew more about her African youth. The photos of her sear, a young girl whose shy and eager smile deserved a longer life.

This country tugs at me. Beyond the obvious, which blares from US newspapers you read, beyond the corruption and larceny and lack of law and torture and oppression and rigged elections is something else, something difficult to articulate, but something about the faces and gentle kindness and laughter of many who I meet here, from waiters to shopkeepers to out-of-work teachers. It sounds clichéd as hell, I know, but there is a spirit of something here, and perhaps I am simply a naive observer with a bleeding heart, but I feel an immediacy that I need to obey.

So I have decided to stay here, at least for a while. An indeterminate while. I can teach or something and it is not expensive to live here. I can comfort Gramps before he goes, keep Gran company, provide what little solace I can. Mom would have liked to know that. I can get distance from behaviors I was not proud of. I can reset, recalibrate, reanimate.

I was looking forward to living with you, having a dad and all. I'm hoping we can still do that one day.

Play easy.

Love,
Innocent

P.S. *Let me tell Isobel. I'll write to her.*

CHAPTER 42

IT TAKES ME three or four readings before the impact of Innocent's email really sinks in.

ARE YOU FUCKING KIDDING ME? YOU ARE MOVING TO SOME FUCKING HELLHOLE OF AN AFRICAN DICTATORSHIP AND LEAVING ME HERE, ALONE?

I look for something to throw. I need to cause pain to a blameless and inanimate object. There is an ashtray on the table, usually kept for Van's proclivities. It is glass, with the name of a Milanese hotel embossed under a logo of indeterminate symbolism. Clearly purloined by a visitor to this hotel, it has found its way to my coffee table, the origins of its journey to this spot unknown. It now flies through the air, propelled by an arm that used to be known as "Mach V" during my baseball career at high school. Even in the passion of the moment I have taken care to aim it at a spot on the wall, not too high, not too low, and a tiny, tiny part of my brain has already wondered whether the appropriate tools for repair still nestle in the hardware cupboard in the basement.

Alas, muscle atrophy and excessive rage have altered my mastery of physics and the projectile veers off the trajectory I had planned and careens into a power switch on the wall, which buckles and sparks, before ricocheting off toward my beloved floor-to-ceiling plate-glass window, my Hollywood-sign-contemplating window. I watch, fascinated in a Charlie Brown zigzagged smile sort of way, as the window bows and then starts to crack and crackle and spread, before explosively shattering and cascading noisily and gleefully down the hillside outside. All of it. The ashtray falls to the floor, on its edge, and in a final act of retribution rolls lazily back to me, clattering into place near my foot. I notice that the graphic for Hotel Dolce Italiano, Milan, is a lemon, I think. This strikes me as mildly amusing until I realize that the TV, which had been silently vomiting up a soap opera, is now dark. I seem also to have fucked the power supply.

I grab my keys and head out the door.

Van is reading *War and Peace* when I get there. Next to his bed is *Ulysses*.

"What the fuck you reading those for?"

He shrugs.

"Trying to better myself."

"You're rich. Why d'you have to better yourself?"

"I don't know. So that people of quality want me for reasons other than my trust fund. Want to get high?"

"Yes. Grab a joint and let's hit Pacific Coast Highway."

"You never say yes. What's up?"

"Fucking Robert Mugabe."

"Robert Mugabe?"

"Yes, Robert Fucking Mugabe."

"That was going to be my second guess."

"Yes. Let's go."

I pull out my iPod and plug it into the sound system in his car. Steely Dan. A song called "Babylon Sisters," from way back when. "Drive west on Sunset . . ." the opening lines, as we do, indeed, drive west on Sunset. Slow, spare funk track. Close harmony voices in the back. Big empty spaces in the arrangement, bracketed by short sighs of incongruous and lustful horns, pregnant with the promise of sex, with these two girls in the car, the Babylon Sisters, on a perfect Southern California day. Like this.

But it isn't. I feel like shit.

"Do it."

Van lights up the joint, an old pro, eyes never leaving the road.

Marijuana is a multilevel marketing scheme, at least for me. A Ponzi scam. There is a series of plateaus. A lovely soft buzz and then the wonder of music and food, as if discovered for the first time. Moving on to a predilection to laugh at everything—the less funny the more we laugh, and then to debate, anything at all. And then to fuck, anything at all, at least anything with an orifice and a skirt. And then to sleep, anywhere at all. And finally, if I get there, the growling paranoia of all sound and movement, all out to get me. At that point, it is like dread on steroids. Which is why I don't generally smoke, because it rarely ends well. I take a niggardly puff.

"So, Meyer, how you doing?"

"Been better."

"How's Innocent doing?"

"Better. He's gone to Zimbabwe."

"Hell, you say. Why?"

"To bury his mother there. Meet his grandparents."

"Ah."

"Yeah."

It takes about twenty seconds for the first threads of MJ to interfere with my neurotransmitters. I switch off the music. I smile goofily at Van and sing the first few bars of "Moon River" to Van. He glances at me, alarmed.

"What's up?"

I switch midstream to "It Don't Mean a Thing (If It Ain't Got That Swing)."

"You making me nervous, Meyer."

I segue into "Ave Maria."

"Stop it, Meyer."

"Got anything to eat?"

"Check the glove compartment."

There is a candy bar in the compartment. Half eaten and with some considerable miles on it. My saliva glands go into overdrive. I gobble it down. It has peanuts embedded in sweet goo and covered in chocolate. I die and go to heaven.

"My dog licked that."

He starts giggling, falsetto and weird.

"Don't care."

"I wiped my butt with that."

Now he really starts laughing. So do I. The falsetto thing is contagious. We are both cackling around high C. He pauses for long enough to get another sentence out.

"Then I wiped my dog's butt with it."

Now we start laughing so hard that it is hard to breathe. Van's face goes purple and he pulls onto the shoulder of the road and beats his steering wheel with his hands.

We fall out of the car, which is perched next to a beach somewhere on the Pacific Coast Highway between Santa Monica and Malibu. There is a lone surfer in the water and few waves. Our laughter slowly subsides in smaller and smaller explosive bursts. We are now silent. The surfer, who has been lying in the languid water waiting for action, suddenly starts paddling furiously as a hopeful and pathetic little swell emerges behind him. The swell catches up to him, now looking prepubescent. It raises him up and he tries to scramble to his feet, only to continue a full rotational movement, his legs suddenly airborne, somersaulting gracelessly backward into the water, arms oscillating wildly for imaginary purchase.

I catch Van's eye now and we know we are in big trouble because we start shrieking so loudly that the poor schmuck in the water, head recently emerged, gives us the finger. The shrieks turn into a rusty, breathless keening as we now lose the ability to stand and collapse to earth, trying to get in enough oxygen to stay alive. I am going to die here, I am sure, killed by inappropriate humor and uncontrolled laughter born of drugs and surrender and wayward sons and dying ex-wives.

When we have recovered, we head out again. I am still hungry and we stop at one of those hanging-over-the-waves patio restaurants and order burgers and fries.

"So enough about me, Van. What's up with you?"

He looks taken aback.

"What d'you mean?"

"How you doing? What's going on with you?"

"Jesus, Meyer, you shouldn't smoke this stuff. I have no idea what you're talking about."

"How's your life?"

"I am going to stab you in the neck with my fork. Try to have a normal discussion. That means music or women."

"OK. How's your woman?"

"Marion? She scares me."

"And this is . . . a good thing?"

"Well, at least it keeps me from straying."

"Et voilà. You have solved the ancient problem of how to maintain a good relationship. Hook up with a scary woman."

"Nah. She's OK, I guess."

"And, ladies and gentlemen, spice up your relationship by telling the lady—you're OK, I guess."

"Get off my back. How's Innocent?"

"Don't ask."

"Why don't you ask him to sit in with us sometime when he gets back. You know, take his mind off and all."

"I did. He's not coming back from Zimbabwe. Gonna find his roots and all."

"Shit. Are we that bad?"

"You're a funny man, Van."

"Damn. Sorry, Meyer. Not a good month for you, huh?"

"You think?"

"How you holding up?"

"Why am I not allowed to ask you about yourself, but you can ask me?"

"Because I don't like talking about myself. Or anything else for that matter. You, on the other hand, revel in self-broadcast."

"Mmmfmm." This is because I had stuffed the entire hamburger into my mouth. If the cow had been on my plate, that would have been gone too. When I finish chewing and swallowing, which seems like an inordinately long process, I resume.

"Well, I'm into the 'why me?' mode. Farzad warned me about this."

"It's a good question."

"Has bad shit never happened to you?"

"Never. Wait . . . I once lost my wallet."

"Gee, that must have been harsh."

"All relative."

"So why me?"

Because I am a student of the fucking odds, that's why. When you understand the basis of statistics, when you realize that there are no systems to beat the casino, when you understand why there is a fifty-fifty chance of two people having the same birthday in a room of twenty-three people, then you understand why you. When you watch while clueless, ignorant, and venal dipshits eat the lion's share, when you understand evolution and its cruel certainties, when you think it can never happen to you, then you know why. When you live a life of rare and relative privilege in a world of arbitrary suffering, sitting atop the pile of aspirants to comfort and peace, averting your gaze from the mayhem below you, then you know why. When you are graced with enough talent to sail effortlessly through math and science and English, and your ears hear the edge of complex harmony, and you have sufficient charm and intelligence and cosmetic luck to attract the affection and respect of many, and you casually piss in their faces so that you can live by your own rules, and not theirs, then you know why you. Then you know why.

I am about to verbalize this marijuana-stained swath of genius, when I am whiplashed onto another plane by a shimmy and swish at the periphery of my vision. Turning my glazed eyes toward the source of this distraction I am met by the disturbingly dark eyes of a young woman, which graze past mine as they sweep the restaurant patio on which we sit. She is with a friend, similarly young and bursting with the brashness of youth. They are between thirteen and twenty-four, depending on one's interpretation and predilection, which in my case is diminished and untrustworthy. I settle on nineteen. They are still wet from the sea and glisten threateningly.

We leer carnivorously at them as they sashay over to the bar and wiggle into tall chairs.

I prod Van with a french fry. "Go and talk to them."

"No."

"Why?"

"'Cause I have a girlfriend."

"Chicken."

"What are you, twelve?"

"So why won't you go over and talk to them?"

"Because I have a trust fund. Other people always make the first move. It's in the preamble to trust-fund-baby bylaws."

I turn around to look at them, now inserting their straws, phallic if skinny, into interesting-looking cocktails. I am not sure if they see me looking. Perhaps. But there is interesting stuff behind me as well. Like the sea. They have noticed, for sure.

I stand up. I am very stoned. I can see this playing out. They are rich kids. They are staying in a bungalow in Malibu. It has two bedrooms and an open-plan kitchen and living area, which faces a rattan-furnished patio. It is all white wood, with pale brown indoor furniture and tasteful abstract paintings, mainly in yellows and blues. There are fresh flowers. And a fruit bowl. She will lead me to the bedroom, without even the pretense of a tour or a drink. It will be warm, perhaps too warm. She will have a thin sheen of sweat on her back as she walks ahead of me, tiny blonde hairs reflecting light, a faint glimmer. I will simply be sweating. She will smile and fall back on her bed, which will be covered by a thick white duvet with girly patterns on its edges, and it will be cool to the touch. She will still have her two-piece bathing suit on, but her legs will be slightly spread, slightly more than they should be. A stray pubic hair or two will protrude.

I now have a hard-on. Marijuana fueled. Explosive. A thing of beauty. I carefully adjust it under the table, using simple physics to flatten it flush against my stiff denim jeans zipper, and to make sure that my white linen shirt is positioned for deniable cover.

"Fuck it. I'm gonna go."

I stand up and wander over to the bar. A last-minute prick of cowardice causes me to adjust direction by a few degrees and head for a space at the bar on their left. The bartender looks up.

"Corona, please." This notwithstanding a perfectly full pitcher of draught standing accusingly on our table.

I glance at the girl on my right. She is staring into her drink.

"Interesting-looking cocktail, that. What is it?"

She looks at me surprised, eyes smiling, lips slightly parted, a glint of corn-fed white teeth radiating. She turns to her friend and then the barkeep.

And in a deep Cockney accent, "Oy, tell this old cunt to fuck off 'fore I kick him in the cobblers. Fooking geezer."

I fall asleep in the car on the way home.

Fucking marijuana. A Ponzi scheme.

CHAPTER 43

IT IS A Saturday night and we are setting up. I am vaguely thinking about playing every solo a half-tone out of key, just to see if a single solitary person notices. But I back down, because Eric Marienthal or Chris Potter or Benny Golson at eighty-fucking-something years old may wander in. And if they do, then just maybe they will say something nice and validate the last thing in my life that seems to be intact.

Everyone in the band seems depressed and gloomy. Perhaps I am contagious. Van is noodling around a riff with some inscrutable time signature. Tim is limbering up with high-speed Celtic violin stuff. Mike is futzing around with the digital mixing equipment, immediately causing me aggravation because the settings are the same week after week. Billy has his feet up on his amp, his bass nestled in his lap, and is staring meaningfully at the ceiling, presumably conjuring up assignations.

It strikes me that a band like this is little more than a weird high-school boys' club. We think that we are important, but we are not. Not really. We have spent a tiny fraction of our lives gaining a tinier fraction more competence than our peers on instruments that play a pitch or strike a skin. Then some of us have gotten together to learn how to march pretty much in lock-step for a few minutes, regurgitating a pale version of someone else's inspiration. All in order to stand on a stage under the pre-tense of a higher status. It is a deformed expression of the evolutionary principle. We get to be envied and obeyed for a short while. It feels good. We think we are making art. We deceive our-selves for a few hours and then we go back to our lives and so does the audience, and that's that. Remember punk? I loved the under-lying principle, which is that you didn't have to bother with learning how to play an instrument at all. Or sing. They cut out the middleman, which was some minimal talent and all that damn practicing. Just get up onstage and assume the position, the clothes, the fucking attitude. That is all it requires. The audience will buy it, they will clap, whistle, go home to your bed. Audiences need heroes, and bands are as good a simulacrum as any. But pre-tenders to serious music, like our little outfit, are little more than sleazy fakirs. I hope we are never found out.

We jostle into position and kick off with a desultory 12-bar, while we attempt to get mojos working and try to remember why we do this, when many other weekend delights beckon.

There is a table of five or six youngsters making a racket. Good-looking, drunk, pumped, up for a night. Screeching and laughing, each one battling for attention. Nothing unusual. But I am not in the mood. And they are right in front of the stage. And they are having a much nicer time than I, and I am full of resent-ment at their uncomplicated lives and burnished youth.

We play through our set—some blues, some tangos, some swing, some Manouche, a klezmer and a Celtic. Van has a goal, he says. He wants the pieces to be so tight that they are driven by muscle memory alone. I differ. Once muscle memory takes over, we will marvel at their polish and mourn at their lack of spontaneity. Tonight, we are on autopilot. I am too dampened to even think about my solos; I just borrow phrases from previous outings and mash them together.

The table in front has gotten louder. I am struck at how a drunken woman can transform from pretty to coarse under the influence, with exaggerated mouth gymnastics and glazed eyes and oversized giggles and undisciplined eyebrows. The men just look drunk and stupid. They are shouting to be heard over the music; it is a distraction to them, an impediment to their awful clatter. We finish on a ballad, an elegy to love entitled "The Wedding" by Abdullah Ibrahim, with a searing sax melody and deep gospel chords. Solos would sully, so we simply deliver the composer's intent as accurately as our competence allows. While I am in the final eight bars, where the climax peaks up to a high-pitch fortissimo, and where deities appear, heads thrown back in bliss at the edges of the simple church harmonies, I can hear the following lovely full-throated refrain from the table, "Blow job, blow job, blow job." I open my eyes, which have been closed as I gamely try to give it my best, and one of girls is under the table, pretending to perform fellatio on a giggling Lothario.

I snap.

I step offstage and walk up to the table.

"Think you can keep it down? It is possible that someone may be trying to hear the music. More likely it is possible that someone may be trying not to hear you."

There is a stunned silence from the table. A young fellow in leather and jeans, tall and broad, with eyes stunned into asymmetry from alcohol, stares at me and then stands up.

"Fuck you. No law against talking."

I am past it now.

"No law against being a tone-deaf, drunk, ignorant asshole either, so fuck you."

I glance behind me. The stage is deserted. The boys have taken their leave into the alley for a smoke.

"You calling me ignorant?"

"No, sorry, that would be a compliment. You are thicker than elephant shit."

A few of the others stand up.

Oops.

Fuck it. I probably deserve a beating. It would color-coordinate with the rest of my life.

A shadow crosses the table. There is a hand on my shoulder.

It is the big black guy from jail. Really big. On a different planet big. My head reaches up to his sternum.

"What, do I have to save your sorry ass twice?"

He looks at the table, the cocked-and-ready drunks.

"My friend the sax player apologizes. But he does have a point: you guys make too much fucking noise. Go to a bar without a band. We all on the same page?"

Everyone looks at him. His arm is thicker than my chest. He makes Tall White Boy look like Anemic Dweeb. They sit down, manage a small scowl, enough to save face. He turns to me.

"You owe me a drink. Maybe I owe you, I don't know." He is not smiling.

We thread through the crowds to the bar. Gordon spots me, comes over.

"Everything OK?"

I am not sure if he saw my near beating or if Big Black Guy concerns him.

"Do you care?"

"No. As long as you're onstage in fifteen minutes."

We find a spot. Or rather, the Red Sea parts as my new buddy approaches. People this big send out their own force field, like the weird change in the air before a thunderstorm. I am reminded, without rancor, of my own youthful insecurities in the large-and-tall department. Grade school rewarded the cheeky and flirtatious, and I thrived. High school rewarded the football team, leaving me pawing for the attention of girls more seduced by brawn than, well, desperate claims of over-imagined intellectual and cultural superiority. Sure, we scored, occasionally, my sports-challenged friends and I. Scored with Goths and Indies and Bookworms and other subcults. But what we really wanted, to be truthful, was Cheerleaders and their skimpy wherewithals. Skimpy clothes, skimpy underwear. Skimpy morals. At my height, nah. The Goths would have to suffice. My new buddy here, looming gigantic like an oak dispensing shade and protection—he knows. High school would have been his zenith.

We sit down. I look up at him, sitting as straight as possible so that I am not talking to his nipple.

"So, you doing OK after lockup?"

"Yeah. Thanks. And you didn't have to do that."

"I felt I owed you something."

"Nah, you didn't. I was just not in the mood for watching some poor white boy get stomped. Normally I don't give a fuck."

I put out my hand.

"Meyer."

"Name's Jonas. I like your band."

"Thanks, Jonas. What are you having?"

"Water."

"I'm buying."

"Water."

"No drunk and disorderly tonight?"

"You never know, maybe later. Why were you in jail?"

"Misunderstanding. They thought I was someone else. Driver's license mix-up."

"Sure, that's what they all say."

"No, true, in this case. What d'you do, Jonas?"

"Anything anyone will pay me for. Which these days, is not much."

"Sorry about that."

"Yeah. This your main gig?"

"Didn't use to be. I am a software guy. But I bust out."

"That was dumb."

"Probably. What was with the drunk and disorderly?"

"Got pissed off."

"With who?"

"With life."

"Right. Know the feeling."

"I doubt it."

"Hey, I may look like a cool sax player in a cool band, but some shit has gone down lately."

"Yeah? I'll show you mine if you show me yours."

"Ex-wife got killed in a car accident."

"OK. Not bad. Better ex than current, though."

"Not in this case. My dad shot up a department store."

"Why?"

"Bored."

"He in jail?"

"Nope, he got off."

"Then it doesn't count."

"Lost my job."

"You told me you bust out. That's not the same as losing it."

"I guess. OK, someone close to me is in trouble with drugs."

"Don't make me laugh, boy. Everybody I have ever known is in trouble with drugs."

"My girlfriend left me."

"Oh, please."

I take a sip of my beer.

"That all you got, Meyer?"

"I suppose."

"You got money in the bank?"

"Some."

"You got people who love you?"

"I do."

"You got friends?"

"Yes."

"You got kids?"

"Yeah."

"You close to them?"

"I am."

"You got health?"

"As far as I know."

"You got prospects?"

"Maybe."

"You're a fraud, man. You life is just peachy. Wanna hear some shit?"

"Yeah, actually I do."

"Big and black."

"So?"

"Most people are scared of me. Especially white people."

"So?"

"This includes people who interview for jobs."

"Ah."

"No education. Grade 10 and I faked that."

"OK."

"No skills. Being a star quarterback in high school don't get you shit."

"Right."

"Long rap sheet. Assault. Drunk and disorderly. Selling dope. Resisting arrest. Gangbanging. Now I'm law abiding and clean, and it don't mean nothing to nobody."

"OK."

"Four children, four moms. None of them speak to me, with good reason. I want to see my kids. Every second of every day. I can't."

"OK."

"No prospects."

"You don't know that."

"Read my lips. No prospects."

"OK."

"You want my life? Wanna trade?"

"Uh—"

"Don't answer. Thanks for the water. Thanks for busting me out. You're OK, Meyer. I'll watch for a while. Maybe come back next week, buy you a drink. Maybe we talk some more. Maybe your shit is as bad as mine. It's all relative. Go play. Make me weep."

CHAPTER 44

THE THING ABOUT Thanksgiving is, shit, it is such a fucking cliché. We are supposed to give thanks, supposedly catalyzed by some complete bullshit about Pilgrims and Injuns breaking bread, presumably a short while before the raping and pillaging began.

So you gather your nearest and dearest to your breast and cook a huge traditional meal and watch football, and then wake up, do the Christmas shopping, and wait for winter. Which doesn't really happen out here in LA.

Given my learned cynicism about all things ritual, it is shiny irony that I love Thanksgiving so much. More than the Fourth of July. More than the Jewish holiday with the apple and honey. More than Valentine's Day. As a youngster, it made me feel American, even though I was anyway. It diluted the whole loyalty confusion that we Jews felt. It made me proud. The weather was always just so. We never fought, unlike all those Thanksgiving movie plots. We just pigged out, the elders got a bit drunk, and then someone would say a toe-curling homily of a speech that was sure to dampen our collective eyes. Then we watched the games with requisite but transient passion. Then we hugged and kissed at the door and fell into an early sleep, at one with our great land.

Which is why I have made a big deal about doing it at my house this year, my first hosting ever. Everyone is coming. I expected at least some weaseling, but even Krystal has accepted (after extracting from me a guarantee that I wasn't seeing someone else, after which she extracted a guarantee from me that I had not fucked anyone since she left, which is true—I expect she will arrive with some high-tech medical kit to test my claims). Only Innocent declines, happy to send good thoughts from Africa where he will have no one to celebrate with. It breaks my heart. I would prefer a cokehead son here than a healthy one there. No, actually that's not true at all.

I experience a great deal of cognitive dissonance on the whole buy-versus-build question. I cook as well as any other single man who grew up in a traditional patriarchal home. Which means a small selection of life-sustaining necessities—sandwiches and eggs and the occasional barbecue. The scale of the Thanksgiving meal prickles my dread response. So many fucking moving parts. Like my life. You need just one small blooper and the whole house of cards comes tumbling down. I have unwisely waved away offers of help from all and sundry, convincing myself that an act as selfless and courageous as cooking and presenting the whole damn thing will absolve me from all forms of vaguely defined guilts and culpabilities, protect me from looming tribulations and calamities, and cause me to be born anew. This is, of course, errant nonsense, but it pleases me to raise the effort to the plateau of some religious awakening.

I furiously browse Google and am immediately swamped with all manner of well-intended advice. I search for the "for dummies" advice and am rewarded with a large swath of step-by-step tactics for the culinarily challenged. I try to go simpler, typing in "thanksgiving meals for the dread-infected-bewildered-recently-bereaved-fool," but alas. Nothing specifically for "people-who-think-cooking-a-thanksgiving-dinner-will-reinvent-their-lives." But I find enough to spend a few hours immersed in a riveting but somewhat alarming craft, which reminds me somewhat of childhood chemistry manuals with their strange ingredients and measures. As soon as I get to the part where I am supposed to produce a hitherto unknown implement called a cooking thermometer to monitor internal turkey body temperature, I start to lose heart. I was sort of hoping that it would be a simple matter of "buy a turkey, put it in a hot oven, take it out two hours later" sort of affair.

Uh-huh. I try to avert my eyes from the non-turkey items, assuming that the bird, the main event, is also the pinnacle of cooking complexity, and the rest is just simple frilling. But the side dishes, garnishes, accessories, extras, traditions, and spares are like sirens. I must read their preparations and, yes, they will kill me. To wit—a herd of ham preparations, a parliament of other poultry options, a convocation of cranberries and chutneys and gravies, a squabble of salads, a pod of potato inventions, a gaggle of green-bean thingamajigs, a sedge of stuffings, a quorum of casseroles, a dole of desserts, a murmuration of mustards and spices. You get the picture. A collective of collectives, alliterated to DEFCON 4.

My surrender is swift and shameful.

"Bunny. Help."

"What have you done now, Meyer?"

"I may have taken on too much for Thanksgiving."

"Uh huh. What do you need?"

"I need you to cook the turkey."

"You can't host Thanksgiving and not cook the turkey."

"I will do lots of other stuff. It'll be our little secret."

"Meyer?"

"Yes?"

"You are a miserable failure at all the important things."

"That I am. Does that mean you'll do it?"

"You are paying for turkey."

"Is what's-his-name coming?"

"His name is Daniel. And no, he is away with his parents in Branson."

"Where?"

"Branson. Missouri."

"Branson, Missouri."

"Yes."

"You can't marry him."

"Why?"

"It's not right. He may take Isobel on a visit to Branson and then she'll have to listen to country music. She could die."

"Your turkey is hanging by a thread, Meyer."

"OK, I retract that. Thanks, Bunny."

One down.

"Krystal. Help."

"What's up, Meyer?"

"Can you make cranberry sauce and gravy and shit? You know. Wet goods. Sauces and stuff."

"Yes. Are you sure you haven't fucked anyone?"

"And stuffing."

"Meyer?"

"No, I haven't. Have you?"

"None of your business. Besides, I'm doing the sauces and stuffing, so you don't get to ask me that."

Two down.

"Farzad. Help."

"I did not marry a blonde American princess to have her cook for you, Meyer. She is mine to exploit, not yours."

"How the fuck did you know?"

"I am a psychologist. We know everything about human behavior."

"Just a salad and a dessert. Nothing fancy."

"OK."

"OK."

Three down.

"Van. Help."

"Why?"

"Because you're my best friend."

"Oh."

"Can Marion make a potato casserole or reasonable facsimile?"

"Marion believes that women cooking for men perpetuates a patriarchal and misogynistic system."

"Shit."

"I can cook a bit. I have to cook for Marion. I usually have to do it wearing nothing but a Germaine Greer apron. It's the penance I pay."

"For what?"

"Uh . . . I'm not sure."

"Can you do it?"

"OK."

"And a green-bean thingee?"

"Fuck, Meyer, you're taking advantage of my soft nature."

"Yes."

"OK."

I should have taken Jim, the HR guy, seriously and gone into management. This delegation thing is a wondrous tool.

CHAPTER 45

I HAVE DONE a creditable job with table-laying and drinks. I have added candles, bought some flowers, done bachelor origami with the napkins. I even prepared a project plan in Excel, outlining every detail, responsibilities, schedules, financial projections, workflows, critical paths.

There is the familiar fist clench in my stomach as I enumerate the risks of turning my first Thanksgiving dinner into a tragedy of Shakespearean proportions. I blot out looming images of alcohol-fueled insults, food poisoning, the long-awaited San Andreas earthquake, an untimely heart attack or stroke or turkey-bone choker. Combustible wood stilt houses. Or the CEO's henchmen appearing at my door with pliers and tape. So many messengers of disruption and chaos.

By late afternoon everyone is around the table. Van and Marion. Farzad and Cherry. Bunny and Isobel. Krystal. All seated. I ping my wine glass with a fork.

"OK. We are gathered here—"

There is a collective groan.

"Wait, wait. It's traditional for the host, who has spent hours over a hot stove . . ."

Hoots, jeers.

". . . to give a short Thanksgiving speech to his guests, in order to make them feel grateful about something or other. I forget. However, on this fine afternoon, I have decided to reverse the tradition and say something that will make each one of you feel shitty in your own way."

Hoots, jeers again. Except for Krystal, who looks at me nervously.

"Krystal, this is me trying to be funny in an alarming way."

"I've never heard of alarming humor," Krystal comments.

"That's why we had relationship problems."

Farzad chips in. "Actually, this would be excellent therapy for my little Meyer friend. He would feel better in inverse relationship to how shitty we feel. But he does not have it in him. He wants to be liked too much."

"Wait," I say, "because my daughter is here, you all have to be nice to me, otherwise she might suffer from all sorts of trauma later in life."

"Daaaad," groans Isobel, "I'm already traumatized by you. I'm fourteen, remember?"

"OK, let's hear it," says Bunny.

So I continue. "As you know, the forces of the universe have conspired to conquer me in greater or lesser degrees over the past while. Most of you have some glancing connection to these events. Which is why I have asked you here today so that we can gang up on the universe and ask it to return my life and demand a guarantee that it never does it again."

"Ah," says Farzad, "I see. It is all about you."

Cherry throws Farzad a glance. "C'mon, let him finish."

"Pass the bread please."

Cherry passes Van the bread.

"You can't eat until I've finished the speech," I insist.

"Why not?" Van asks.

"I dunno. Seven years' bad luck?"

"So talk."

"First, a toast to those absent. Innocent, who is excavating new experiences in Zimbabwe, including getting to know his maternal grandparents, who are old and fading. May he provide succor, enrich himself, and return safely."

I raise my glass, as do my guests.

"To Innocent," I continue, "a fine young man on the cusp."

Murmurs of assent.

"And then there's Grace. She was buried in Zimbabwe, and nobody has spoken for her here. So I say simply this—she lived up to her name."

I stop, fearing loss of control. I take a deep breath. There are many things I would like to say about Grace, but they are not for this audience, around which relationship baggage is liberally scattered.

"To Grace."

There is an awkward silence, as everyone takes a sip.

"And now to the nub of the matter. Life is like a box of chocolates . . ."

Groans, vomiting sounds.

"OK, OK. Seriously. It seems as though adversity has its own rewards. A bad thing smacks you upside of the head and when your ears have stopping ringing and you've had a nice cup of coffee, you get to reflect long and hard on the thing that whumped you and then you try to fit it into the greater scheme of things. Not saying that everything happens for a reason and all that nonsense, it's more that with hindsight you can sort of integrate the thing into the story of your life so that it makes sense."

"Whoa," Farzad says, "I am the psychologist here."

Cherry nudges him, "Farzad, let the man speak."

"My incessant pedant Farzad here talks about the threaded life," I continue without looking at him, "about life being a tapestry woven by the person who lives it, and that it is our responsibility to make it pretty. Nice thought, Herr Doktor, but I am off on a different, uh, thread here, if you'll excuse the pun."

I realize that I am still standing. I sit.

"The villain is expectations. When life veers off the track of our expectations, we get unhappy. Even though we know that we are really habituated at forming unreasonable expectations. So, in hindsight, we can simply convince ourselves that we should have had more prudent expectations, and voilà, the story of our lives starts to look rational again, if not downright reasonable."

"Um . . ." Bunny pipes up. "Can I object?"

"Mom! This isn't court," Isobel says.

"Can you change the food rule?" asks Van. "I'm really hungry."

Marion looks irritatedly at Van. "No, you can't change the food rule."

"I agree with Van," says Krystal. "It sounds like we're settling in for a long exposition here. The no-food rule is hereby overruled. All in favor?"

All hands go up, expect for Marion, whose face is pinched into an attitude of quiet fury. I expect that she is here under duress. Presumably she'd rather be at home being spanked.

Everybody climbs in simultaneously. Attention is diluted, hunger ascendant, philosophy of life descendent.

"And that, folks, is it," I say.

"No, I want more," Farzad insists. "Something good enough for me to steal for professional purposes. You were just on the edge of something there."

I am trying to work out if he is being sarcastic.

"Nah, I'm done. But one more little exercise and then we can gossip viciously about people who are not here. Each person here needs to tell us something that they are thankful for, and something that they are not."

"Jesus," says Bunny. "Why can't people just have normal get-togethers anymore. All this sharing. It's pornographic."

"I have always been pro-pornography actually," I respond.

"Typical male comment," sighs Marion.

"Marion, lighten up." I want to do this. "I'll start. I am thankful for, uh, rebellious daughters and wandering sons. I am not thankful for car accidents."

Cherry's next. "I'm thankful for plump Iranian husbands and I am not thankful for, um, let me think, yes, most other Iranians."

"I am thankful," Farzad retaliates, "for robust and disobedient American wives, and I am not thankful for psychotropic drugs dispensed by psychiatrists who tell their patients that they will get better when they won't unless they come and lie on my couch for a few years and talk to me."

Nobody else volunteers.

"Bunny, mother of my child . . ." I prompt.

"Not playing."

Hoots, jeers, raspberries.

"Please, Mom. For me?" Isobel's on my side.

"You first then," says Bunny.

"Thankful for cute boys—"

"Aaaargh," I groan.

"—and not thankful for cute boys," Isobel continues without breaking her stride. "Who I hate right now, but it's not any of your business. I will Facebook Innocent about it later."

"OK," volunteers Bunny, "I'm thankful for small mercies, not thankful for large ones."

"Oh, that's cute," I say.

"Thankful for women." Marion's playing along. "Not thankful for Republicans."

Van rolls his eyes.

"What about Republican women?" I ask.

"Thankful for trust funds. Not thankful for, uh, hmmm. Let me see. Bad musicians who get famous because of their hair. Or teeth. Or clothes," says Van.

"Am I the last?" asks Krystal. "OK. Thankful for our host, who invites ex-girlfriends to Thanksgiving dinner. Even if they are still angry with him. Not thankful for relationships. I am going solo from here on."

The sound of spooning and cutting and clinking consumes the table. There is a combinatorial explosion of food-related conversation, which morphs neatly into the pros and cons of diets (with Farzad arguing persuasively for the benefits of gluttony).

"Eat, be happy, then die."

This sort of ends that conversation, given that no one wants to press home the glaring fact of Farzad's proximity to obesity, but perhaps he is on reasonably solid philosophical ground here. My experience of diet-conscious people is that they are generally boring and brittle and occasionally melancholic. Farzad suffers from none of these maladies.

This segues nicely into a conversation about the US health system and it's seemingly inexorable path to unaffordability. The table is immediately divided along party lines, with those leaning to the left (led by the humorless Marion) arguing for a Canadian-style national health system, and those on the right (led by the delectable Cherry) arguing for the supremacy of the market system. The debate is spiced with tangents into the legal system and the insurance system and, inevitably, human rights. Stock-standard stuff, except for Marion's increasing frustration at not being able to drive home her point of view. The degeneration into *ad hominem* attacks is rapid.

"The trouble with you people," says Marion, refusing to capitulate, "is that you believe that the rich have a God-given right to better health care."

"Would be easier to accept your point of view if you weren't driving a BMW bought for you by a rich boyfriend," says Cherry, a little harshly.

"I offered her the Tesla," says Van, "but she exhibited remarkable self-discipline."

Dagger glance from Marion to Van.

Isobel's clearly exasperated. "Why are you all fighting?"

"It's not fighting, darling. It's called debating. Reasoned debate. Passionate debate. Which often ends in someone being killed in other countries, but here in the US we seldom take it beyond serious injury."

We move swiftly onto safer territory, which here, perched high above the city, is generally celebrity gossip and disgrace. This is Los Angeles terra firma. We snipe and nip at Scientologist superstars and bulimic divas and messy divorces and closeted gender preferences. We dissect illicit affairs, underage scandals, underperforming box-office receipts, drug convictions, crumbling careers, snarky up-and-comers. We gorge ourselves on how the mighty have fallen and who is down and who is out and who has been caught, nabbed, shamed. With each succeeding humiliation our eyes shine brighter, our souls lifted and made whole by stories of misfortune and retribution. And we do it without irony or shame, barely registering the quickening of our hearts and the drool on our chins.

And so the conversation settles into the percussive and unhurried chirrups of friendship. I miss Grace. I want her here. Her absence is clamorous, but I settle back into the warm hum of the moment and enjoy it with a sense of unalloyed peace.

But being at peace almost always fills only a small moment in time.

CHAPTER 46

IT SEEMS TO me that life should have a narrative arc, like a work of driving fiction in which there is a third-act climax and the tying up of loose ends that leaves us with a sense of resolution, of pieces fitting, and behaviors and consequences explained and put to bed. My little inarticulate rambling to my Thanksgiving guests was meant to open this debate, triggered by my series of unfortunate events and the bewilderment they have engendered.

But the everyday events through which we meander are nothing if not untidy. It is a great irony that the stories and books and films and TV shows that we seek to amuse and inform us are shoehorned into neat paradigms while our lives conform to exigencies of an entirely different kind.

Fuck it. Before all of this shit started I simply plodded along, putting one foot in front of the other, my mind largely empty of anything, guided only by the gods of small pleasures. Now I have become a clumsy contemplator, sprouting sidewalk philosophies about the meaning of life. I have always thought that people indulging in these sorts of self-indulgent musings should be shot to protect the rest of us. But I seem to have become one of them.

I head down to Hollywood Music to buy reeds for my saxophone. I like hanging out there. The owner is a grizzled old rocker who goes by the name of Wasted. About forty years ago he played guitar with some of the names of the time (Jackson Browne, Allman Brothers, Deep Purple, Joe Cocker), and ricocheted from the Roxy to the Whiskey to the Troubadour to the grand Hollywood Bowl, doing the *carpe diem* dance. And when the public taste gave breeched birth to the monstrosities of New Age and Disco and Punk, when guitar solos became a scarlet letter, he hung up his kit and opened a small store in Hollywood. He stocked it with some Stratocasters and plectrums and Marshall amps and Jefferson Airplane sheet music and watched the hopeful pour through the doors to bask in the smell of varnish and skin. Today the store is legend and he still holds court—gray, bejowled but sparkling, the old man of popular music.

The store itself is an order of magnitude larger than his original store, a marvel of pop architecture and creative utility. Nobody who is anybody shops anywhere else, and there is rumored to be a secret lounge on the second floor that continues to be homage to excess, where drugs and groupies are on permanent appointment to serve the promise of rock 'n' roll, even now in this jaded time. I have never been invited in, which is fine, because Wasted seems to have grown fond of me nevertheless, having heard me play during the years when all seemed possible. He is happy to shoot the breeze whenever I visit.

"Yo, Meyer, how's it hanging?"

"Wasted, my last friend on earth, it's the roller coaster of a life. Know what I mean?"

"You heading up the hill or down the slope?"

"In the middle of the Loop the Loop right now. Not sure which way is up. How's business?"

"The Internet, surprisingly, tickled my *toches*."

He has learned a good deal of Yiddish. Told me it sometimes comes in handy.

"How's that?"

"Live is the last thing left, baby. Everyone wants to play live because that's where the money is. I supply the nuts and bolts. Wanna head upstairs to the inner sanctum? Have some coffee or something?

"The inner sanctum? To what do I owe?"

"I have a soft spot for aging musicians. I am the fucking old man of aging musicians. The kids out there are young enough to be my grandchildren."

"Wasted, I'm only forty. Still a chicken to you."

"Nope, you have the weary eyes of an old fuck. Let's go."

We traipse up a flight of stairs, down a dark corridor and through a bland door. Inside is a bar, deep soft fabric couches, a pool table, pinball and video machines, a kitchen and chef, an oversized Jacuzzi. There are a couple of rooms off the side, closed doors with names. The Freddie Mercury Room. The Amy Winehouse Room. The Karen Carpenter Room. The Kurt Cobain Room. The Keith Moon Room. The Jim Morrison Room. Casualties all. I expect that excess happens behind those doors. There are huge posters on the wall, historical treasures—a Buddy Holly from the '50s, a Stones concert poster from the '60s, Led Zeppelin and Dylan from the '70s. Hundreds of autographed photos from the feted to the forgotten. Oh, and a few desolate but gorgeous young women, who look hopefully at me before losing interest as my age and anonymity become apparent. Wasted heads off to the cappuccino machine, pours a twin.

"Need anything special?"

"Like what?"

"A joint. A bump?"

"Nah. I'm good."

"That's what I like about you, Meyer. Been there, done that. Past it. Like me. You playing at all?"

"Yep. Tangos and swing and klezmer and shit. At The Beast Belly."

"Nice. Something different. Original stuff?"

"No. Just unusual."

"You got a day job?"

"Not anymore."

"What were you doing?"

"I'm a software guy."

"Hmmm. How good?"

"I can program any computer you name into multiple orgasms."

"You looking for a job? I could use you on the floor. This stuff is way beyond me now."

"Thanks, Wasted, but I'm taking it slow right now. Planning to plan my next move."

He nods slowly while lighting a cigarette. He gestures at one of the young women.

"Nadia, come over here. I need you."

A willowy young thing unfurls herself from a couch and wafts over. He taps behind his neck.

"A shoulder massage, love."

She steps behind his seat, drapes her long fingers over his shoulders, and starts kneading. Her face is without expression, almost robotic, as though it contains no moveable muscles. She is impossibly beautiful—statuesque, alabaster skin, large green eyes with just a dark hint of decadence in the skin below, marine-cut short white hair, swan neck, sharp angled jawline.

"Nadia here is from Russia. Or Belarus. Or Kazakhstan. Or some fucking place. She wants to meet a rock star. Don't you, darlin'?"

There is no reaction at all.

"She also speaks almost no English. I haven't a clue how she got here, where she sleeps, what her story is. She just sort of arrived one day, and now she spends most of the day up here, watching MTV, looking at fashion mags. Occasionally a muso takes a fancy and she disappears for a few days, sometimes more. I don't pay her, she gets to eat for free. The other girls around here are about the same. They are basically groupies. The spoils of rock 'n' roll."

I smile at her. She smiles back. Maybe she is not a robot. Although with visual recognition systems these days, you never know.

Wasted turns around to look at her and then points at me.

"This Meyer. He big star."

She looks at him, then looks at me uncertainly, and then smiles again. She has impossibly large teeth through which a small tease of vermillion tongue protrudes. I feel a small flutter of lust and disgust. The disgust part is buried deep, something about taking advantage of the lost and lonely that rattles me, perhaps something about the proximity of this girl's age to Isobel's. In the old days, lust usually won out. I have more trouble with it now.

She continues with Wasted's massage, now stealing looks of interest in my direction. I tear my attention away from her before unspeakable images of dark and wet undo me.

"So, Wasted. You miss the action? The bands?"

"I did at first. The store was just a way to pay bills while I planned my next band. And then it just took over and I started making money. And I didn't have to travel and I found a girl and settled down. A few times. Anyway, it's not as though I'm not close to the action."

"What about the whole performing thing? Don't you miss that?"

"Meyer, you are a wise man. You could have asked me if I missed making music, which would have been the wrong question, and, no, I don't miss making music because none of us really makes music, at least not like Miles or Mozart. We're circus acts. We satisfy a need. So, do I miss performing? Yeah, you bet. Standing up there while a bunch of assholes who don't know shit from Shinola adore you? What's not to miss?"

"Know what you mean."

"At the end of the day, all of us, even the most fucking superstar asshole, know that we are going to get old and ugly and that nobody will remember us a hundred years from now, except possibly as a footnote in some pop-history coffee-table book. We will never be discovered by future generations as Shakespeare or Chopin or Monet or Ellington were. A guy like Martin Scorsese knows he'll be taught at film schools for a long time to come. But you think they will dedicate music college classes to Adele? Snoop?

Madonna? Gaga? Footnotes, man. Who remembers Deep Purple? Uriah Heep? Luther Vandross? Chicago? Joni Mitchell? Crosby Stills? The Clash? The Ramones? The Sex Pistols? These guys could once fill any stadium in the world. Now dead and buried. And it has only been a couple of decades. Go to any high school and mention these names. You'll get nothing. Nada. You know what it all comes down to, Meyer? The stadiums and the crowds and the screaming?"

"Sex?"

"Yeah, sex. In the big sense. Fucking the fans. Fucking your parents. Fucking the man. Fuck you, fuck you, fuck you. Fuck responsibility. I don't give a fuck. Just wanna fuck. That's what it is, Meyer. Kids in a candy store gorging themselves before they throw up."

"No exceptions?"

"Far and few, man, far and few. Yeah, some of the guys can play pretty good, a couple write lyrics that maybe will be remembered. A few songs become anthems for the age. Some of the famous musos use the platform to do politics and good works and shit. But most of it? Circus performances, like I say."

"That why you stopped?"

"What? No! I fuckin' loved it. I miss it every day. This music store is not maturity. This is my compromise, man. Not a bad compromise. But nothing gets close to standing up there and tearing through a solo and spotting this one teenager in the second row whose face is all shiny and smooth and you just know she's going to be on the end of your dick later. It's just that primal, man."

Wasted. He has it all sorted out. Found a wormhole through the universe. Given up on his dreams and replaced them with reasonable facsimiles. And he stills gets to smell the greasepaint. I envy him.

That's what I want to do. Find a reasonable facsimile of the life I want and step inside. I bet it will be all warm and snug in there.

CHAPTER 47

I AM SITTING in my house browsing job sites on the Internet without much enthusiasm. I give up and start fucking around on the web. I do this more often when I am depressed. My current set of circumstances exceeds that considerably. So I meander off to sites whose content is so depressing that by comparison my problem might recede. Economics, for instance. What could be more distracting than a spot of deep economics, peopled by experts who are certain to be more battered than I. I am particularly fond of economics blogs. Years of reading abstruse arguments about monetary policy and debt reduction and quantitative easing and stimulus packages and employment statistics and stag/in/deflation have achieved little in the way of personal edification, but they have armed me with few impressive buzzwords and a certainty that no one, particularly economists, has the foggiest idea how to get us out of this mess. These people, all armed with PhDs from our most august institutions and a quiver of formidable mathematics, seem to be unable to agree on which formulae will solve the world's manifold economic problems.

Not only do they disagree with each other, they disagree with prejudice, insulting each other with alarming abandon, throwing statistics at each other like deadly weapons. It is like watching cage fighting. There is blood on the floor. This somehow pleases me. One of the smarter bloggers, a happy pessimist by the name of John Mauldin, has a neat theory that if economic problems get bad enough they tip over into a singularity, a word borrowed from physics, where the laws of economics no longer apply, much like the breakdown of traditional physics in a black hole. This pleases me even more. And if the smartest people in the world are drowning in bewilderment and laws no longer apply, far be it from me to expect more, given the comparative puniness of my own concerns.

Gordon, the proprietor of The Beast Belly and my last handhold on normalcy, calls.

"Bad news, Meyer."

I wait. The silence is like deadweight. I hear a cackle deep in the recesses of my damaged ego.

"I sold the place. Going back to the Midwest. Gonna marry my childhood sweetheart."

"As we all should. What's the bad news? Although I can guess . . ."

"New owner. He's gonna turn it into a cabaret place."

"HE IS *WHAT*?"

"A cabaret place."

"A FUCKING CABARET PLACE? SHOW TUNES? FUCKING SEQUINS AND FALSE EYELASHES?"

"I guess. Sorry, Meyer. You were my first. You never forget your first."

"When?"

"This Saturday is your last gig."

"Perfect."

"Sorry, Meyer."

"Why are you selling?"

"I never came to LA to make it, Meyer. That's just a fool's game. I came to have some fun. I did that. Made a small pile too. Time to move on, to have a family. It doesn't take a genius to know that. You should think about it before you are too old."

"I did it when I was too young, actually. Got a couple of families already. That's the thing. It's all about timing. Sounds like you may have it right. OK, I'll tell the guys. See you Saturday."

I call Van.

"Gordon's shutting down. It's our last gig."

"Huh. Want to come over and get high? Marion's out protesting something."

"No, thanks. So what d'you think?"

"About what?"

"THE FUCKING END OF THE GIG! *JESUS!*"

"Stop shouting. It is what it is. It's always temporary. We'll find another."

"Why does everything have to be temporary?"

"Not everything is temporary."

"Name one thing."

"The universe."

"Firstly, the universe is temporary. But that's another story. I am talking about temporary here and now. Lifetime scale."

"OK. How about aging?"

"Aging?"

"Yeah. Not temporary, it goes on till you die."

"You're deep, Van."

"Thank you."

"I have to go put my head in the oven for a while. I will see you on Saturday."

"OK."

Everything is temporary. Yet another cheerful thought to consume me. No, wait. Dread is not fucking temporary. It is fucking permanent. Why can't dread be temporary like all the good stuff?

I am struck by a lacerating sadness now. I crawl upstairs and get into bed. It is barely noon. They are taking everything away from me. It is a plot of conspiratorial dimensions. Like Bush blowing up the Twin Towers. JFK. The Protocols of Zion. That's it—anti-Semitism. This is an anti-Semitic plot carried out by dark forces bent on my destruction.

I vaguely remember a story I once read in which the plot was that the earth was actually a toy in some alien's living room. The alien kids would come home from school and fuck with people and weather and wars and disease and would watch what happens. Then they would laugh uproariously at pratfalls and other unintended consequences. Sort of like The Sims. Eventually they get bored and go off and have dinner with the parents. Finally, there is a fight between two of the youngsters vying for time on the earth toy and the loser stomps on the toy out of spite, breaking it into a million pieces.

The story is startlingly apposite. Someone is fucking with me. I expect the crew to jump out and shout "*Candid Camera!*" any moment now. No amount of intellectual rigor can explain all this. It is all a game. It will end soon. Then we will all go out and have a beer and a laugh.

I call Isobel on her cell phone.

"Hi, sweetie."

"Hi, Daddy."

"What's up?"

"Nothing."

"Why do all teenagers say that?"

"Because it's a dumb question. You have to be specific, Daddy."

"OK. Do you have a boyfriend?"

"Not that specific."

"OK. How's school?"

"Fine."

"The answer 'fine' is even worse than 'nothing.'"

"Because it's another dumb question, Daaaaad."

"OK. What was your last test?"

"Math."

"How did you do?"

"84."

"Really?"

"Really."

"That's great, sweetie. What else?"

"What else what?"

"How's your mom?"

"Fine."

"Aaaargh. Dumb question, right?"

"Yes."

"What do you think of Daniel?"

"He's OK. He's pretty nice."

"You'll let me know if he gets creepy?"

"Daaaaaaaad!"

"Sorry, that was out of line."

"OK. He's not creepy. He's pretty cool."

"As cool as me?"

"Never."

"You know I'll always love you. Always. It's not a temporary thing. It goes on forever. No matter what. Not temporary. Permanent."

"I know, Dad."

"OK?"

"OK."

"Love you, sweetie."

"Love you, Daddy."

Not Isobel. Not Innocent. But everything else is fucking temporary. Especially the good stuff.

Grace would know how to behave. She always had the sort of demeanor that would calmly deconstruct crises into piffling minutiae. She would have words of succor. She would have composure and balm. She would have wisdom. She would think her way through the problems and the obstructions and then act swiftly to clear the debris.

Am I rose-painting her? Have I elevated her unrealistically? Is my memory of her aggrandized and inflated into a comic cliché? Perhaps. Perhaps.

But I miss her with searing clarity.

CHAPTER 48

THE NEXT DAY Hyman Meyer dies. I receive the call at 5 a.m., jolting awake to the handset's shrill and alarming insistency.

"Is this Joshua Meyer?" No more is necessary.

My father is dead. He has not died in his bed. He has not died at the home. He has been found lying on the sidewalk, miles away, with a small suitcase under his head. The suitcase contains two pairs of underwear, a swim suit, pajamas, a Hawaiian cotton shirt, a white T-shirt, a pair of shorts, sandals, a beach towel, a toothbrush, a razor, a spare set of dentures, and a comb. And his passport together with an obsolete 35mm Olympus camera. There is $500 in his wallet.

The sidewalk on which he died is outside a travel agency. A travel agency that specializes in cruises. It is miles from the home. They have a discounted "Singles Special" to the Bahamas advertised in the window. Nobody knows how he got there.

I fly to Miami that same day, trying to make the strict twenty-four-hour burial rule imposed by some of my less considerate ancestors. I take a taxi to the GoldLife Jewish Senior Living Center. I am met there by earnest-looking staff and a rabbi, a bedraggled-looking fellow who seems uncomfortable in the role.

I am always deeply interested in rabbis and priests and other men and women of the cloth. They all seem so out of their depth, acting as conduit between their flocks and the All Powerful. I can't imagine the horror of that role. What if you wake up one day with a bad headache and go and minister and advise, and do a suboptimal job, thereby sending people to fates terrible and tortured? It's almost like being a doctor, who can at least take out insurance against the consequences of bad advice and incorrect dosages. In this line of work if you make a mistake, you are in eternal shit.

I take a walk with the rabbi.

"I am sorry for your loss."

"Yes, thank you. Death duty, huh?"

"I beg your pardon?"

"Did you know my dad?"

"No, I didn't. Apparently, he was pretty secular. He didn't attend synagogue."

"So what are you going to say?"

"I was hoping to get a background from you."

"But that would be cheating, wouldn't it?"

"What do you mean?"

"You can't pretend to know him if you don't."

"If you wish it, I will simply say the prayers. The Kaddish."

"In what language? Hebrew?"

"Yes."

"Does God understand English?"

"I suppose."

"So why Hebrew?"

"Tradition and ritual."

"Perhaps we shouldn't say any prayers. As you say, he was pretty secular."

"We have to, Joshua."

"Why?"

"Because they won't bury him unless the service is done."

"Ah. Pretty strict, these burial authorities."

"I suppose. But the history behind this is long and rich."

"I've had a tough couple of weeks, Rabbi. Do the whole thing. Hebrew is fine. Say a few words if you like."

"Tell me about him."

And I do. I tell him that fathers like mine are rare. I tell him that men whose goodness is manifold and whose flaws are superficial are to sons as water is to plants. My father, I say, died at the right age. Perhaps he died for the right reasons. But he died at the wrong time because I had not told him enough how much I loved him, and had he lived forever I still would not have had enough time.

I tell him that sons need heroes, not the sort who fly with capes across screens or who pitch perfect games. Not one who can conquer the curse of polio or one who can put together the notes of an ensemble horn section in a way that arrests the heart and enflames the emotions. Sons need a quiet hero. A man who will protect them without condition or recompense, who will revel in their every small victory. For whom pride requires no ingredient other than the line of blood.

I tell him that I have heard that when a father dies, the son finally becomes a man. I tell him that it's bullshit. Sons become men when they have fathers who are men, men to whom they can raise their gaze and find someone who does right. When he sees someone for whom family is sacrosanct and for whom life is to be gently and humorously lived.

If the son sees all of this and stills fails to become the man of his father's example, then he deserves the sorry state of his fucking life.

I tell him that all dread leads here. This is the end point foreboding.

We men wheel the pale and plain pine coffin along the well-trodden cement paths of the cemetery, just the few of us—a couple of ancient residents of the institution, some of the management, and those cemetery employees press-ganged into service, giving us just enough pallbearers to keep the coffin rolling. This old patriarchal ritual, of men handling the heavy lifting and the mourning women walking behind, dates to an age where such things were commonplace. It seems spectacularly anachronistic now and at the same time solidly bolstered by immutable traditions that have gotten us from there to here, the tribe still vibrant and intact.

The rabbi has done some intoning at the reception building, Hebrew words spilling out like so much gravel, sounding to my secular ears as strange incantations from an alien world. I have been to a number of Jewish funerals. Their effect on me is strangely calming, even in the midst of bereavement and grief, my secular contempt and bruising cynicism evaporating in the face of the primitive ancestral call.

There are perhaps ten mourners in all, not counting the press-gang—mainly a shriveled group of aging men and women whose attendance at these events must by now be a familiar ritual, a series of practice runs for their own hour upon this final stage. As we walk we pass countless headstones, mostly modest in keeping with tradition, bearing witness to names that ring familiar to us all. Morrie Sachs, Loving Husband, Father and Brother. Born 1912. Sarah Rappaport, Beloved Daughter, Born 2012. Rebecca Stern, Harry Rosen, Jerry Baum, Kerri Frankel, Cohen, Cohn, Kohan, Levy, Levine, Name-stein, Name-sky, Name-berg, Name-witz, Name-off. And everyone in between, collected here in the presence of familiars, names cast in stone, memories whispered and receding.

And then, the lowering of the coffin and that ancient sadness, the Kaddish, the prayer for the dead, the translation of which is opaque, but whose cadences and cries and imprecations and blessings comfort me in ways I do not understand, even as I stand here, weeping without restraint.

My father was going to take that cruise. He was going to meet a pretty girl, he was going to marry her, have a couple of kids, start a career, buy a house, live happily ever after.

Death took him away from his dreams.

Death took him away from me.

CHAPTER 49

MY HOUSE BURNS down while I am on my way to my last gig.

I am driving down Beachwood Drive to The Beast Belly to say goodbye to yet another part of my life. As I reach the bottom of the canyon and into the maw of Hollywood, the fire engines turn in from Franklin, rushing past me, cacophonous with sirens and sure-footed omen. I glance in the rearview mirror. High on the hill, below the "D" of the Hollywood sign I can see smoke and flames. I don't bother to turn around. There can be no other home for whom this particular bell tolls. It can only be the worst of imaginings, because that is what I am—a receptacle for the worst of imaginings. A toy for a toddler to smash.

I conjure it up. The fire will start in the alcove outside the kitchen, where the power supply and distribution board parse out their goodies. A small mouse will have happily chewed through an important rubber-coated length of copper, leaving it dangling under gravity, swaying to and fro, making contact with conductive materials, sparking, combusting. A small flame at first, greedily seeking sustenance. Finding a splintered corner of the fucking woodframe, perhaps. Or lint, collected in a clump from years of intermittent and neglectful cleaning. And then an exponential acceleration of rage—flames leaping and cackling, jumping to ever greater challenges, curtains, carpets, chairs, tables, eventually reaching my bedroom, sprinting to cupboards and drawers, destruction now an urgent and inviolable intent. My passport. My clothes, neatly hung on plastic hangers. My shoes, including the cowboy boots I wore when I played behind Guns N' Roses in a stadium gig twenty years ago. My books with handwritten inscriptions from my parents. My music. My piano. My bed, sadly unmade. Toothbrush. Hairbrush. The dirty clothes hamper. My tax forms. Spare car keys. The computer. My beautiful piano, a battered old Steinway baby grand, procured at an auction subsequent to the death of an old German professor. Medals, certificates, awards, degrees. And then the photo albums. The one of me and Rebbe and Mom and Dad on a beach somewhere, my mother smiling, hand carelessly draped on her husband's bare shoulder, while her three-year-old twins shriek with laughter at some photographer's antic. The one of me at the Hollywood Bowl playing with Mark Knopfler in the early 1990s. Backstage with Lauryn Hill. The one in a bar, sitting in with Rickie Lee Jones. At a party with Grace, Innocent tucked in against her chest, a sleepy look of happiness on his face. The one of me and Bunny and Isobel, just before her big starring role in the school play, her smile wide, eyes apprehensive. Objects large and small, each with its own story to tell, the threads of Farzad's tapestry. I see it clearly, the ravage dying down, the house slowly crumbling down the hillside, my life becoming embers.

*   *   *

The bar is heaving, packed, spilling over onto the patio and street. Word has gotten out, and these are witnesses to the end of an era. Gordon comes over.

"Hey, Meyer. So this is it."

"You are fucking up my life, Gordon. Why does anyone and everyone insist on fucking up my life?"

"It's not about you, my friend."

"Ha. But it is. At least it should be. And if it's not, I want to know why."

The band is setting up, a mood of inappropriate celebration abounds. Mike the drummer is fucked up on something, his eyes not really focusing clearly. He generally plays well when he is flaming as long as he doesn't head over his pharmaceutical tipping point. Tim is grinning at nothing in particular, his violin/accordion virtuoso status making him much in demand, a bulwark against the curse of musicians' stress. Billy is nonplussed, predatorily scanning the audience for sexual possibilities.

I gather the forces into an alleyway conference.

"So. We gonna look for another gig or fold it and become street people?"

Tim offers, "I think we're at the end of the road. Time for new beginnings. I have a shot at a live TV gig. Steady pay, steady hours, great band. Been thinking I'm gonna do that."

"Really? Who?"

"*The Ned Curtis Show.* Studio band."

Ned Curtis is the next big thing, according to those in the know. Talk-show format. Alternative hip guests from new media, music, tech, theater, comedy—the spicy and colorful fringes of everything. Ned is young and funny and smart and a comer. The studio band, whose name is Global Economy, is eclectic and musically literate, and a critical part of the show. A younger and hipper version of Paul Shaffer's *Late Show* band. A gig like this is the pot of gold at the end of the steady gig rainbow. I am instantaneously riven with lacerating and cruel jealousy. I revert to a moment of childishness.

"Gee, nice of you to let us know."

Tim shrugs. I relent and give him a buddy shove.

"Jackpot. Lottery. 77 Virgins. The Excalibur Sword. Royal Flush. Damn, Tim, that's great."

Tim just grins and shrugs some more. Every musician who has ever dreamed of stardom but understood its mocking mirage has at some point remolded his aspirations to include this. It's like being offered a high-paying gig at Google after toiling in the hell of go-nowhere start-ups.

I turn to Mike.

"You, Mike?"

"Yeah. I suppose all things must pass. I've been thinking about some travel. Go play drums in Africa or Asia. Somewhere where it's not that easy to score drugs, you know? I need some clean time."

"Billy?"

Billy is the youngest of us, about twenty. He is wiry and handsome and boyish. He can trade on things that we can't.

"Happy to play another gig with you guys, but I guess I should look around. Play some kids' music, dance stuff. Find some teenage singer and write some songs with her. Maybe hit the big time, who knows."

I nod. Van puts his arm around me.

"You and me, Meyer. Till the end. Fuck these guys. We'll form a Simon-and-Garfunkel thing, fill Central Park."

"Uh huh. Can you sing?"

"Yes. Badly. Can you?"

"Yes. Even worse."

"OK, maybe not Simon and Garfunkel. But something."

I look at all of them. Part dreamers, part fuck-ups, part musicians, part along-for-the-riders. Part part-timers like me. It is a strange bond between band members. The coming together of these parts for a few hours of smoke, mirrors, and occasional magic. Then off to our lovers and wives and children and broken toilets and tax returns and other bloodless concerns until the next time.

"Let's go and tear the roof off this place."

There is a mood of abandon in the bar. The Santa Anas have gone; now it is just hot. Deep, thick, dry, unrelenting Los Angeles summer heat. I scan the audience. There are a lot of familiar faces. Some friends. Bunny, Krystal. Even Farzad has made the trek from Santa Monica, looking mildly astonished at the tightly spaced pointillist crowd, colorful Hollywood dots in a youthful collage.

We launch into the set, pushing our high-energy stuff to the front of the playlist, surfing the energy of the crowd. The auspiciousness of the occasion, the specter of an uncertain future, the sense of an ending seem to push us. A hard tailwind, warm and insistent. The band is cooking, heating up, becoming the best it can be. There are no loose notes, the ensemble sections an impermeable unstoppable juggernaut, perfectly shaped, riding high above the rhythm section—the sax, violin, and guitar melded into a rainbow-colored single polyphonic instrument, cogent and oratorical. I glance at Billy and Mike—they are in the rare zone—eyes closed, stitched together in lockstep, building a rail over which the rest of us ride.

And the solos! Even Van, who stays away from front and center, is having his say—long bent notes at the top of the guitar neck held like grief until a glissando down to middle octaves and a scurry and explore across the chords ending low down on the E string, a whisper, a croak of farewell.

Tim is all satire and innovation and good humor: a Celtic jig across the blues, Yiddish klezmer across a country rock standard, a tango mash on top of a Nirvana cover, Arabian scales over Britney Spears.

We reach the end of the set, one more. I turn to the band.

"What's the saddest shit we know? The saddest song ever written?"

Everyone sort of looks thoughtful.

"'Oblivion.' Piazzolla. Seems appropriate. That's where we're going."

And so we drop down, soft, almost whispering, the traditional four percussives on one/two-and/three/four, setting up the melancholic tango underpin. We let the vamp build, with Tim on accordion inventing partially arpeggiated scaffolding, the instrument's sad and thin voice keening softly. We continue to build, holding off from the melody launch until I step up to the microphone and hit the low G, roughhewn and breathy, and we are in.

And then I lose myself, just as I have lost the rest. The job, the son, the house, Grace, Dad. I lose myself, eyes squeezed shut. And somebody else takes over, steps in, relieves me of myself. I hear notes and cadences and timbres and phrases that I have never heard before, beautiful and haunting, the melody reborn, shaped into curves and edges that shock me, that wash me clean. And then the solo. Slowly now, languid, notes collecting into phrases, phrases into stories with beginnings and middles and endings, smooth and easy, no repeat of old tales, no cowardly borrowings and half-formed ideas, just small and curious excursions from the majestic melody, nibbling at its edges, catching its echoes, while it holds the center, still commanding its exquisite authority.

We come around again and the band carefully puts the song to bed, gently, laying it down to sleep as if a newborn child. The last note is played and fades. I open my eyes. There is quiet in the audience, as though they have heard something and are trying to find its source. This is new. They were listening. Somebody claps. Someone whistles. The applause slowly builds to a roar.

My eyes are drawn to a table near the back. It is dark, I can't make out the faces. One of them stands up. The light spills over him. A handsome black face, light skinned, deeply intelligent. I would know it anywhere. He is looking straight at me and frowning. It is royalty. It is the king. It is Wynton Marsalis. The apogee of musical erudition and creativity.

He claps lightly.

Then he nods slightly.

Then he smiles gently.

Wynton Marsalis. Clapping and nodding and smiling. Just enough to grace me. Like a benediction from on high.

And then he mouths a word. I read it as certainly as if he were whispering in my ear, as surely as if he had commissioned a billboard on Sunset. His lips caress the sharp opening consonant, tongue darting to the top teeth to support the second syllable. The word he utters is "Pretty."

I look down at my feet. They seem so light. So I tap a foot. And then the other. First the toe and then the heel. And then I am dancing. Alone. Arms outstretched, head thrown back. I can see the open pipes and the overhead stage lights and the wiring, and through it, to the night sky, sparkling and winking like an infinity of semaphores. And I am dancing, dancing, knees pumping, hips swinging, swiveling around, shoulders pumping, back arched, bouncing up and down on my private stage, head bobbing this way and that. I can hear laughter and clapping and whoops. I switch to an Irish jig and then a Russian Cossack leg thing and then a faux tap dance, the twist, a broken breakdance, and then I let loose, tearing around like a dervish, jumping, swaying, soaring, spinning, until the sweat is pouring, my breath in rasps, my muscles spent. I look up, through the roof, through the smog, through the clouds. Up to the dark sky, sparkling with stars and hope. And in my ecstasy, I can hear Rebbe, laughing the light sprinkles of a childhood giggle. Dancing. Dancing for my loves, my lives, my losses, my legacies.

Dancing to a music only I can hear.

But still, I am dancing.

ACKNOWLEDGMENTS

I LIVED IN Hollywood for a large part of my adult life. The city of LA has a distinct personality, one that I came to understand through the alchemy of random experience and ill-considered jaunts. I thank this city and the exceptionalism that struggles (and often succeeds) to emerge from the fog of ordinariness.

I have also played saxophone for many years, sometimes for money, sometimes for fun, and when fate smiles, for both. The band in this book is based on the band *Ensemble Borsalino*, which I played with in 2011/12. Our powerhouse drummer, Michael Canfield, was stone cold sober. Rian Malan, our guitarist (and writer of substantial notoriety) does not, alas, have a trust fund to protect him. Peter Sklair, our excellent multi-genre bass player, was not a sexual predator, or a predator of any sort. Timon Wapenaar, our violinist and accordionist, now living in Spain, is a giant musical talent. He is accurately portrayed—I hope that he will not sue. *Ensemble Borsalino* catalyzed this book, and I am deeply grateful.

To the legions of technology nerds I have known—you have always been my heroes.

Thank you to my agent Tom Miller, Cal Barksdale, and the Skyhorse team, my sister Vicki, and the warm supportive embrace of Kate, Alex, and Joe Sidley.

The academic paper to which I refer in Chapter 3 is from the American Association for Artificial Intelligence: DJH Brown and S Sidley, "The Expression of Aesthetic Principles as Syntactic Structures and Heuristic Preferences and Constraints in a Computer Program That Composes Jazz Improvisations," in *Artificial Intelligence and Creativity: Papers from the 1993 Spring Symposium: Technical Report SS-93-01.*